THE GAME

BECCA JAMESON

THE GAME COPYRIGHT © 2016 BY BECCA JAMESON.

All rights reserved. Printed in the United States of America. No part of this book may be used or reproduced in any manner whatsoever without written permission except in the case of brief quotations embodied in critical articles or reviews.

This book is a work of fiction. Names, characters, businesses, organizations, places, events and incidents either are the product of the author's imagination or are used fictitiously. Any resemblance to actual persons, living or dead, events, or locales is entirely coincidental.

Book and Cover design by Vanessa North
Print ISBN: 978-0-9863360-8-9
eBook ISBN: 978-0-9863360-7-2

THE GAME

BECCA JAMESON

Contents

Chapter One	9
Chapter Two	15
Chapter Three	28
Chapter Four	57
Chapter Five	66
Chapter Six	74
Chapter Seven	89
Chapter Eight	103
Chapter Nine	119
Chapter Ten	133
Chapter Eleven	140
Chapter Twelve	158
Chapter Thirteen	172
Chapter Fourteen	187
Chapter Fifteen	198
Chapter Sixteen	218
Chapter Seventeen	231
Chapter Eighteen	244
Chapter Nineteen	273
Chapter Twenty	281
Chapter Twenty-One	295
Chapter Twenty-Two	310
Chapter Twenty-Three	317
Chapter Twenty-Four	328
Chapter Twenty-Five	341
Chapter Twenty-Six	367

Chapter Twenty-Seven	378
Chapter Twenty-Eight	395
Chapter Twenty-Nine	418

Chapter One

"Oh my *God*, Cheyenne. Did you hear who's speaking at the fundraiser this afternoon?"

I twisted my neck around to peer over my shoulder at Stacy. "No. I'm guessing it's someone important?" I'd been swamped all week preparing a new marketing campaign. The last thing I'd paid any attention to was the rundown of who was going to be at the afternoon's event.

It wasn't that I was indifferent. I was as enthusiastic as anyone about raising money to provide better computers in the local schools. I was simply drowning in work. It was only Monday morning, and already I felt like the week was getting away from me.

Stacy's face lit up, her eyes wide and her smile huge. "David Moreno," she finally declared as if he were the president of the United States.

I froze, my head seemingly stuck in its cocked position as I continued to stare at Stacy, unblinking.

"You know, David Moreno, the CEO of Alexander Technologies. Surely you've heard of him."

Oh I'd heard of him all right. I knew him far better than I was willing to admit.

Riley.

David Riley Moreno. His close friends knew him as Riley.

I finally licked my lips and nodded. "Yeah. I know who he is."

Stacy giggled. "Judging from your expression, I'm gonna assume you aren't immune to his good looks. He is smokin' hot." She fanned herself with one hand. "I think I'd die if I got close to him. Do you suppose he's an asshole? I mean, he's so freakin' rich." Her voice faded as she swung around to face her computer screen.

I eased myself back to face my own desk, unseeing.

Great. Just what I needed. Riley in my personal space. Hell, the last thing I wanted was for that man to take up space in my *head* for the next six hours before the fundraiser. I had a shit ton of work to get done between now and then.

I lifted my fingers to the keyboard but continued to stare distractedly at the screen.

Dammit.

Finally, I slumped in my seat and closed my eyes. My fingers shook as I yanked them to my lap. I took a deep breath.

Stacy wasn't kidding. Riley was sex on wheels. So were his best friends, Cade and Parker. Any one of the three could turn heads by themselves. When they were together, the world seemed to freeze on its axis.

Considering my best friend Amy was about to marry Riley's friend Cade, there was no way I would be able to avoid the man forever.

I'd met Riley only one time, but it was memorable. The man had been at Cade and Amy's engagement party six months ago. I nearly drooled when I met him, and we had several beers together before he disappeared into thin air.

I never spoke to him again.

The thought of seeing him today made my stomach roil. I shouldn't have made a big deal out of it. I mean, who the hell cared that we shared some laughs and a few dances at a mutual friend's party?

I did.

I had liked him. A lot.

We had fun.

Granted, he'd also come out of an engagement himself only a few months before the party, and I could totally understand him having cold feet after the way his ex-fiancée treated him. From what Amy had told me, Christine was a real bitch. Shocking really, considering how down-to-earth and kind I found Riley to be.

And then he vanished without a word.

Amy had been so involved with Cade that night I doubted she realized how much time I spent with Riley. And I never mentioned it to her.

I knew I wasn't in his circles. Hell, he was ten years older than me, owned his own fucking technology company, and ran in wealthy circles. Technically, he owned three companies. Alexander Technologies in Atlanta was just one. He and his friends, Cade and Parker, also owned two others—one in Nashville and one in Charlotte.

In contrast, I was a recent college graduate with a master's degree in marketing, a pile of student loans, and a

The Game

sparsely furnished apartment.

But that had been six months ago.

I'd now been working for Talent Marketing Group in downtown Atlanta for over a year. I loved my job, and I made good enough money to chip away at the loans and invest in enough furniture to at least entertain my friends. Compared to other recent college graduates, I considered myself lucky.

Compared to Riley Moreno, I was inept.

I did *not* need to run into the man who had taken up residence in my dreamworld for weeks on end. All that could possibly come from such an encounter would be more dreams of what had become an imaginary romance with the elusive sexy Riley.

I pressed two fingers into each of my temples and squeezed my eyes tight. Closing them didn't block out images of that man leaning over my naked body with the ever-present smoldering look in his eyes—visions I'd conjured in my head that had no basis in reality.

We hadn't even kissed. All we'd done was drink a few beers and hang together. It had never made any sense to me. Riley knew other people at the party. And yet he spent the evening with me as if I were the only woman in the room. His attention had focused solely on me. Even his gaze hadn't strayed. I was the center of his universe for several hours.

    And then he left to use the restroom and never returned.

Chapter Two

It was after four in the afternoon when I made my way to the first floor, hoping to duck into the fundraiser and keep myself as inconspicuous as possible. I knew my presence was expected, and I didn't want people to question my absence, but if there had been any way for me to slink out of that building and drop a check in the mail, I'd have leaped at the opportunity.

The last thing I wanted was to run into Riley ever again in this lifetime. I was mortified by his departure from the engagement party and had no desire to face him and deal with the awkwardness that would forever define our first encounter.

Of course I knew I'd have to see him again. After

all, he was Amy's fiancé's best friend. Their wedding at the very least would bring the two of us together.

But that was still a few months away.

I wasn't prepared to face Riley today.

The moment I slipped into the enormous event room, Stacy spotted me from the stage. She waved me toward her, undoubtedly thinking any woman in her right mind would jump at the opportunity to get as close to Riley as possible.

I was not a woman in my right mind.

And furthermore, the man himself was currently speaking to the audience from the podium. When I heard his voice, my gaze shot from Stacy to the stage.

The first time I'd seen him, he'd been dressed casually in khaki pants and a deep blue shirt that drew attention to the intensity of his blue eyes. Today he was in a suit—charcoal gray—and he looked even more breathtaking. His shoulders appeared even broader in the suit jacket, and the perfectly starched white shirt made him look incredibly tan. Even his tie, the same blue as his eyes, was hypnotic. No wonder everyone in the room was focused on him.

I flattened myself to the wall just inside the door, wishing I hadn't worn heels. Anything to keep me as invisible as possible would have been appreciated.

I was mesmerized.

His blond hair looked exactly the same—slightly long. I suspected it was intentional. It curled at the ends, making him look younger than his thirty-four years, begging a woman to run her fingers through it. Playful.

I didn't hear a word he spoke. Instead, I concentrated on the cadence of his voice, the way he leaned into the podium passionately, the broadness of his shoulders...

Lord, I needed to get a grip.

I was supposed to be hurt, angry, pissed. Instead, I was aroused.

I gripped my thighs together as the tone of his voice made my panties wet with no effort on his part, wondering if everyone in the room was as aroused by his voice as I was.

I didn't even glance around the room. To do so would deny myself of even one moment of his magnetic personality. And if this was all I ever had of David Riley Moreno, I intended to suck the moment for all it was worth to store the semi-encounter in the back of my head for later.

And who was I kidding? I would have wet dreams

over this man more times than I could count over the next several months.

This was a disaster.

Finally, Riley pushed off the podium, thanked the audience for their participation in a community service that was dear to his heart, and walked off the stage.

Instead of leaving the room through a side door as I expected, he turned to skirt the edge of the audience, heading toward the back—toward *me*.

Stacy must have nearly wet herself when he went by, but I didn't look in her direction to confirm. My eyes were glued to Riley, and I pondered an exit strategy that wouldn't draw attention to myself and would allow me to avoid the encounter that would occur in about ten seconds.

An earthquake would've been more than welcome.

I held my breath, flattening my palms to the cold surface behind me as Riley wove through the crowd of spectators who hadn't managed to procure a seat. He smiled at several people, shook hands with a few, and spoke to a handful.

I wanted to glance away, dig for something in my purse, or pretend to drop something at the exact perfect moment to avoid all contact, but I stood like a statue instead, not breathing, my eyes pinned to the man who'd taken my heart out of my chest in mere hours and then stomped on it, leaving the smashed bits on the floor all those months ago.

The second his gaze found mine, I knew it immediately—he hadn't seen me until that moment. He faltered as he inched through the crowd, and then he smiled.

I pursed my lips, determined to be as cordial as possible and to keep our encounter brief and pleasant.

At the last second, a woman stepped in front of me and wrapped her long, thin fingers around Riley's bicep. "Riley. So nice to see you. I didn't realize you'd be speaking at this event." Her voice was syrupy sweet, and her face held a mask of fake happiness.

I would never understand people like her, but my mind told me she was Riley's type. If I had been told to point out someone in the room to match him up with, I would have chosen her. She was willowy and tall with her dark hair pulled back in a tight professional bun. Her designer suit cost more than my rent. And the jewelry dangling from her ears, neck, and wrists was undoubtedly real diamonds and gold.

Riley looked shocked. Uncomfortable. He glanced

at me and licked his lips before returning his attention to the wealthy woman leaning into his space. "What are you doing here?"

She smiled. "I should ask the same question. I just moved here. I've got several interviews lined up."

"To Atlanta. You moved to Atlanta," he deadpanned. "You expect me to believe you just happened to have moved to Georgia and ran into me purely by coincidence."

I wanted to flee. This was my opportunity. But I couldn't resist listening in on this conversation. Whoever this woman was, she obviously didn't have Riley's stamp of approval.

Interesting.

Her skin tightened around her eyes as they widened, and she flattened her free hand on her chest. "Riley. I can't believe you would think so ill of me. Atlanta's plenty big enough for both of us. And besides, we should bury the hatchet, get together for drinks, remember old times."

Whoever this was, she had known Riley well in the past. She even called him by his nickname. Most people in the room knew him as David Moreno.

Riley reached with his opposite hand and peeled

her hand off his arm. "Not going to happen. Make sure we don't cross paths again. I'm not interested in whatever web of deceit you're selling." With deliberate intent, he eased her to one side and stepped between her body and mine.

Too close. I inhaled his scent, a combination of the same aftershave from six months ago and Riley. It shocked me that even blindfolded I would know that scent.

Riley.

As if to save face, the rich woman muttered something about it being so nice to see him and that she'd be in touch soon. Her gaze penetrated me for several seconds before she strode away, her head held high as though she'd won that round.

Judging by Riley's dismissal and the fact that he completely ignored her final words, she had won nothing.

"Cheyenne." He stepped closer into my personal space and reached out to stroke his fingers from my shoulder to my elbow. The touch was so intimate, I wished I hadn't left my jacket upstairs. My sleeveless blouse left my bare skin exposed.

The warmth from his fingers melted a piece of me, forcing me to smile while at the same time I wanted to reach out and slap him. This wasn't the place for such a scene. I intended to be the bigger woman in this game.

On the heels of the woman he just summarily dissed, I intended to come out ahead.

So I smiled. "Mr. Moreno. Nice to see you. Your speech was inspiring."

He flinched, his shoulders slumping at my formal approach. And then he winced. "Yeah, I deserve that."

Shit. I would have preferred no mention of the past. I shrugged. And then I tugged my elbow free and stepped to one side. "I'm sure you have places to be." I nodded toward the door.

He cringed this time, but ignored my gesture. "Do you work here?"

"Yes." I stepped closer to the door myself, determined to put an end to this awkward meeting. If I could manage to keep the syllables to a minimum…

"I knew you were in marketing, but you never mentioned what firm you worked for."

I smiled, offering nothing else.

Riley blew out a breath. "Listen, Cheyenne, is there someplace we could talk?"

I shook my head. "That isn't necessary."

He narrowed his gaze on me and stepped closer.

The Game

His proximity chipped away at my resolve. As if he put off some sort of pheromone that drew me in closer.

The room buzzed around us as everyone clapped and cheered for the next speaker. I didn't even know who it was. That's how tuned in I was to one channel—Riley. "It's water under the bridge. No worries." Why did he have to smell so damn good?

Riley frowned. "I know you don't mean that."

"I do." I straightened my spine and met his gaze, dragging up every ounce of willpower I had to end this fast. I even held my breath to avoid breathing in his aftershave, his brand of soap, his personal musk…

"I was an ass."

I tucked my lower lip between my teeth and bit down to avoid responding.

Why wouldn't he just leave? I didn't need this. I didn't need his apology. And I certainly didn't need him in my space, filling my nose with his scent and my vision with his unbelievably broad chest, smooth face, and blue eyes.

Riley glanced around finally, taking in the audience behind him. "Do you need to stay? Could we leave?"

My eyes widened. Leave? With him? Hell no.

"That's not a good idea." I pasted on a broader smile. "I'm fine, Riley. Really. You don't need to worry about me. I'm a grown woman. I'm over it."

That was so far from the truth, it was a wonder I was able to utter those words. Sure, I was over it, if by "over it" one meant that I had stopped masturbating by hand to visions of this sexy man and had switched to using a vibrator to speed up the process. If "over it" entailed me not dating anyone since I met him because any man who approached me didn't measure up.

Yep. I was so "over it."

What I knew was that if I gave him a chance, I would fall under his spell in a heartbeat. It unnerved me. This man who already infiltrated my dreams—both during the night and during the day.

Riley held my gaze, scrutinizing me with an intensity that made me fidget. With only a few inches between us, his eyes shot back and forth between mine. "Right." He chuckled. "I wasn't born yesterday. No woman wants to be treated the way I treated you. I'm not an idiot. You'll hold that grudge for the rest of your life. And I don't blame you. But I'm asking for a chance to explain myself. An explanation I should have had the balls to offer that night instead of leaving you there without a word."

He was right. I simply stared at him, a little stunned. Did I want to allow Riley to explain himself?

I blew out a breath.

Did he really have an explanation that went beyond jackass? Maybe he'd had cold feet? Maybe he'd still been hung up on his ex that night? Maybe he'd had another girlfriend at the time?

Lord. I shouldn't cave. He was lethal.

"So again, is there someplace we can talk?"

I stuck to my previous resolve. "I'm not having this discussion with you in my office. No. And I'm telling you it isn't necessary. You've apologized. I accept your apology. Can we just leave it at that?" A chill ran down my arms. I needed to get rid of this man before I started shaking and embarrassed myself.

"I'm making you nervous."

"No shit." Those two words fell out of my mouth unbidden.

Riley smiled again. Damn but he looked like a god when he smiled. I had loved watching his face light up the first time I met him, and it was no different today. "Okay, I'll respect your wishes inside your workplace and under the circumstances. I've blindsided you. But we aren't done. I'll call you tomorrow."

I bit my lower lip again. No way in hell did I want him to call me tomorrow or any other day of the year.

I had to be honest with myself. It wasn't so much that I was afraid he couldn't possibly have a legitimate excuse for his behavior.

Nope.

What I feared was that he *did*. And if that was the case, what would keep me from caving and going out with him again?

What would keep me from having my heart broken when he walked away a second time?

I knew my vulnerabilities when it came to Riley Moreno. He had the power to destroy me.

Riley reached to cup my face with his palm, tugging my lip from between my teeth with his thumb. He inhaled deeply, his eyes shutting for a moment. And then he released me, turned, and strode from the room as fast as he could manage to get through the last few people and out the door.

I didn't breathe while I watched him walk away, his perfect ass encased in designer suit pants, swaying. Every muscle in his butt and thighs was firm and tight.

I licked my lips, imagining running my hands

over all the planes of his body.
>Fuck.
>I was doomed.

Chapter Three

I was on pins and needles the next day. Would Riley actually contact me? The chances were slim. After all, his track record was zero.

Stacy grilled me for fifteen minutes when we arrived in the morning. For the first time since I'd started at Talent, I hated not having my own office but rather a cubicle in a room with the other consultants.

"Cheyenne, I can't believe you never told me you knew Mr. Moreno. I mean, surely you know him. It looked like you two were in a deep discussion." She chatted on, leaning against the partition between my cubicle and hers, fully inside my small space, making it impossible to avoid her. "So where do you know him from?"

    I lifted my gaze to hers. "We met at a party months ago. Not a big deal. I'm surprised he remembered me." That last bit was a lie, but I was surprised he *cared* that he remembered me.

    "You're so calm about it." Stacy beamed. And then she giggled. "What's he like? Don't you just want to rip off his shirt and see if his pecs are as firm as they look?"

    I rolled my eyes. "I hardly know him. And I haven't given any thought to his bare chest." That was also a lie. A blatant lie.

    Stacy pushed off the wall. "Who was that other woman fawning over him? She looked like she'd be happy to lick his feet clean, and then she slipped quietly away as though someone had killed her puppy. And the glare she gave you… Girl…"

    "I have no idea." Whoever it was, she knew him well. And what did I care?

    "I don't know how you can be so nonchalant. He's like an elusive god. I'd give my right arm to have him stroke it like he did yours yesterday." She nearly moaned, and then she righted herself. "Damn, I gotta get back to work. We'll talk later." Finally, she left me alone to return to her own cubicle.

BECCA JAMESON

    I stared at my computer screen—the one I hadn't turned on yet—and tried to control my emotional upheaval and my shaking hands. With a deep breath, I concentrated on my workload and attempted to stuff Riley to the farthest corner of my brain.

    And I succeeded to a certain extent, burying myself for hours in my current project, ignoring the time and even skipping lunch while I was on a roll. I was currently working on an advertising campaign for a large cell phone company—Link. It wasn't unheard of for the hours to slip by while I plastered myself to the screen in front of me. After spending the morning contacting the customer to ensure I had all their current logos and artwork on hand, I spent the afternoon playing with possible new slogans and a fresh look.

    It wasn't until my phone buzzed on the corner of my desk near the end of the day that I stretched my neck and reached to grab the cell. There was a text.

    I stared at the device in my hand, blinking for several seconds.

    Cheyenne, I want to apologize properly. Please let me take you out. Friday night?

    The man added a smiling emoji to the end of his text.

The Game

I squeezed the phone so tight it was a wonder it didn't shatter.

My instinct was to not respond at all, but he was so persistent about this that I doubted my lack of response would deter him.

What if I'm not available Friday night? I finally texted in return.

Make yourself available.

I groaned. When had he become so high-handed? And why was his persistence so hot? I should be angry instead of fidgeting in my seat attempting to take the pressure off my pussy by adjusting my dress pants.

I stared at my phone in my hand for several seconds, my fingers shaking too much to respond.

Please? he texted next.

Okay. Why? Why was I doing this to myself? The only thing that could possibly result from me going out with Riley would be heartache and disappointment.

:) You want to give me your address?

How did you get my phone number?

Touché.

I knew it would be easy for him to get my address from Amy. I was certain that was how he'd gotten my cell number.

Sure enough, Amy called ten minutes later. "What's up between you and Riley? I didn't realize you two knew each other so well."

"We don't," I countered too quickly. "I just ran into him at the fundraiser yesterday—huge shindig to get computers in the hands of more students in city schools. Apparently Alexander Technologies is involved. Guess he's trying to be polite. We should make nice since our friends are getting married and all." I didn't want to get into my feelings for Riley any further with Amy. I was embarrassed to be so enamored with the guy. A complete fool.

"That's sweet."

"You know me." Too well. That was the problem. If she could see my face, she'd know I was lying through my teeth.

As it was, this was going to be the longest week of my life, and it was only Tuesday.

****

At five minutes before eight Friday night I stared at my reflection in my bathroom mirror, wondering if I'd gone overboard or not.

Riley didn't seem the type to hang out in seedy bars in jeans and a T-shirt. I assumed high-end was more his style, so I'd wiggled myself into my favorite tight little

The Game

black dress and heels that I was well aware made my calves look fucking awesome. I knew this because Amy and Meagan told me every time I wore them.

The decision to go this route hadn't been easy. I'd put on jeans and a tank top first, thinking I could perhaps deter Riley from insisting we go out if I wasn't dressed the part.

But that idea had the potential to backfire on me if Riley decided to follow my lead and invite himself into my apartment instead. The only thing worse than sitting across from him at a bar would be sitting next to him alone in my apartment on my couch.

And then there was my hair. For years I'd worn it in a cute bob. I'd been told countless times my thick blonde locks fell perfectly around my face. Too perfectly I imagined. I was tired of the image. So, over the last year, I'd let it grow out. It now skimmed my shoulders in loose curls I'd stopped trying to straighten months ago.

Meagan said it made me look softer. Amy said I looked more human. She was teasing, but she'd always insisted I looked like I stepped out of a painting.

Tonight I had taken the time to blow-dry the thick curls into submission, and I'd pinned the front section on top of my head, leaving a ringlet on each side to hang across my cheeks. It looked fantastic. Too bad it was essentially wasted on Mr. Riley Moreno.

My makeup was the same as always, subtle—mascara, eye shadow, light foundation, lip gloss. I'd had it down to a science since about sixth grade. It worked for me. My girls told me so. So I didn't fuck with it.

When the knock sounded at my front door, I flinched.

Show time.

Holding my breath, I made my way to the front room, peeked through the hole in the door, and then turned the knob when I confirmed Riley was indeed standing on the other side.

I was in far more danger opening the door to this man than perhaps a serial killer, but I did it anyway, unable to keep myself from following my curiosity.

Riley was smiling when I opened the door, but his smile widened as he took me in.

I was simply relieved to find him wearing a suit instead of jeans. At least we matched.

"You look gorgeous, Cheyenne." His voice was deep and sincere, and he leaned forward and kissed my cheek.

I blushed, surprised by both his intimacy and the

THE GAME

chill that raced down my spine and left goose bumps on my arms. Why did this man affect me so thoroughly?

He stroked my elbow next. "I'm glad you dressed up. I didn't have time to go home from the office. We'll go to Sky."

Sky. I'd been there only one time before and that was right after Meagan, Amy, and I finished our master's degrees and splurged on an evening at the most exclusive nightclub in the area.

"You ready? Need anything?"

I reached for my clutch on the stand next to the door and nodded. "This really isn't necessary, you know."

"It really is." He took my arm to guide me down the hall of my third floor apartment. My front door shut behind us like a gong, sealing my fate. If Riley thought he was going to lure me out for an evening of entertainment and then leave me to find a cab home, I would kill him and never flinch at the repercussions.

"I swear I'm not usually such an ass, Cheyenne," he said as we waited for the elevator.

"I'll take your word for it." What else was I supposed to say?

"You don't have to take my word. I'll prove it. And I don't blame you for the way you're looking at me either. I deserve your distrust. If I were you, I might have dead bolted the front door and ignored my knocking. Thank you for giving me the opportunity to make things right."

How he could possibly make things right? But the man was insistent, so I decided to guard my heart closer this time and let him do what he needed to do to clear his conscience.

I was surprised to find a sleek black Mercedes parked out front, and even more shocked to see a man climbing from the driver's seat to round the car and open the rear passenger door. He was tall and slender. His hair was sparse and mostly gray. He tugged his suit jacket down as he walked. When I met his gaze, he gave me a small smile that made his eyes twinkle and a nod. "Evening, Ms. Decard."

He knew my name? Interesting… I smiled back at him.

"Cheyenne, this is my driver, Les Charles."

I shouldn't have found it odd that Riley had a driver. After all, Cade also had a driver. I wasn't sure Amy had been behind the wheel of a car since they moved in together last Thanksgiving.

Before that, Riley had been the CEO of The

The Game

Rockwood Group in Nashville, Cade had been at Alexander Technologies in Atlanta, and Parker was at Edgewater Inc. in Charlotte.

For a moment, I regretted my decision to wear the short black dress that hugged my body a bit too tightly. I tugged the hem as I slid into the back seat of the car, worrying the entire time I'd given Riley a bit too much of a view.

He didn't say a word, however, as he slid in beside me.

I fidgeted as we took off, unable to keep my hands still in my lap, wringing them.

Riley surprised me by setting his hand on top of mine and squeezing. "I swear I don't bite. Relax."

I blew out a breath and turned my head to meet his gaze, tugging my hands away to escape his touch to no avail. In fact, his fingers were so long, they grazed my bare thighs at the juncture, precariously close to my sex.

Riley stared down at me. "Why do you have to be so damn alluring?"

I blinked. *What the…?*

He smiled, a slow grin that spread across his face, lighting it up. And then he rolled his eyes and turned to face the front, leaning his head against the seat. His hand tightened around my balled fists, and I took a deep breath.

If I was so attractive, why the hell did he leave me high and dry that night?

The drive wasn't long, thank God. We sat in uncomfortable silence. Perhaps he didn't want to speak in front of his driver.

I tried to relax and stared out the window, but I saw nothing. My entire focus centered on the long fingers dangling against my inner thighs, occasionally stroking the sensitive skin there.

When we pulled up to Sky, Riley gave my hands a gentle squeeze and finally released me. The damage was done, however. My panties were wet, and a ball of need had grown incrementally between my legs as we'd driven.

Riley eased from the car first and reached to help me.

I flushed as I scooted closer to the door, silently berating myself for choosing this particular dress. This was my fit-to-kill outfit. What the hell was I thinking wearing it out with Riley?

It was too short, too tight, too sexy. I didn't want to feel sexy. I wanted to go back home where I was safe from men like Riley who could spike my arousal and then

The Game

walk away. I had begun to abhor being as horny as I was right then, especially since the only man who brought out that side of me was Riley, and the bastard could do so without being in the room. He'd managed to control my body on many occasions in the last six months, and I'd never once seen or heard from him.

Goddamn it.

By the time I stood on the sidewalk next to this imposing man who loomed over me at over six feet, I was pissed. More with myself and my inability to control my reactions to him than anything else.

"You okay?" he asked, tipping his head to one side, his brows furrowed.

"Of course," I lied.

Riley hesitated for a moment, gazing at my face. Finally, he sighed and took my hand, turning to head into the bar.

All my attention focused on the feel of his fingers gently wrapped around mine. His grip was softer than it had been in the car. And he stroked his thumb over the back of my knuckles, distracting me maddeningly.

I let Riley lead me into Sky. It was crowded. We wound through a throng of people until we emerged at the far side. I shivered when I glanced at the table I had sat at last time I was there—the night Amy had shared a drink with Cade.

The place had seemed so intimidating at the time. We were recent graduates pretending to be older and wealthier. Man, how things had changed. I had my head above water financially for one thing. And Amy was engaged.

I had only been on a few dates in the last six months. No one I met measured up to the evening I'd spent with Riley, and I was beginning to worry about my sanity.

A waitress waved toward Riley to follow her.

I wasn't surprised. Cade Alexander owned this bar. Riley and Parker would receive the same level of service as Cade any time they entered.

In moments we were ushered to a high round table. Riley leaned over to say something into the waitress's ear, and she nodded and smiled. She turned and sashayed away as fast as she'd led us to the table.

Riley pulled out a stool and then glanced down at my frame. "Can you manage?"

To get on a stool? I wasn't an idiot.

His reservations weren't altogether unwarranted, however. Luckily my seat faced away from the crowd

THE GAME

because I was sure anyone walking by would have gotten an eyeful of my crotch as I hefted myself up, using the rung as leverage.

I wiggled around on the seat, making sure my ass was covered, and set my clutch on the table.

Riley grinned but said nothing. He slipped onto his own stool without incident. In fact, his butt was nearly at the level of the seat to begin with. "I ordered us a bottle of wine. I hope that's okay."

What if it wasn't? I nodded. I'd never been a huge fan of wine, but since Amy had met Cade, I'd learned a thing or two about good chardonnay. She'd developed a palate for the expensive stuff. After sharing several bottles with her over the months, I'd learned to enjoy the rich fruity flavors and oak undertones.

"So, tell me about your job. I knew you were in marketing, but I didn't realize you worked for Talent Marketing Group. Do you still love it?" Riley set his elbows on the table and leaned toward me. His gaze never left mine, not even to glance around the bar.

Like the night I'd met him, his attention was riveted on me. No one else existed.

My heart pounded. The sensation was both heady and disconcerting. When I was with him, he was all mine.

He focused one hundred percent on what I had to say.

As flattering as his attention was, I wasn't here for small talk. I needed answers. I could not allow this man to toy with my heart. I simply wasn't built for brief trysts. I would fall for him; and he would hurt me.

"Why are we doing this exactly?"

"Having a drink?"

I narrowed my gaze. "Having anything."

Riley's shoulders slumped. "I wanted to apologize. I owe you that much."

"You *did* apologize. Monday. And I accepted. And you don't owe me." I didn't falter from my stance. My guard was up high. Insurmountably high. My traitorous body might have had other ideas, but my brain was smart enough to know I needed to keep my distance from this man.

Why was he torturing me?

Riley grabbed my hand to hold it against the table top. He stared down at my fingers and rubbed them again with his infuriatingly tantalizing thumb.

I tugged against his grip, just as I had in the car, and Riley held steady again also.

"Your skin is so soft." He lifted his face. "Hell, all of you is soft."

The Game

"I've never considered myself soft."

He smiled broader. "Yeah. I can see that."

The waitress returned with a bottle of white wine. She removed the cork and poured a splash into one glass.

Riley released my hand to taste the wine, and I immediately tucked both hands in my lap. He nodded at the waitress as she settled an ice tub on the table to keep the wine chilled.

When he nodded at her, she filled both our glasses and then walked away.

He leaned forward, elbows on the table, and held my gaze. His face was unreadable. Serious. His eyes bore into me, slightly squinted. His lips were a straight line.

I fought the urge to squirm. The man was so unbelievably sexy, and his entire attention was once again focused on me as if we were alone instead of sitting in a noisy, crowded bar. My emotions were all over the place. It was impossible to ignore the magnetic pull he had on me when I was with him. And I didn't want to feel that tug.

I took a sip of the chardonnay and nearly moaned. It was that good. A hint of citrus teased my taste buds. Riley knew his wine.

This man would hurt me.

If I let my guard down, I'd be sorry. And I couldn't avoid letting my guard down. He stripped it away with just a look. I couldn't stop him. The only way to ensure I wouldn't get hurt would be to keep my distance.

I knew I shouldn't have agreed to this night out. And really, I hadn't agreed. He'd strong-armed me.

If this thing between us were normal, I would relax and let it progress naturally. He obviously liked me. That wasn't the problem. The trouble was we weren't in the same circles. We didn't have enough in common.

Just because Amy had pulled it off with Cade didn't mean the rest of us normal, everyday, middle-class ladies could snag us a millionaire and live happily ever after. It didn't work that way.

I could date him. I could even sleep with him. But I knew it couldn't go further. And under normal circumstances, that would be fine. I was single. Unattached.

But not with Riley.

I'd known from the moment I first laid eyes on him that my feelings for him wouldn't be controllable. He had a pull on me that drew me to lean his direction, and I needed to rein it in.

I did not want him to know how I felt. Ever.

The Game

I didn't want anyone to know.

Just sitting across from him was dangerous. And if I'd had any doubt, all I needed to do was remind myself of the moments I'd seen him yesterday and the drive over here in the car.

Yeah.

I was screwed.

"I can't do this, Riley." I drank more wine, enjoying the fruity taste immensely. Why did the man have to be such a wine connoisseur on top of everything else?

He sighed. "I wasn't in a good place last time we met."

"I know. Amy told me about your fiancée and the breakup. I get that. But this isn't about you, Riley. This is about me. *I* can't do this."

His brow furrowed. "What? Go out for a drink?"

"Go out for an *anything*. With you. This is a bad idea."

He pursed his lips for a moment and then spoke again. "I was a coward that night we met. My actions were stupid. We had a great time together. I was an asshole."

"And I said I forgive you. Now you need to let me go."

"What if I don't want to let you go?"

"You don't have a choice. I'm telling you. I. Can't. Do. This." I enunciated each word.

He ignored me, shaking off my words as if they were inconsequential. "I haven't been able to get you out of my head since that night." He reached forward with one hand to stroke the tips of his fingers across my cheek.

I drew back out of his reach, but not fast enough.

He let his hand fall to the table. It lay too close to me. I could still feel his touch on my face, the way he'd stroked my knuckles, the way he'd held my hands together firmly in the car.

With every second, I was falling. Too hard. It both strengthened my resolve and made me melt. His gaze bore into my soul, digging a hole I would never be able to escape. "Riley, we're from two different worlds. I would never be able to run in your circles."

"Cade and Amy are no different. They're making it work."

"Cade and Amy have been through the roughest times of anyone I've ever met. Hell, she left town and changed her name to get away from him. Not exactly what I'm looking for in a relationship."

"But they're fine now. Better than fine. They're

the strongest couple I know. Who's to say we can't do the same thing?" He held up a hand. "Not that I mean to get ahead of myself. I'm just suggesting you date me. Let me take you out. Movies. Dinner. We have a connection. I want to explore it. I'm not asking for forever. I'm just asking for now."

"And that's the problem, Riley." I lowered my voice. I was deadly serious. I needed to make myself clear, and the only way I knew to do it was to be honest.

Not that he had been honest about why he left me at the engagement party, but this wasn't about him.

"I'm not following," he said.

I downed the rest of my glass and reached for the bottle.

Riley beat me to it, grabbing the chardonnay and filling my glass. "Talk to me."

I blinked, taking another fortifying sip. "Since you're so persistent, let me spell it out for you." I was putting myself out there. I didn't care. I needed him to understand and respect my boundaries. "I can't do casual with you. I'm irrationally attracted to you. You'll hurt me. And you'll ruin me for other men."

There. I said it. The most awkward conversation of my life. Now I just needed him to let me go.

"Riley. Darling…" The syrupy sweet voice coming from behind me made me cringe. And if that wasn't enough, the woman who accompanied the voice glided right up to the table between us, grabbed Riley's arm with her tiny hand, and leaned in to kiss his cheek as if they were the closest two people on the planet.

The same woman from Monday afternoon. Was she stalking him?

And this was why I couldn't date this man. I needed no other proof.

My stomach pitched forward while the woman stroked down Riley's arm and settled her perfectly manicured fingers on his forearm. I tucked my own dull nails into my palms to hide them.

I glanced up and down the woman's body to confirm my previous suspicions. She was filthy rich. She wore a tight off-white dress that made my best little black dress look shamefully inadequate. Her nearly black hair was pulled back from her face in a perfect coif once again, every single strand accounted for. She couldn't possibly have done that to herself. Did she have a hairstylist living in her house? She was tall, slender, and perfect. Like a model.

I would never be able to compete with that. I

never wanted to. Something about her made me cringe.

And she was touching Riley.

No. This would never work. Jealously ate a hole in me so fast I couldn't breathe. I didn't like the feeling.

This woman knew him. Way better than I did. He was ten years older than me. He'd been wealthy beyond measure for that long also, so obviously he would know lots of women. I didn't want that money or the hoity behaviors that went with it.

I needed to get out of Sky and never come back.

The woman tossed her head and smiled at Riley. Too strained. She made my skin crawl.

I gripped my glass so hard it was a wonder it didn't shatter. I wanted to peel her fingers off his forearm. Could she not see he was with me?

And this was why Riley and I would never work.

Riley's gaze slid from mine to hers, his face hard, his teeth gritted. "What the hell are you doing here, Christine?"

Christine? Seriously? His ex-fiancée?

"I just moved here from Virginia. I told you that. In fact, I got a new job. I start next week." She beamed.

"Are you following me?"

I took a long drink of my wine, set it on the table,

and clenched my hands in my lap. If I drank much more, I wouldn't be able to make sound decisions.

Riley looked uncomfortable, which wasn't surprising. I didn't know all the details about their relationship, but I did know she truly was a bitch. She'd been partially responsible for coming between Cade and Amy and almost destroying them. That was why Riley broke things off with her in the first place.

Why the fuck did she move to Atlanta? Just to torment him? Did she want him back?

She giggled. "Don't be silly."

Riley's face turned a deep red. "I'm with someone, Christine. Glad to hear you're doing so well. Now, if you'll excuse us."

Christine was undaunted. She started petting him. *Petting* him. And she turned her face to glance at me as though she hadn't noticed me sitting there before. She pasted a fake smile on her face and tipped her head to one side. "Oh. Hi. You look familiar." She tapped her lips with her free hand. "Do you work at my dry cleaners maybe? Or wait, maybe it's my spa. Are you a receptionist at Beatrice's?"

My eyes widened. Riley had been engaged to this woman? I mean, I knew she was a vicious bitch. I knew

The Game

she'd said horrific things to Amy, but hearing about her and witnessing her firsthand was entirely different. I wanted to slap her, and I'd never hit anyone in my life.

Riley stood, jerking his arm out of her grasp. "Christine, I don't know what you're trying to do, but go away. It's over between us. It has been for a year. I can't imagine why you'd decide to move to Atlanta, but you need to stay away from me."

She leaned into him, a pout on her face. "Oh, Riley. Don't overreact. I love Atlanta. And I'm moving here because this is where I got a job. Don't worry. I won't keep you from your evening with this little toy of yours." She flicked her gaze to me, glancing up and down as if I weren't worth the dirt on the bottom of her shoes.

She smirked then and stepped closer to me. Shocking me, she touched my face.

I flinched back, but from my perch on the stool, I didn't have much room.

"Your skin is so delicate. It must bruise easily and last for days when he spanks you." She shivered. "I can't imagine what happens when he uses a flogger." She grabbed my wrist next and flipped it around before I could stop her. "How does he keep your wrists from getting marked?" She turned toward Riley, dropping my hand. "Did you get some softer cuffs, my love?"

Riley lurched forward and grabbed Christine by the arm. He turned her around without a word and marched her through the crowd.

I lost sight of him quickly. My entire body shook.

What the hell just happened?

Her words swam around in my head. Flogger? Cuffs? Spanking? What the fuck?

I gripped the edge of the table with both hands until my knuckles turned white. I needed to move—get the hell out of Sky, grab a cab, and go home. But I didn't trust my legs to function properly yet.

A chill raced down my spine. I felt dizzy, perhaps from the wine, perhaps from the insanity of the last five minutes.

If I'd had any brain cells, I would have left the bar before Riley returned, but I clearly had none, so I nearly jumped out of my skin when Riley's hand landed on my shoulder.

I lifted my gaze to see his face.

He was on the phone. "Yes… No, I'm not fucking kidding. She was right here in Sky… Yes, I spoke to the manager… He was very apologetic… No, you don't need to fire him… I'm sure I made myself clear. That bitch

The Game

won't be coming through the doors of Sky again... Right. Okay." He flipped the phone shut and turned to face me.

"Jesus, Cheyenne. I'm so sorry."

I shook my head.

His fingers on my shoulder burned into my body. All I could think about was the way he'd grabbed Christine's arm and marched her out of the room. Had he also beaten her when they were together?

I yanked myself free of his grip and jumped down from the stool, legs wobbling "I need to go." I backed up, running into a passing waiter almost instantly.

The man steadied me from behind with a touch to my back. "Sorry, ma'am."

I twisted around to smile at him, but my mouth wouldn't work to form words or acknowledge his statement.

He furrowed his brow. "You okay, ma'am?"

"Can you get me a taxi?"

Riley interrupted behind me. "That's not necessary. I'll have my driver take you anywhere you want to go."

I didn't look at him as I turned and grabbed my clutch from the table. I didn't acknowledge him again as I shoved my way through the crowd toward the entrance.

There were twice as many people in Sky than had been there when we'd entered.

    I burst through the front door and gasped for air.

    Riley was right behind me. "Cheyenne, let me explain."

    I spun around to face him and held up a hand. "No. Please. Just let me go." My fingers shook in the air.

    "Sir? Did you want me to take you someplace else?" The voice of Riley's driver at our sides made me turn toward him.

    "I'd love if you would take me home. Riley is staying."

    The man glanced at Riley, who nodded. "It's okay, Les. You can come back for me later."

    Les nodded and took two long strides to the car at the curb. He opened the rear passenger door and stepped to the side.

    "Cheyenne."

    I twisted toward Riley. "Please. Just let me go. This was never going to work anyway. I've told you that a million times. Thanks for letting me use your driver. Don't call me."

    Riley ran both hands through his hair until it was a messy blond disaster that made him look younger than his thirty-four years. I could almost feel sorry for him. His eyes were wide. His face was red. And he started to pace a few steps in both directions in distress.

Did it have anything to do with me leaving? Or was it because he was worried about the things I'd just learned?

I didn't care. I just wanted to get the fuck away from him.

"Good bye, Riley." I slid into the back seat and held my breath until the driver shut the door.

The man rounded the car in a hurry and sped off before I glanced out the window.

A tear ran down my cheek unbidden and uncalled for.

I would not cry over this man. It was stupid.

I'd only seen him on three occasions. He wasn't worth it.

And if anything Christine said was true, he was abusive.

I closed my eyes. My mind ran all over the place as the vibrations of the car lulled me enough to calm my shaking body down.

There was no way Riley was abusive to Christine and Amy didn't know it. Hell, Amy had given Riley my phone number and then my address. No way in hell would she do that if she thought Riley would harm me.

Something didn't compute.

I took deep breaths and held on to my composure by a thread all the way back to my apartment.

I could do that. There was plenty of time to fall apart when I got there. Here in the limo with no one but Riley's driver watching was a bad idea.

Chapter Four

The moment I entered my apartment, I turned the deadbolt, dropped my purse, kicked off my shoes, and padded toward the bathroom.

I needed to get out of my dress before it suffocated me. I needed a hot bath to stop my limbs from shaking.

I turned on the faucet over the tub, stripped out of my clothes, and pulled my hair up in a band on top of my head.

When I slid into the water, I sighed.

I closed my eyes and leaned back as the water rose around me.

The shaking wouldn't stop.

I was a ball of nerves.

Confusion wrapped around me, weighing me down. What the hell had Christine been talking about?

The woman was certifiable. How could Riley have ever been engaged to such a raving bitch? And he'd known her for over a decade. How could he have planned to marry a woman who would speak like she did to any other living human?

More proof that I had made the right decision when I told him I didn't want to date him.

I worried about my own sanity for being ferociously attracted to a man who found someone like Christine worthy of one minute of his time.

I took a deep breath. That crazy woman insinuated he beat her. That he would beat me too. In fact, she'd acted like he already had.

If he were abusive, why was he friends with Cade? And why hadn't Amy told me about Riley? Jesus, she'd known I was going out with him tonight. She might not have known I spent the evening with him at her engagement party, but Riley got first my number and then my address from Amy and Cade.

I lifted my arms out of the warm water and rubbed my temples.

Maybe Christine was lying.

The Game

That was certainly possible. She was obviously insane.

I needed to speak to Amy. And I dreaded the idea at the same time. I just wanted to go to bed and sleep for a week. Or at least for the weekend. I was suddenly exhausted.

When the water grew too cold and my skin was sufficiently wrinkly, I hauled myself out of the bath, wrapped in my favorite huge fluffy towel, and headed to the kitchen. I grabbed a bottle of water and then dug my phone from my purse on the way back to my bedroom.

It buzzed in my hand. When I swiped my thumb across the screen, I smiled. At least a dozen texts from Amy.

Of course.

Riley would have called her.

It buzzed again, this time an incoming call which I answered. "Hey."

"Girl, I've been calling you for an hour."

"Yeah, my phone was in my purse. My ass was in my tub soaking." I padded back to my room, dropped my towel, and climbed under my covers. Naked wasn't my usual sleeping style, but I just wanted to get under the blankets and ask Amy about ten thousand questions.

"So, what happened?"

"I'm guessing you know more than me since you're calling, but in a nutshell, Riley took me to Sky and tried to talk me into dating him, and then his certifiable ex-fiancée leaked her venom all around, and then I left. I'd be so grateful if you'd fill in the blanks."

"I didn't realize you were interested in Riley." Naturally, that's where Amy would choose to start the conversation.

I wasn't surprised. I blew out a breath. "We spent the majority of the evening together at your engagement party in April. I never told you because at the end of the evening he left without a word, and I never heard from him again."

"Why didn't you tell me?"

I shrugged, although she wouldn't be able to see me. "I don't know. It was sort of embarrassing. I mean, he's one of Cade's best friends." I lowered my voice as if someone could hear me. "I fell for him, Amy. He's smoking hot. He's polite, attentive, sexy. His smile melts me. I knew I had it bad for him within a few minutes of meeting him. And then he walked out on me. I didn't want to say anything."

"So, you saw him at the fundraiser Monday and

The Game

he asked you out?"

"Basically."

"Ah. That makes sense." She sounded excited.

"More like told me, but whatever. I knew it was a bad idea. I shouldn't have gone. He didn't really give me much of a choice though."

Amy giggled. "Yeah, that sounds like Riley. He's bossy. So, he took you to Sky and that tramp was there?"

"Yep. And she said some very interesting things. I had already told Riley I didn't want to see him again before she showed up." My memory flooded back. "Fuck. In fact, I even showed him my hand."

"What do you mean?"

I rubbed my palm down my face. Damn it. "I told him I was too attracted to him to date him."

"Is that even a thing?" Amy laughed again. "What does that mean?"

"It means I can tell he would break my heart if I let him. I don't fit into his world at all. And I can't control my libido around him. I just want him to jump my bones. It's unnerving how fucking sexy he is and what he does to me."

Amy's laughter was muffled as she must have covered the phone and then spoke to Cade. Then she was back. "We need to talk."

"We *are* talking."

"No. I mean really talk. There are things I need to tell you."

"Please don't tell me he's some sort of abuser, because if you do, I'll kick your ass for giving him my number."

"What? Of course not. Why would you think that?"

I inhaled deeply. "Some stuff Christine said."

"What the fuck did she say?"

"She implied that he was abusive."

"What?" Amy's voice rose to a near scream. "That fucking cunt."

"Yeah. That describes her."

"Riley would never lay a hand on anyone in anger, Cheyenne. Trust me."

I winced. He'd grabbed Christine's arm and dragged her from the bar.

"What exactly did she say?"

"Some shit about spanking and flogging and handcuffs. She thought my skin looked too sensitive to endure that sort of thing. I don't know. My adrenaline was pumping so hard by then, I might have misheard her. She was probably just spewing shit to try and shock me or get me to leave him. And that's fine. She can have him."

Amy didn't speak again for several seconds.

"Amy?"

"Yeah. Listen. Are you sitting down?"

"I'm in bed." I tried to flatten myself and release my tense muscles to no avail. "Just say what you need to say. I'm a big girl."

"He's not abusive, Cheyenne. He's a Dom."

"A what?"

"A Dom. A Dominant. Someone who practices BDSM."

"Okaaay. Seriously?"

"Yeah."

"And you know this why?"

She hesitated again.

Oh. Fuck me. "Cade is too."

"Yes."

"Jesus, Amy." I gripped the phone so hard my hand hurt.

"It's complicated. But don't judge me without educating yourself. It's not what you think. I love it."

"You mean you let Cade hit you and tie you up and stuff and this is a good thing?" I was stunned. This wasn't the girlfriend I thought I knew.

"It's not like that. It's consensual. And trust me, it's fucking hot."

"Uh-huh." My hand shook now. Who was this woman?

"God, Cheyenne. I wish I were there so I could take three days to explain it better. Listen, I'm not talking about abuse. I'm talking about submission. I willingly give my control over to Cade when we play, and he in turn rocks my world. I've never experienced anything so fulfilling."

I knew Amy well. "Amy, you never experienced anything at *all* before Cade. He was your first. How the hell can you possibly know what sex might be like for the less deviant." I was seriously concerned.

"Please. I know it's a lot to take in, but just calm down and look into it. I'll make arrangements for us to come down there next weekend. Don't freak out on me. Google BDSM and read about it. I don't want you to think I'm not making my own choices. I'll show you what it's all about next weekend. Okay?"

"Show me?"

"Sure. I'll have Cade take us to a club. You can see for yourself."

The Game

"A club? You mean a fetish club?"

"Yeah."

I wasn't sure I liked this plan at all. But on the other hand, I didn't want to ignore whatever one of my best friends was involved in if only for the sake of making sure she was safe. There was no fucking way some man was going to boss me around or tie me up, but the entire idea had become moot. My attention had shifted to Amy's safety. Not my own. "Okay."

"Okay? You'll look into it?"

"Yes. For you."

"Do it for you. Not for me."

Whatever…

Chapter Five

Cade and Amy took a half day from work the following Friday and drove to Atlanta from Nashville. Amy worked for The Rockwood Group. Cade owned it. They were still living in the condo Riley had purchased several years ago. When the dust settled after Riley broke up with Christine, and Amy and Cade reconciled their issues, Riley and Cade had agreed to swap homes and cities and jobs. It was a win-win for both parties. Amy wasn't willing to leave her new job in Nashville, and Riley needed to get as far away from Christine as possible.

When Amy explained all of this to me months ago, the story had been so convoluted it was difficult to follow, but I assumed I had the gist of it correct.

The Game

  Cade and Riley jointly owned three technology companies with their third partner, Parker, in Charlotte. I had only met Parker briefly the night of the engagement party. He'd arrived later, and Riley and I had already hit it off and were several beers into the party.

  To say the last week had been long and informative would be an understatement. I did spend a lot of time in the evenings reading everything I could get my hands on about BDSM. I was still extremely leery about Amy's lifestyle choice, but at least I no longer feared for her safety. Apparently most people practiced a very consenting form of dominance and submission.

  I did find myself squirming a few times as I read, especially when I saw pictures of people tied up and submitting to the hands of their Dom or Domme. It was titillating. I couldn't deny that much.

  I was grateful Riley left me alone. He didn't call or text once.

  I knew Amy had spoken to him and asked him to give me some time.

  The layers of issues I had with Riley piled up until the mountain was too high to climb. Nothing had changed about my feelings for him in the sense that I still had the hots for him on a purely base level. Now I had to add bondage and dominance to the list of things he enjoyed.

My hand shook as I tried to apply mascara. I kept smudging it and having to wipe it off my eyelid.

Amy and Cade were going to arrive any minute, and I wasn't ready. I wasn't sure I would ever be ready.

When the doorbell rang, I jumped.

"Jesus, Cheyenne, get a grip," I muttered under my breath.

I made my way to the front of the apartment and opened the door.

Amy burst through, dropped her bag, and pulled me into her embrace. "Missed you."

Cade stepped in behind her, an indulgent grin on his face.

I loved the way he looked at her—like he was the luckiest man alive. There was no way in hell Cade was abusing Amy in any way. I didn't believe it. On the other hand, I tried not to ponder what the two of them did together behind closed doors. It was their business, and it gave me the heebie jeebies.

My entire body relaxed as Cade shut the door. I didn't realize how nervous I'd been until I set my eyes on my friend and her fiancé and reassured myself she was

THE GAME

happy and adored.

Amy grabbed my hand and tugged. "Come on." She picked up the large bag she'd carried in and lured me toward my hall. "Let's get dressed. I'm going to rock your world."

I glanced down at my outfit. "I *am* dressed."

Amy rolled her eyes. "Not for where we're going."

Whoa. I glanced back at Cade, who rolled his eyes and shook his head. "I've created a monster."

When we got to my bedroom and shut the door, Amy dropped her bag on my bed and unzipped it.

"Where exactly are we going?"

"To a party. It's actually a private party. I know I said we'd go to a club, but friends of Cade are having a fetish party at their house tonight, so even better." She beamed as she unzipped her jeans and tugged them off her body, giggling. "Cade hates it when I wear jeans."

"Really?"

"Yeah. That's why I do it." She winked at me. Who was this friend of mine? I stood rooted to my spot, watching her pull her T-shirt over her head and grab things from the bag.

I hadn't changed clothes with Amy since college. She hadn't owned any underwear as sexy as what she wore

69

now. "Damn, girl. That's seriously sexy lingerie you have on."

She lifted her brows.

"Cade." I stated. Of course. "So…holy shit." I lost track of my line of thinking when Amy pulled a miniscule piece of material out of the bag and slinked into it. It was a dress, sort of. But it left nothing to the imagination.

"You like it?" She glanced down as she smoothed the material over her hips. It was black, thin, short, and revealing.

I stepped closer. "You look gorgeous. But damn. That's a lot of skin." The front hung low enough to expose the cleavage created by the lace bra she wore. The back crisscrossed over her skin, hugged her perfect ass, and landed barely below the globes.

Amy pulled out another dress. "This one's for you."

I held up my hands. "Wait. No way." I was dressed in a skirt and blouse and my fuck-me heels. That was bad enough for a night out with people I didn't know at a fetish party. I didn't need to make it worse.

"Yep. Come on. I bought it for you the other day. It'll fit you perfectly, and you'll make heads turn."

I stared at the item she held up with both hands

The Game

to display it more precisely. The top was halter style, the material so thin it would barely conceal my breasts. "I don't think I want to make any heads turn at a fetish party. Shit. You can't even wear a bra with that."

"Nope." She held it out. "Come on. I can't wait to see you in it."

I reached for the dress tentatively, figuring if I at least tried it on, I could prove she was crazy and get us one step closer to "hell no." "Fine. But I'm not leaving the house in that."

I laid it on the bed and undressed. When I popped my bra off, I shivered. This was insane.

Amy was right. It was exactly my size. It fell luxuriously over my skin. The material was so soft, I hardly noticed I was wearing anything.

Amy circled behind me and tied the top at the neck.

I inched over to my full-length mirror. It was a deep midnight blue, almost black. The silky material covered the parts that mattered most, barely. My breasts felt completely exposed. My nipples rubbed against the dress with every step. It hugged my slender stomach and then ended with a full skirt that hung obscenely short over my ass.

"There is no way I'm wearing this."

"Of course you are. It's fantastic. I'm jealous actually." Amy rounded me and stepped between me and the mirror. She held up a thong with two fingers. "Change into this. It matches the dress. Most female subs don't wear panties, but I knew you'd balk at the idea."

I scrunched up my nose. "I'm not super fond of thongs, Amy."

"Yeah, but do it this time. Trust me. You'll love the feeling. It's not like you're wearing jeans or something that will push the strap up in your ass. It's a dress. Trust me. You'll feel incredibly sexy with your ass bare. Just knowing what you don't have on under a dress can raise your arousal."

"And why would I want to be aroused?"

Amy shrugged. "Never know. Just being prepared." She grinned.

I slipped out of my normal bikini panties and stepped into the thong. It was little more than a few pieces of lace with a triangle that covered my most intimate parts.

And then I stared at myself in the mirror, taking deep breaths. "This is crazy, Amy. I don't belong in the fetish world."

The Game

"That's what Riley thinks. Let's prove him wrong."

My face flushed. "But he's *not* wrong." My hands shook as I adjusted the front of the dress. Every single movement brushed against my nipples. They stood at attention, sensitive and tight.

Through the mirror, I glanced at Amy. She was still smiling. "Just give it a try. I'm only asking you to go with us and watch. What's the worst that can happen?"

Chapter Six

My entire body trembled as I followed Amy and Cade through the front door of their friend's house. A man greeted us. He shook hands with Cade. Amy stood demurely next to her fiancé with her head bowed.

My trembling turned into a shudder as Cade set a hand on the bare small of my back and ushered me forward. "Cheyenne, this is Master Dillon. This is his house."

"Welcome." Dillon smiled broadly. "I'm sure Cade gave you the rundown, but it's pretty simple. House rules are easy. Safe, sane, and consensual is number one. Whatever safe word you choose is fine, but *red* trumps in my home. No piss play. No scat play. No blood.

The Game

No permanent marks. Other than that, have fun, look around, enjoy."

He swiped a hand farther into the foyer.

I held my breath. My head spun from that ridiculous list. Piss? Feces? Blood? Was he kidding?

"Amelia. Gaze on the floor. I'll handle Cheyenne from here."

I swallowed as Amy nodded. She'd gone by Amy for as long as I'd known her, but I'd heard Cade call her by her full name on many occasions. Apparently he liked it.

Cade took my elbow and led me farther into the house. Voices grew louder as we stepped into a giant great room filled with about two dozen people. Except for the unusual attire of many of the guests, it looked like any other party—people standing around talking in groups, drinking, snacking.

Cade leaned in to speak to me again. "You'll notice most of the submissives keep their heads bowed. It's normal if they're playing. Some of them may not speak much either. No one expects that of you tonight. Take everything in. I know it can be overwhelming at first, but watch."

I let my gaze travel around the room. Many of the women were dressed in similar revealing clothing. A few wore less. Two of them wore corsets that left their nipples exposed.

I swallowed hard. My heart beat fast.

Why was I here?

No way in hell was I going to date a man who wanted to control me. No matter what I'd read on Google, I couldn't see myself turning my will over to anyone—not even Riley.

My stomach clenched at the thought of Riley as a Dom. I closed my eyes for a moment and pictured him standing over me, his gaze boring into mine, his mouth a firm line. *This is what he does?*

I squirmed, shocked by my reaction to the thought of him controlling me. My pussy tightened and wetness leaked out to soak the tiny swatch of silk between my legs. I wanted to cross my arms over my chest, but decided that would look absurd.

Instead I gripped my hands into fists at my sides.

"Would you like a glass of wine?" Cade asked. "I don't let Amelia drink more than one glass when we're playing, but I'll go grab you each a drink if you want."

I nodded up at him. "Or the bottle," I muttered. This was like a game. An orchestrated game that consenting adults "played" in order to improve their sex?

The Game

He chuckled, kissed Amy on the forehead, and cupped her face. "At ease, baby. I'll be right back."

As Cade wandered toward the kitchen area, Amy stepped closer to me. "What do you think?"

"I think I'm in shock."

"When we get our drinks, we'll go downstairs. That's where the real action is. You can watch a few scenes."

"There's more?"

She giggled. "Of course. The basement will have areas staged for playing."

I could imagine what she meant. And it made me even more nervous. "How often do you do this sort of thing?"

"Parties? Not that often. Once a month. Maybe twice. We practice D/s at home."

I blew out a breath. *At home.* "How…exactly? If you don't mind me asking." I turned to face her more fully.

"I don't mind. Most evenings I submit to Cade. He makes decisions. I don't question him."

"Why?"

She smiled. "Because the sex is out of this world."

I stiffened. I would be lying to myself if I couldn't

see that. Just being in this room made me feel aroused.

"Does he spank you?"

"Sometimes. But not for punishment anymore."

"Anymore?" What the…?

Amy giggled again. "He tried to discipline me with spankings early on, but I liked it too much. Now he uses time outs when I'm disobedient." She shrugged. "And realistically that isn't very effective either. I spend most of the time wiggling in my spot, needy. The only thing unpleasant about it is being ignored. I hate being ignored."

I shivered. My best friend of over six years was dropping one bomb after another at my feet. I wondered if I ever knew her at all.

Her shoulders lowered. "I know this is a lot to take in, but just relax and look around. Open your mind. You might find aspects of BDSM you enjoy more than you can imagine."

I found that hard to believe, but on the other hand, I'd be lying to myself if I pretended I wasn't horny. In theory it was all well and good, but that didn't mean I would let anyone order me around.

Not even Riley.

****

The Game

I tried not to spill my wine while Cade led us downstairs. It was darker in the basement, and the atmosphere was extremely different. The first thing I noticed was how much quieter it was. People were standing around in groups on the edges of various scenes, but they were almost reverent.

A St. Andrew's Cross caught my attention. Cade left us to talk to someone he knew, and Amy and I stood to the left of the scene and watched.

Amy whispered in my ear. "The man on the cross is a sub."

"Oh." *Of course.* There was no law that said submissives had to be female. Duh.

"The guy circling him is a Dom. Not his own Dom, but an experienced one who people often request a scene with."

"You can do that?"

"Yep. As long as all parties agree. Cade wouldn't let another man lay his hands on me in this lifetime, but not everyone's Dom is as possessive."

I could see that with Cade. Even though I hadn't known he and Amy practiced BDSM, I had known Cade was attentive and almost overpowering. Now that I knew more about their relationship, it all made more sense.

Cade returned and threaded a hand into Amy's hair. "Amelia, I reserved a spanking bench for you."

Amy's expression sobered. "Yes, Sir."

Cade lifted an eyebrow. "I thought it would be easier for Cheyenne if she watched you participate. You okay with that?"

Amy nodded. "Yes, Sir."

I cringed at the way she said *Sir*, but I also knew it was part of the role playing. I just wasn't used to it—and certainly not coming from Amy.

I wondered how much clothing she would wear. Some of the women in the room were completely naked. It shocked me to picture Amy doing something like that in public. It was one thing for her to submit to her man at home, but here? Naked? Exposed to everyone? Yikes.

Cade led Amy away from the cross before I got a chance to see what the Dom had in mind. I followed behind my friends, watching the way Cade led Amy by the neck, possessive and loving at the same time.

Again, a rush of arousal spread through my body. Just watching Amy submit to Cade made things happen to my body that were entirely unexpected.

As we entered another room, Cade nodded toward the wide open doorway and met my gaze. "Stand wherever you're comfortable." He took my glass and set it on a high bar table just inside the door, undoubtedly noticing how badly I was shaking.

I leaned against the frame of the door, gripping it with one hand so tightly my fingers turned white. I needed to brace myself to avoid collapsing.

Cade slipped his hand from Amy's neck to her back, and then he settled his palms on her hips and lifted her onto the bench. It was like a small padded picnic table. The "table" portion was only about six inches wide. Her legs spread over the center and landed on padded areas on both sides. Her elbows did the same next to her head. She leaned on her right cheek, her hair falling over her face enough to curtain her from the room.

Apparently Cade didn't want her face covered, however, because he tucked the thick brown locks behind her ear and then kissed her cheek. He said something into her ear next. She smiled and nodded.

I melted a little more as Cade moved around her as if this were a performance. *A game*, I reminded myself.

My breaths were shallow as Cade stroked his palms up Amy's thighs and drew her skirt up over her ass. He set the loose material on her lower back, leaving her ass exposed to the room.

I was both shocked and horny. Holy shit this was hot. Every move Cade made increased my arousal. I squeezed my legs together, but nothing helped. It unnerved me that I was so turned on by this lifestyle. Was everyone as aroused as me? Or was I some sort of pervert?

The first time Cade's hand landed on Amy's skin, she flinched. So did I. And a rush of wetness released from my pussy. The second spank drew a soft moan from my lips, and I bit into the lower one to stifle the crazy reaction.

Several more spanks landed in succession across Amy's thighs and ass. Her skin turned pink. It looked warm. Cade stroked his palms down the backs of her legs and then up to grasp her butt cheeks, caressing them, molding them with his hands.

Amy's mouth hung open. Her eyes were closed. She looked like she could come at any moment.

As the next spank made contact, a hand landed on my bare lower back. I nearly jumped out of my skin, twisting to see who was behind me.

Riley.

His face was unreadable as his gaze met mine. In fact, I knew he was trying to read *me*. He pressed harder on my back and stepped into my space. He hesitated

The Game

about two seconds, and then his gaze darted to my mouth, and he leaned in and took my lips with his own.

The kiss was instantly deep and smoldering. I turned slightly to more fully face him, and he crowded me against the wall. His legs straddled mine as he consumed me with his mouth.

I grabbed his waist, angling my head to one side as he gripped my chin and directed my face.

His tongue plunged into my mouth to dance with mine. When he sucked gently, my knees buckled. That's how powerful the kiss was.

Riley pressed his body into mine to hold me upright. His free hand landed on my waist, spanning to cover the naked skin of my back with several fingers. All but his thumb.

His thumb landed just below my breast and stroked maddeningly against the lower swell.

I moaned, unable to stop the sound from escaping into his mouth.

His cock pressed into my belly, the huge length of it teasing me.

By the time he pulled back and released my mouth, I was a pile of goo. I had no muscle mass. He set his forehead against mine and searched my eyes. "Jesus,

Cheyenne."

I sucked in a deep breath, licking my swollen lips. "What are you doing here?"

"I was about to ask you the same thing."

"I came with Cade and Amy."

"I see that." He nodded subtly behind him where I assumed Amy was still getting spanked. "They failed to mention you'd be with them." He stroked his thumb over my bottom lip. "You're so fucking sexy." His eyelids lowered, and he took a long deep breath. "Did you know that every man in this room is staring at your hot body in that dress?" He plucked at the material just over my breast.

I fisted my hands in his shirt at his waist. "I might kill Amy."

"I'm betting she didn't know I was coming either. Cade told me they were coming. Not a word about you, however." He searched my eyes again. "I assume you've never been to one of these before."

"Why would you assume that?"

He smirked. "You were gripping the doorframe as if it wouldn't stand up on its own, and your eyeballs were bugging out of your head."

"How long have you been watching me?"

The Game

"Long enough." His thumb grazed the underside of my breast again. "Long enough that I couldn't stop myself from taking your mouth."

I inhaled deeply. My nipples puckered. My breasts felt heavier.

"Long enough to know I needed to claim you before anyone else moved in on you." Riley glanced down at my chest and moaned. He released my face and lowered his hand to grasp my waist on the other side until both hands now held me firmly beneath my breasts. "Hell, I can't even manage to feel sorry for kissing you like that. You're like a drug. Potent."

I arched into his touch. For so long I'd wanted him to touch me, kiss me, hold me. And now that it was real, I wasn't disappointed. His kisses were much better in person than I'd even imagined when I masturbated.

"I'm sorry about last weekend. Christine's a bitch."

"Yeah."

"I take it you called Amy and got the entire scoop."

"I did." It was so hard to concentrate on his words with his damn thumbs grazing my boobs. The soft silky material of my dress rubbed like sandpaper against my nipples. I tried to find some brain cells. "Why didn't you just tell me? Is this why you left me at the engagement party?"

"Yes." His hands rose higher, cupping my breasts. "Oh God, Cheyenne. I love how you respond to me."

I lifted onto my tiptoes, thrusting harder into his palms.

Suddenly he covered my breasts and pinched my nipples between his thumbs and forefingers.

I yelped at the shocking sensation. No one had ever pinched me like that.

"Oh, baby. You make me so fucking hard. Do you have any idea how sexy you are?"

I didn't respond.

Riley released my nipples but continued to graze them with his thumbs. "I need to see you."

I furrowed my brows. He was looking right at me.

"Naked, Cheyenne."

Naked.

If anyone would have told me I'd be in this position ten minutes ago, I would have laughed in their face.

Now?

Now I wanted whatever Riley requested.

I nodded, shocking myself.

The Game

Riley moaned. "Jesus."

I wasn't sure what upset him, but a tight expression took over his face. He released my breasts and stepped back, his hands still on my waist to steady me. "Have you seen enough yet?"

I blinked. That question was loaded.

"Of the party, I mean. Come home with me."

Should I? Leave with this man I'd only met on three occasions? None of which had ended well.

I leaned around him to find Cade lifting Amy off the bench. He set her on the floor and she inched toward us. "Riley. I didn't realize you'd be here."

"My fault, baby," Cade said as he tucked an arm around Amy's middle from behind. He kissed her shoulder. "I told him."

Amy grimaced at me. "You okay?"

"She's fine. Relax. I'll take it from here." Riley's voice was firm.

Amy inhaled sharply and then pursed her lips. She met my gaze.

I didn't have any idea what to say. My mind was still focused on Riley's words. *I'll take it from here.*

"I'm not sure public is the best place for Cheyenne to find her footing." Riley stepped to my side, one hand sliding around to flatten on the small of my back.

I was quite sure public would *never* be the best place for me to find *any* footing.

Amy nibbled on the corner of her bottom lip, not taking her gaze off me. She started to speak, her mouth opening, but Cade silenced her with a finger to her lips. "Let Riley handle this, baby. You know him. He's not going to do anything stupid."

She nodded, but her eyes still questioned me.

"She'll call you tomorrow," Riley said to Amy. Without another word, he turned me around and led me from the room and back toward the stairs. My legs were wobbly, but he kept his hand steady around my waist, guiding me expertly through the house and outside.

Chapter Seven

When we stepped into the night air, I took a deep breath as though the inside had been void of oxygen. Riley turned toward me and tucked a curl behind my ear. "You okay?"

I nodded. I wasn't sure, but I wasn't *not* okay either. I was so damn horny, that was all I could really concentrate on. I was no longer sure I cared about much of anything but wrapping my body around Riley's and sating my lust. I'd been drooling over the man in my head for half a year. It was time I actually got some.

Riley slid his hand down to grab mine and led me down the steps toward his car. His driver leaned against the hood and jumped to standing as we approached.

"Sorry, Les. I know I said I'd be a while, but I changed my mind. You can take us home now."

Les opened the back door, and Riley urged me forward.

I climbed into the back seat and scooted over to make room for Riley. He followed me. The second he was inside, before Les had even shut the door, he leaned over me, cupped my face, and kissed me again.

This time he was even more thorough than the first.

I melted into the seat as he thrust his tongue into my mouth. His lips were soft but demanding. He nudged my lips wider and proceeded to devour me.

We only separated when the car started moving. I found my hand on Riley's forearm, gripping tight.

He eased back against the seat, rubbing a hand over his face. He grasped my hand and settled our tangled fingers on my lap.

We rode in silence for several minutes, but when Riley stroked the skin of my inner thigh, I fidgeted.

"Sit still, baby."

I froze. Insanity. Three commanding words and I instantly rose to a new level of arousal. How was this possible?

The Game

Was I submissive?

How could I have not known this about myself?

Something about his tone and the deep pitch of his voice lulled me under his spell. I wondered again how it was possible I hadn't known this about him.

The car continued, smooth and silent. What did his driver know?

I flushed as I glanced at the front seat. Les's gaze was straight ahead, paying no attention to us in the back.

How many women had Riley brought home like this?

My leg bounced as nerves wormed their way under my skin.

Riley released my hand and flattened his palm over my thigh. "Cheyenne. Sit still. You drive me crazy wiggling around."

I inhaled sharply and held my breath.

Riley held my bare thigh. My skirt, which had been too short to begin with, rested way too close to my pussy, barely covering me in any sort of decent way. His hand lodged between my thighs, his pinky reaching toward my sex.

He turned and met my gaze. His expression was unreadable.

And then he smirked and shook his head. "You're like a genie escaping from a bottle. How did this happen?"

I had no response. I couldn't answer him any more than he could.

The car pulled to a stop in front of Riley's house, and we climbed out. Riley said something to his driver, and the man got back inside and pulled away.

I stared at the front of the house. I knew about his house. It had been Cade's before he and Riley swapped. Amy had learned everything she knew about submission inside this house.

And now it seemed I might follow in her footsteps.

Riley ushered me forward. He pulled his keys out of his pocket and let us in. When the door shut behind us, he glanced down at my hands. "Did you not have a purse?"

"No. Cade said I wouldn't need anything. I left it at home."

Riley nodded.

Shit. I didn't have anything. Not even a phone.

Riley stepped closer. He cupped my face and flattened me against the door. "Don't worry. You can use my phone to call Amy and let her know you're okay.

The Game

Relax. I'm not going to harm you. I'm just going to show you the ropes. See what works for you."

I didn't move. His lips were so close to mine. I wanted him to kiss me again.

He stepped back instead, tugged his phone from his pocket, touched a few things on the screen, and handed it to me. "There. Send Amy a text. She probably won't answer right now, but at least this way she'll know where you are and how to get in touch with you."

I took the cell from him with shaky fingers and quickly sent my friend a text. When I finished, Riley took it back and stuffed it in the pocket of his jeans again.

I hadn't considered what he was wearing yet. The man was so fucking sexy in jeans it made my mouth water. He wore a tight black designer T-shirt also. It displayed his pecs to perfection, making him seem larger than life.

"Come." He took my hand again and led me through the foyer and deeper into the house. When we reached the living room, I glanced around. It was attached to the kitchen. Both rooms were done in grays and blacks and whites. It was luxurious and inviting at the same time.

Riley led me to the center of the plush carpet and

released me. He circled me slowly. Finally, he leaned down and removed my heels one at a time, setting them under the coffee table. "You're unsteady. I don't want you to fall." He righted himself and then sat on the coffee table.

I fisted my hands, not sure what else to do.

"Stand tall, baby. Shoulders back. Clasp your hands at the small of your back."

I followed his instructions, a tight ball forming in the pit of my stomach. Need.

"Spread your legs wider."

I stepped out, shakily. This was so surreal.

My mind raced. All I could think about was the need growing inside me, keeping the scrap of lace between my legs wet and threatening to leak around the edges.

Not for the first time, my chest felt tighter than normal. With my arms behind me, my breasts jutted outward, the nipples puckering once again.

"Look at me, Cheyenne."

I met his gaze.

"If I had known…" He hesitated and then shook his head. "When I met you, I had no idea you were so submissive."

"I—"

"Don't deny it. I know it's a new and foreign

The Game

concept for you, but don't try to refute it. It's real. You're living proof. I bet you're so wet right now, my hand would come away soaked if I reached between your legs."

I bit my lip. He was right.

"Don't do that. Let your lip go. Open your mouth."

My lips trembled as I obeyed him. "I'm nervous."

"I know, baby." He leaned forward, putting his elbows on his knees.

"And unsure."

"Expected."

"Are you going to hurt me?"

He gasped. "Never."

"I mean spank me or whatever. Amy said Cade spanks her. He also makes her stand in a corner. That sounds so absurd to me right now, I'm shaking."

"I'm not going to spank you tonight. And I would never hurt you. The only time I will ever lay a hand on you will be for your pleasure or to discipline you."

More wetness when he said the word "discipline." I shuddered at the implication. A tear crept unbidden into the corner of my eye. What was happening to me?

Riley jumped to his feet and stepped in front of me. He brushed his finger across my cheek to catch the tear. "Baby, don't cry. Calm down. Deep breaths. I know it's overwhelming, but that's because it's so new. Unexpected. I'm not going to maul you. I'm just giving you a taste of what to expect if you stay with me."

Stay with him... I wasn't sure what he meant by that exactly.

"You okay?"

I nodded, and he stepped back. "I'm going to pour you a drink, to help calm your nerves. Don't move."

Riley headed across the room and into the kitchen area of the enormous great room. He rounded the phenomenal island and ducked down beneath the counter. I bet he had a wine fridge under the surface where I couldn't see.

Sure enough, he stood and reached for a fancy electric cork screw. Moments later he had two glasses on the counter and was filling them with white wine.

Taking one glass in each hand, he returned. "You can let your hands go, baby." His voice was gentle as he held out a glass.

I took it, trying not to shake, and then sipped the wine. It was delicious.

"You like it?"

"God yes." Or maybe I needed a drink so badly

anything would have been welcome. I doubted that, however. This bottle of wine was probably more expensive than the last ten bottles I drank put together. And judging by the taste, I was definitely right. Who knew it made that much difference?

Riley sat on the couch this time, leaning back, kicking his shoes off, and propping his feet on the coffee table. "I want you to remain standing to keep you in the zone. But don't lock your knees."

I didn't know what that meant, but I took another sip and tried not to shake so badly that wine sloshed out of the glass.

"I'm sure you have questions."

"About a thousand."

He smiled. "Let me try to answer some of them." He ran his finger over the rim of his glass. "I'm a Dom. You were rudely informed of that fact by Christine. I'm sorry about that. She's obviously got issues. She was also a horrible sub. I have no explanation for why I wasted so many years with her."

I flinched. I imagined I too would make a horrible sub.

"In retrospect, I should have seen the signs. Hell, Cade knew she was a fraud. He should have told me. But then again, I had blinders on, so I might not have listened to him."

I took another drink, letting the cold liquid soften me a bit more. I wasn't sure it was working. "Why did you stay so long?"

He ran a hand over his face. "I'm an idiot, apparently."

How could he not know?

"She played a game. She was only in it for the money. She faked like she cared about me the entire time. When I started in this lifestyle, she followed. She didn't submit to me well, but she tried. I thought it was enough."

I nodded and took another sip. It was going down too easily.

"After we split, I knew she had been faking. I Dommed for other submissives over the next few months. They were nothing like her." He closed his eye and then opened them. "And then I met you."

I held my breath.

He smiled. "God I wanted you. From the moment I saw you, I wanted you. But I knew you weren't in the lifestyle. And I knew you were way too innocent for this scene." He grinned. "Obviously I'm a poor judge of character."

I watched his face.

"I thought about taking you home that night and having a normal sexual encounter. I thought about dating you. I even pictured changing my ways to accommodate your innocence. But it would have been a lie to fuck you as if I were vanilla without saying anything. So, I took the coward's path.

"I walked away from you that night because you were so damn perfect. And so young. And so naïve. I wanted you. Badly. I'd only been single for a matter of months. You were so full of life. Fun. Youthful. Gorgeous. You looked like you walked off a fucking magazine every time I saw you."

I said nothing. He had more to say. And I wanted to hear it. That was a line I'd heard before. It didn't faze me.

"By the end of that evening, I wanted to fuck you senseless. So badly I knew I wouldn't be able to control myself if I didn't get the hell out of there. So I ran. Like a coward. I left you sitting there wondering where the hell I was. I'm an asshole. And I'm so sorry."

"You could have just told me."

"Yeah. I should have. But then again, what if I

had stood there at Cade and Amy's engagement party and told you I was a Dominant? And I wanted you to submit to me?"

I nodded. He was right. That wouldn't have gone over well.

"And then there was the fact that you knew nothing about Cade and Amy's arrangement. It wasn't my place to tell you. That was up to Amy." He glanced up and down my body until I felt naked. "Hell, you're still so fucking innocent. I can't believe I'm even entertaining the idea of dominating you."

I shuddered again. My body was under his spell. I wished he would stop talking about dominating me. Every time he said a word, it went straight to my pussy.

"I've thought about you non-stop since that night. I've masturbated in my shower more times than I can count."

That did it. My knees buckled. I lowered myself to the floor and set my glass on the coffee table. I slumped forward, putting my hands on the carpet in front of me.

Riley watched me. He didn't comment. Instead he kept talking, his voice lower, softer. "When I saw you at that fundraising meeting the other day, I swallowed my tongue."

"Me too."

"I wanted to yank you into a closet and fuck you senseless."

"Me too."

He groaned. "Don't say that. I'm trying to be a gentleman."

I couldn't imagine why.

"I'm not going to fuck you, Cheyenne."

I jerked upright.

He shook his head. "I mean it. Not tonight. I don't think I can ever go without you after I take you. You're like a drug to me. Once I taste you, I won't be able to let you go."

So don't.

"I'm a Dom. That isn't going to change. I've known it for years. I need a woman who can submit to me. I realize now I would have been miserable even under the best of circumstances with Christine. She was a horrible submissive, mostly because she was faking it. You… You might be submissive."

I stared at him. Was I? Really? Or was I just so fucking horny and I'd lusted after him for so long that he seemed like an Adonis? Maybe he was an asshole inside. Maybe I couldn't be what he needed.

"I'd like to explore that possibility. Would you do that for me?"

I swallowed the lump in my throat. "Do what exactly?"

"Submit to me. Try it out. See if it works for you."

"Yes." It was the only possibly answer. I stated that one word firmly.

Time stood still. Seconds ticked by. Finally, Riley spoke. "I feel like I've won the lottery."

"Maybe *I* have."

Chapter Eight

Silence stretched forever it seemed. We stared into each other's eyes and breathed heavily. I wasn't sure what to do next.

Finally, Riley cleared his throat. "Stand up, baby."

I struggled to my feet and resumed the stance he'd put me in before. I clasped my hands together in front of me.

He stood also and stepped around the coffee table to circle me again. When he came up behind me, he clasped my wrists and tugged them apart. "Set them at your sides. Don't move them."

I let my arms hang loose at my sides.

Riley flattened his palms on my bare back and

stroked my skin. Goose bumps rose in their wake. His fingers eased around to my sides and slithered under the material covering my breasts. In painstakingly slow motion, he gently cupped my breasts. "This is the sexiest dress I've ever seen."

"Amy got it for me," I choked out, fighting the urge to moan as my nipples puckered under his thumbs. I arched into his hands.

"She's got good taste." He smoothed his hands over my breasts until he reached my shoulders. "Dip your head, baby."

I lowered my gaze to the floor.

Riley untied the silk at my neck—the only thing holding the dress up. When he released the two ends, the entire dress slid to the floor, leaving me in nothing but my thong.

I flinched, fighting the urge to cover myself. My breath caught at the cool air in the room and the extreme exposure.

Riley stepped between my legs and flattened his palms on my belly, pinning my arms at my sides. His lips landed on my shoulder. "Jesus. Your skin is perfect." He spread one hand up to cup a breast. The other inched toward my pussy and paused just above the tiny strap of my thong.

His cock pressed into my back.

His top hand left my breast to spread over my neck. He pressed on my chin to push my head back onto his shoulder. "How many men have you been with?"

The question was unexpected. I sucked in a breath. My head swam.

"Cheyenne. How many?"

"Two," I whispered.

He hissed. "When?"

I swallowed. I was all but naked. The sexiest man I'd ever set eyes on had his arms wrapped around me from behind, holding me against him possessively, and he wanted to discuss my other partners?

"When, Cheyenne?" His voice was softer. Gentle. He stroked the thin skin at my neck.

"One in high school. One in college."

"How long ago?"

"Four years." I hated admitting that. It made me look ridiculous. But he didn't give me much of a choice.

He blew out a breath. "Jesus." His lips landed on my bare shoulder again. He nibbled a path to my ear and sucked my earlobe into his mouth. "I'm going to make you forget both of them."

"That won't be hard," I muttered, letting my head loll against his shoulder.

He smiled. I felt it against my neck. And then his forehead landed on my shoulder. "You're going to be the death of me."

"I hope not."

Riley released me so quickly I teetered. He rounded to face me, leaving about two feet between us. "Clasp your hands behind your back again."

I managed to obey him somehow, grabbing one wrist with my other hand.

"Shoulders back. Breasts high."

I held my breath as I did his bidding.

"So fucking sexy. You have the most perfect breasts I've ever seen." He reached out and flicked one nipple.

I flinched as it jumped to attention.

"And so responsive." His fingers danced down my belly toward my pussy. "Did Amy buy you this thong too?"

"Yes."

He smirked. "Then you aren't particularly attached to it?"

"No…" What did he have in mind?

The Game

He slipped one finger slowly under the thin lace on one hip and tugged hard. The thong broke easily. He collected it in his hand and brought it to his nose, inhaling long and slow. "You smell delicious."

I nearly died. No man had ever so blatantly brought my panties to his face. Heat crept up my cheeks.

"Spread your legs wider."

I stepped out, though it was difficult. I was concerned about the ability to remain upright again.

"Are you wet for me?"

"Yes."

"May I check?"

I wanted nothing more. "Please." My pussy clenched in anticipation.

Riley made no move to touch my sex, however. Instead he circled me again and stood behind me. Had he only been asking out of curiosity? Did he know the question made me even hornier?

Undoubtedly.

"Your ass is so fine." He cupped the globes and massaged them. Just as quickly, he released me and rounded back to the front.

He blew on my nipples until they stood at attention once more.

The wetness between my legs was out of control. I was going to come without any contact if he kept this up. Maybe I was indeed incredibly submissive. The concept was still foreign to me. "Touch me."

"When I'm ready. Not when you ask." He lifted his gaze. "Submit to me. Give me the control, Cheyenne. Then you won't have to make requests. Turn over the reins. You already know how good it will be, don't you, baby?"

"Yes." He was right. I'd never been so fucking horny.

"It gets so much better."

"Why?"

"Why what?"

"Why do you want to dominate me?"

"Because I love the way you look when you're so needy you can hardly stand up. I love knowing I've made your pussy so wet it's leaking down your legs. I love the flush across your chest and the sharp points of your nipples from my words alone."

Was that what submission was all about? Because I was on board for all of that.

"BDSM is all about power. It's really simple. When we play, I want you to give your power to me.

The Game

Submission is very misunderstood. The Dom doesn't hold the power. The sub does. You have to give it to me. I can't take it. If you don't hand over the power willingly, that's a different game altogether. I'm asking you to give me that control."

"All the time?" I licked my dry lips.

"No. Only within the time periods we agree to."

I could do that. It was possible. Or at least the results would be something I couldn't give up if I wanted to.

"Don't think too hard. You aren't making a decision tonight. I just want to play with you. Give you a taste. Let you think on it."

"I need you to make love to me."

He leaned down and kissed my nipples, one at a time. "I know. And I'm not going to fuck you tonight, baby."

I flinched. Was he for real?

"It would kill me if I slid into your pussy and then you changed your mind. I can't do it. And I won't. I'm going to rock your world as if I had though."

Oh. My. God.

"Submit to me."

Wasn't I?

"Submit to me, Cheyenne. Give up your control. Let me show you what it's like."

"Okay."

"I won't leave any permanent marks on your body. You have my word. Let me take you someplace you've never dreamed of."

"Okay," I repeated. I was naked in the living room of the man I'd lusted after for six months. It wasn't like I could deny him anything.

"When we play, I want you to call me Sir."

This was like an intricate game. "Okay…Sir." I shivered. The word was foreign on my tongue.

"Not *okay*, but *yes*, Sir."

I licked my lips. "Yes, Sir," I whispered.

"Good girl." He kissed my lips briefly. "Do you know how hard my cock is, Cheyenne?"

"You could show me," I teased.

He chuckled. "Wouldn't you like that?"

"Yes."

"Yes, what?"

"Yes, Sir," I amended.

"That's better. I like the way it sounds coming off your lips."

"I heard Amy call Cade Sir earlier."

The Game

"Yes. He's a pretty firm Dom himself. From what I hear, she gives him a run for his money, but he puts her in her place."

"She said she enjoys spanking and he stopped using it for punishment. I can't even wrap my head around that idea."

"You will." He danced his fingertips down my chest, teasing my nipples.

I clenched my butt cheeks together at the thought of him hitting me. "How do you know? What if I hate it?"

"I can read you well."

"What if I'm not submissive enough?"

He chuckled again. "You're so submissive. There's no chance it isn't enough."

I shivered. "Then why not just sleep with me?"

Riley smoothed both hands down to my thighs. "I'm not the one who needs to be sure. You are."

I blinked. "I've never been more sure of anything in my life."

"Oh, I know you want my cock inside you. What I need is for you to be certain you can give it up to me on a daily basis without warning and through submission. I'm not the one with doubts. You are. You're thinking if you play your cards right, I'll fuck you. But it won't work that way. When I'm certain you know you're mine and you're willing to give up your free will to me in the bedroom, then I'll take you. Not before."

"Just in the bedroom? We aren't in the bedroom now," I taunted.

"Semantics."

"What about the front porch? The car? The back of the movie theater? How far does your bedroom extend?"

He grinned wide. "Baby, my bedroom extends to wherever we want. I'm a good judge of what you're able to handle. Trust me."

"Make me." I had no idea why I blurted that out, but as soon as the words left my mouth, Riley's face grew sober. He took my hand and turned around, leading me from the room, down the hall, and through the second door on the left.

I glanced around, realizing this had to be his bedroom. I sucked in a breath when I saw the king-sized bed. Wide slats on both ends of the missionary-style bed spoke to their possible uses. I flinched and rubbed my wrists.

"Lie down on the bed sideways, Cheyenne. And

The Game

spread your legs wide for me. I want a good view of your pussy."

I climbed onto the mattress, shaking like a leaf. His dirty talk pushed the edges of my sanity, shocking me while driving me wild with need. I lay down on my back, drew my knees up to my chest, and spread them open.

"Good girl. I like how you obey me without pause. That will earn you a reward. Now hold your knees high and wide with your hands, baby. Open."

He knew exactly what he was doing. I had no doubt. At this point, a slight breeze could set me off.

Riley stepped closer. His gaze landed on my pussy. No one had ever scrutinized me like that. The two men I'd slept with years ago had been more like boys. The first one, Jacob, had been a virgin also. We'd floundered together, the experience a total fail. The second man I'd slept with had only cared about himself and getting his own rocks off. The moment he came, he was done. Neither man had left me wishing for another round.

Until I met Riley, I had very little interest in having sex with anyone else.

Now I was literally shaking under the gaze of a man I knew could fulfill any fantasy I'd ever had…and then some.

Riley set one finger on my thigh and stroked it toward my center.

I bit my lower lip, pleading silently for him to touch my clit. Anywhere really.

"You're so wet, baby." He grazed his finger through my folds, making me arch my ass off the bed in response. "Stay still. Let me explore."

"Riley…" I purred his name.

He lifted his finger. It glistened with my juices. And then he sucked it into his mouth and moaned. "Delicious." His gaze met mine. "Let me shave you."

"What?" My eyes bugged out.

"Let me shave you, Cheyenne. I love the look and feel of a smooth pussy. I promise you'll love it too. The bare skin leaves you feeling exposed. It will ensure you think of me often when we aren't together."

I wanted him to make love to me.

He wanted to shave me?

He grinned. "I promise it will drive you wild."

I licked my dry lips and continued to stare at him. My hands shook where they held my legs open. I'd never shaved down there. I trimmed, but I had never taken a razor to my sensitive skin. How could I let someone else do it?

Was he testing me?

It was just hair. Who cared?

Finally, I nodded. "Okay." My voice was small and squeaky. I was freaked out.

Riley turned and left the room. I released the grip on my thighs and let them lie parted on the bed. My nipples hardened further as the air circulating in the room brushed over them. I crossed my arms over my chest and squeezed my breasts against my body. The pressure eased some of my tension and left me feeling slightly less exposed.

Riley returned. "Arms above your head," he commanded. "Don't cover yourself."

I tentatively released my breasts and lifted my hands toward the headboard. My chest rose with the action. I thought I would faint under his gaze.

He set several items on the bed and then tapped my hip. "Lift up a little, baby. Let me slide this towel under you."

I dug my heels into the bed and lifted. As I settled back down, Riley squirted a glob of shaving cream on his palm.

"I'm not sure…"

He met my gaze. "That's the entire point. *I'm* sure.

Let yourself relax into my care."

I swallowed and closed my eyes.

The second his hand landed on my pussy, I moaned. I was going to come. There was no way he could possibly shave me without making me come. And that idea embarrassed me.

"Stay still, baby." His fingers stroked through my hair, spreading the shaving cream around. "I know you're aroused. Control the need. Let me work."

My entire body went rigid as he pressed my legs open wider, my knees bent at an angle that left me too exposed.

"Don't move. I don't want to nick your skin." He held me steady with one hand, pulling my skin tight. With the other hand, he dragged the razor over my mound.

I held my breath.

Every stroke across my skin left me more naked.

Riley worked in silence from top to bottom. By the time he was done, I was a ball of need ready to explode. The only thing that kept me from coming was his avoidance of my clit. He didn't touch the bundle of nerves until he was completely finished, and then only to clean me up with a warm, wet cloth.

The Game

I moaned as he wiped my skin of the last of the shaving cream. The air in the room hit my freshly bared skin and caused my clit to jump to attention.

Riley set his tools aside, wrapped in the towel, and danced his fingers over my nudity. "So soft. So unbelievably sexy." He tapped the hood of my clit, making me jump. "So responsive. Now you really deserve a reward. I'm so proud of you." Before I knew what he had planned, his mouth descended. Instantly his lips were wrapped around my pussy, sucking, licking, teasing.

My hands shot forward to press against his head. It was too much. I was too sensitive. Or perhaps I was just shocked. No man had ever gone down on me. Hell, I hadn't ever given a blow job either.

Riley ignored my hands threaded into his hair and gripped my thighs, holding them wider, pinning me to the bed.

I squirmed to escape his mouth, mortified at the way he moaned around my pussy.

When his tongue thrust into my sheath, I screamed. "God. Riley. Oh. My. God." I pressed harder against his head. I was going to come. Like a tidal wave, the sensations crashed around me, building with each second.

And then he sucked my clit into his mouth and flicked the tip rapidly with his tongue.

I shot off immediately, my pussy pulsing, grasping at nothing. My clit throbbed inside his mouth as he continued to torment the little nub with his lips and tongue. He didn't ease off until I was completely sated.

With one final reverent kiss to my center, he lifted his face. "Cheyenne, that was the single sexiest thing I've ever seen in my life. Thank you." He blew across my sex, making me flinch.

My hands slipped from his head to the bed at my sides. I didn't have the strength to close my legs. He was the first man to see me come.

Riley, still fully clothed, climbed up my body, nestled between my legs and held my head between his hands. "Stay. Be mine. Let me show you what my world is all about. Give me the weekend. Then you can decide."

Chapter Nine

I awoke with a start. Something was caressing my nipple. I reached up with one hand and found another larger hand covering my breast.

Riley.

I flushed. He brought that out in me often.

My back was snuggled against his front where we lay spooned on our sides. His top leg was lodged between mine, forcing my knee to be bent high.

And his hand was stroking the skin of my breast, his thumb rubbing across my nipple in a steady rhythm.

I arched into his touch, wetness leaking between my legs. My fingers grasped at his on top of my chest.

"Riley…"

"Mmm." He nibbled a path up my neck to my ear. "Even your skin is sweet."

I writhed beneath him.

He held me tighter, pinching my nipple and then plucking it outward. The sharp pain was immediately eased when he released the tip and thrummed it again. "Love the little noises you make."

"I need you. How long is this moratorium on sex going to last?"

He chuckled. "Not going to fuck you. But if you need me inside you, I'd be happy to oblige between those sweet lips of yours." He smoothed his hand up my chest and ran his thumb across my bottom lip.

I hesitated. I'd never given a blow job. What if I didn't do it right?

"No one's been in here, have they, baby?"

I shook my head. My tongue slipped out to lick my lips, bumping into Riley's thumb.

He slid his thumb into my mouth. "Suck, baby."

I drew him in, swirling my tongue around the tip and sucking.

Riley moaned. "Jesus. That's all there is too it." He plucked his thumb out. "Enough practice."

I twisted around until I was on my back, facing

him. The dim light from outside filtered through the window. We hadn't closed the blinds when we went to sleep.

I wondered what time it was, knowing it was the dead middle of the night. We hadn't been asleep long. Nevertheless, I felt rested and wide awake. The prospect of tasting Riley's cock had me on full alert. "I'd like that."

He grinned, his eyes rolling. "You're killing me." He flopped onto his back and hauled me over the top of him. "I won't do anything to control you this first time. Don't feel pressured. This isn't a demand. Just do what feels natural. If you don't like it, stop."

I sat next to him, my gaze wandering down his naked chest and lower. The sheet had pulled away. He'd hardly given me a chance to ogle his body before we went to sleep. I'd been sated after the shaving and ensuing intense orgasm. When Riley had slipped into bed to spoon at my back, I'd snuggled closer and let him envelop me. The most I knew about the size of his dick was from feeling it pressing against my butt.

I shoved the sheet completely away from him and then crawled lower to sit next to him. His cock bobbed in the air, fully erect and significantly larger than either of my two previous partners. When he did finally take me, the stretch would be tight.

Setting my hands on his belly and thigh, I leaned forward. I flicked my tongue over the tip of his cock first, gathering the leaking precome and tasting his essence. Salty. The desire to possess this man with my mouth in the same way he had done to me consumed me.

I didn't hesitate. I closed the distance and sucked him deep into my mouth.

Riley's hand landed on my head. His fingers burrowed into my hair. "Jesus. God. Cheyenne." His voice trailed off.

The tone of his voice gave me the strength to continue. He was aroused. I did this to him. I stroked the thick vein on the underside of his cock with my tongue as I pulled off and then sucked him back in.

"Baby... Lord. Slow down. I'm going to come too fast."

I didn't frankly care how fast he came. In fact, I loved the power I had over him. And it was only fair after the way he'd consumed my pussy last night. I let my cheeks cave in as I sucked him in deeper.

Riley groaned loudly. His body stiffened beneath my hands. He gripped my hair and tugged on my head. "You need to release me baby. I'm going to come." His words were gritted out. And I had no intention of obeying that command. Somehow I didn't think he would mind this particular disobedience.

When I lowered my face to consume him more fully, he released my hair and stroked the back of my head instead. "Ahh, baby. Jesus." His cock stiffened further, and then he came, his come shooting down my throat.

For a second I was shocked by the force, and my gag reflex kicked in, making it difficult to breathe. And then I swallowed in rhythm with each pulse of his cock, suckling his length until he was spent.

He didn't go completely flaccid. Instead, his shaft remained almost rigid inside me as I slipped off. Sudden embarrassment slammed into me. I didn't even know why. I'd sucked him off. He hadn't complained. In fact, he'd seemed to rather enjoy the act. I had no explanation for the flush creeping up my cheeks.

Riley reached for my face, cupped both sides, and nudged my head to lift. "Look at me, Cheyenne."

I lifted my gaze.

"That was unbelievable. I'm so honored."

I nodded.

"Come here."

I crawled up beside him, my face level with his.

He pulled me into his side with a hand wrapped around the back of my neck and angled my lips to his.

The kiss was powerful. Our first kiss, last night at the party, had been all-consuming. This one was different. It reached deep inside me as if he were communicating with me through our lips. I lifted my top leg and threw it over his. My pussy ground into his thigh. The instantaneous renewed arousal shocked me.

He deepened the kiss further, sucking my tongue into his mouth and then thrusting his own into mine in a way that made me long to have him inside me. Teasing. Tempting. Torturing me.

When I pulled back to gasp for air, I realized I had been grinding my pussy against his thigh. I was soaked, my clit throbbing with need.

I gasped and stopped moving, biting the inside of my cheek at the arousal that pulsed through my body. No way was I going to beg him to fuck me. But it was hard.

"Don't stop." His hand slipped down to my bare ass and pressed me against him. "I love the little noises you make when you're aroused."

I lowered my gaze. No way was I going to masturbate against his leg. Not now that I was conscious of the act.

The Game

"Cheyenne, I want you to come. Continue."

I shook my head. "I'm good."

Before I had even a second to catch my breath, Riley bolted to a sitting position and hauled my small frame across his lap, face down.

I gasped. My belly rested on his legs. My breasts hung over one side. I pressed into the mattress with my hands, trying to lift off him, but he held me down with a hand to my back.

His other hand smoothed over my ass. "I have rules, Cheyenne."

I held my breath. What was he going to do?

"I want you to submit to me. I want you to get the full experience this weekend. In order to do that, you have to let go and obey me. If not, we'll have accomplished nothing."

I whimpered and squirmed against him, hating that in this position of submission I was more aroused than I had been grinding my pussy against his thigh moments ago.

"Do you understand?"

I nodded. Though I wasn't sure what I was agreeing to.

"Words, Cheyenne."

"I understand," I lied.

He pinched my ass, making me squeal. "What I want to hear from you is 'yes, Sir.' In addition, I never want you to lie to me. I won't tolerate lying."

"I… Yes, Sir."

"I'm going to spank you now."

I stiffened, another whimper escaping my lips. "I'm not sure I'm ready for that."

"That's okay. *I'm* sure. And in the future, you'll think twice before you lie to me."

"I didn't—"

He cut me off. "Stop while you're ahead, baby. Never tell me you don't need to come when I can clearly see you do. And never insinuate you have understood a directive when it's obvious you have not. If something isn't crystal clear to you, ask for clarification."

Damn he was astute. "Yes, Sir."

"Take a breath and let it out."

I managed that simple task.

His hand lifted off my cheeks and landed a sharp stinging slap.

I winced.

He rubbed the spot with his palm. "Did that hurt?"

The Game

I shook my head. It shocked me, but it didn't really hurt.

"See? It's all in your head. Concentrate on my palm against your skin. Nothing else." He landed another blow.

I flinched, but it wasn't as bad as the first.

A third spank met with the junction of my thighs and my ass cheeks, shocking me with the powerful combination of pain and pleasure so close to my sex. I moaned before I could stop myself.

Riley chuckled. "Don't come, baby. You don't have permission to come while I'm punishing you."

A deep burn crawled up my face.

He held me firmly against his lap and continued to spank me three more times.

My pussy pulsed with need. My face ticked with embarrassment.

And then he rubbed my ass with his hand, molding the tender flesh.

I slumped against his thighs, letting my breasts press into the mattress, my forehead against the sheet. I fisted my hands at the sides of my face, breathing heavily.

Riley lifted me, turned me around, and cradled me against him like a child. He brushed the hair from my face and tucked it tenderly behind my ear. "You did well, baby. I'm proud of you."

I blinked up at him, my emotions all over the place.

"What are you thinking?" He smiled. "And be honest."

"That's humiliating."

He nodded. "That's the idea. It wouldn't be an effective punishment if it wasn't."

"I didn't like it."

"Good."

I bit my lower lip. This was the strangest conversation I'd ever had. The man—this Dom—was rocking me against his chest in the middle of the night after spanking my bare ass for lying to him.

Crazy.

His hand landed on my thighs. "Spread your legs, baby."

I braced myself against him and wiggled to free myself, wishing he would put me down. The arm wrapped behind my back held firmer. "Open for me. Don't make me repeat myself, Cheyenne."

As if I were a puppet, I spread my sex open.

Riley reached between my legs and stroked his

fingers through my pussy. "So wet. Jesus, baby. You're so needy."

He pushed two fingers into my sheath and curled them forward so they pressed against my G-spot.

I writhed, reaching forward to grasp his hand and push at it. The last thing I wanted was for him to realize how horny I was right after being spanked.

"Let go of my hand, baby."

I tucked my face against his chest and dug my heels into the mattress.

Riley held steady with his fingers deep inside me. "Move your hands away, Cheyenne." His voice was firm. Commanding.

I let go, my fingers shaking.

"Good girl. You need the release. It's perfectly normal after being spanked. Sometime I'll grant that need. Other times I'll leave you needy. You will not choose."

I shivered, uncertain what to do with my hands.

"Pinch your nipples for me, baby. Bring them to stiff peaks while I fuck you with my fingers."

I shuddered.

He reached deeper, too slowly, his palm flattening against my pussy, the base grinding into my clit and holding steady. "Nipples. Make them hard. Don't hesitate."

I lifted my shaky fingers to my tits and caressed them. They seemed far more sensitive than reasonable. A low moan escaped my lips as I took each nipple between my thumbs and forefingers and squeezed.

"That's it. You keep them hard, and I'll keep fucking you." His hand moved again, pulling out and thrusting back in.

I tried to lift my pelvis, arch upward, but to no avail.

He held me steady and fucked me fast and hard with his hand. In seconds I was at the peak. His thumb landed on my clit and pressed.

My head rolled back against his arm. Like a completely wanton slut, I pinched and plucked my own nipples for the man—partly because I enjoyed the slight sting of the pain, but also because I wanted to come so badly it overrode any other thought.

And then I was right there, my body rigid, my heels pressing deeper into the mattress. My mouth fell open and I shattered, moaning with every pulse of my sex as though there were a connection between the gripping of my sheath and the sound from my lips.

The Game

"That's it, baby. That's a good girl." He leaned down and planted a kiss on my forehead. "So sexy. You're like a breath of fresh air. When you come, it's like it's always the first time."

I pursed my lips. He didn't need to know I hadn't come many times in life and never with a man.

"Fuck. Nobody has ever made you come before."

I squeezed my eyes shut. He was way too astute.

"Not before me last night." He rocked me forward and backward, removed his fingers from my sex, and cradled me closer. His face buried in my hair. "I won't survive this thing if you leave me," he mumbled. "I thought I could hold my sanity in check if we didn't have sex. But I'm too far gone already. I can't let you go."

I let him rock me. He wasn't the only one who wouldn't survive. I could never leave him. At the moment I couldn't imagine separating from him to brush my teeth or shower. I had a lot to learn, and I wasn't sure I would like all of it, but leaving wasn't an option. I would learn his ways.

Already he'd driven me to the highest peak imaginable. And he hadn't used his cock on me yet. I was lost to him. No man would ever measure up. No man would ever look into my eyes with the same deep longing

BECCA JAMESON

I had seen in his since the first moment we met months ago. No man would ever be able to make me come on demand like he'd done. My body melted into his. I belonged to him entirely.

I just hoped I could survive.

Chapter Ten

When I woke the next time, I was alone, tangled in the sheets of Riley's bed. My entire body ached deliciously. My ass stung, but not in a bad way. It seemed to have a direct connection to my pussy which instantly flooded with renewed wetness.

I moaned as I shifted against the bed. My entire body tingled and my hand wandered down between my legs to press against my pussy. I'd turned into a nymph. I didn't recognize myself.

"As sexy as that is, stop rubbing yourself, baby."

My eyes shot open. I wasn't alone after all. I lifted my head and blinked into the brightness from the sun streaming through the window. Riley sat in a chair a few feet from the side of the bed. He leaned forward, his elbows perched on his knees, a mug fisted between both hands.

I smelled coffee. How had I not noticed that immediately?

"I wasn't…"

He lifted an eyebrow.

I swallowed and dropped back onto the bed, burying my face in the pillow. What was with my incessant need to lie all of the sudden?

"Let's not start with the lying again this morning. I'm not oblivious. You won't be able to get away with it. Unless you want to spend the day with an ass too sore to sit on, I suggest you rephrase whatever you were about to say."

I remained mute.

"Let me help. 'I'm sorry, Sir. I shouldn't have attempted to masturbate against the sheets. My orgasms belong to you. I won't touch myself or rub against other objects without your permission and approval.'"

I gasped. My heart raced. I could feel it beating as though it would explode out of my chest. I didn't lift my face to meet his gaze. Instead I gripped the sides of my pillow with both fists, trying desperately to ignore the

The Game

throbbing in my clit. It amazed me how the man could control my body with his dominant words.

"Come here."

I hesitated, knowing it was a bad plan.

"Cheyenne," his voice was lower, authoritative, "come here. Now."

I lifted my body as if I weighed a ton and dragged myself off the side of the bed to stand at his side.

My entire frame shivered. I was naked, exposed, and so fucking aroused he would easily see the wetness pooling between my legs.

"On your knees."

I lowered to my knees at his feet, still not meeting his gaze. I kept my head bowed the entire time.

"Grip your hands behind your back, baby." His voice was steady. Easy. As if he were asking me to flip on a light or grab him a cup of coffee.

I did as he instructed, gripping one wrist with my other hand tightly.

"Spread your knees wider."

I inched them out one at a time, biting my lip again. My hair fell over my face.

"Perfect. When we play, I want you in this position first thing. It helps align your mind properly. It's humbling and submissive to kneel before me."

He was right. And dammit it was effective.

There was no denying I was indeed submissive. To deny it would be insane. I wasn't sure I liked it yet, but it was a simple fact.

"Look at me, Cheyenne."

I reluctantly lifted my face to meet his gaze.

"Good girl." His brow furrowed as he concentrated on me, his gaze wandering up and down my body as I held my gaze on his face. Finally, our eyes met again. "I told you I have rules. You'll follow them today. You'll follow them for the next thirty-six hours. You'll follow them because I'm asking you to give this a shot. You'll follow them because you can't help yourself. You'll follow them because you're submissive."

I inhaled sharply, renewed moisture gathering between my legs and dripping down my thighs. "Yes, Sir."

"Repeat after me. I will not lie to you, Sir."

"I will not lie to you, Sir."

He lifted one brow. "I mean that, Cheyenne. You need to stop trying to hide your true emotions and cover them up with piles of fibs. If we can't be honest with each other, we have nothing. This sort of relationship is based on honesty. Without that, we can't make this work."

The Game

"Yes, Sir."

"You're not permitted to masturbate without my permission. Ever. When I feel like watching, I will direct you. When you aren't with me and you feel the urge, deny it. Do. Not. Touch. Yourself. Are we clear?"

"Yes. Sir."

"Yes what?"

"I won't touch myself without your permission," I whispered, humiliated at having been caught pressing my hand against my pussy.

"I would ask that you keep your pussy shaved, but I enjoyed doing it myself, so I think I'll continue to do it for now."

I shivered. The act had sucked brain cells from my head. I wasn't sure I would survive another round of that intense scrutiny.

"Ordinarily, if you agree to be my submissive, we won't live under the same level of intensity I'm going to demand for the next two days. But under the circumstances, I want your total obedience in all things until I take you home tomorrow night. I know it's a huge step. But I want you to have all the facts when we part so you can make a decision without any surprises."

"Yes, Sir."

"Is there anything you need from your house that you can't live without?"

I shook my head. I didn't even have my phone. But who was I going to call? "No, Sir."

"Birth control?"

I flushed. "I've never taken it. There was no reason."

"Okay. We'll stick with condoms for now. But I abhor them. If you choose to stay with me, I'll want you to get on the pill."

"Yes, Sir." My face was doomed to remain red for the rest of my life. I wasn't accustomed to such frank discussions about private matters.

"I want you to text Amy from my phone several times today and let her know you're okay."

"Yes, Sir." What if I'm not okay?

He chuckled. "You're like an open book. Often I can read your expression. So, don't text her. I'll give you some privacy to call her. I'll even be generous enough to give you time to talk things over with her. She's been living the lifestyle for a while. She might be able to help you sort through your feelings."

"Okay."

"I'm going to push you today. I want you to give

it your all."

"Yes, Sir."

A pause filled the air.

"Are you wet, baby?"

"Yes, Sir," I mumbled.

"You'll get over the embarrassment fast. I want you to know your body. Know your needs. Know when you're about to come and be able to stop it if I say so. And part of that is being able to express yourself and your needs to me. I know it may seem otherwise, but I'm not omniscient. You have to speak up."

"Yes, Sir."

"Eventually it won't faze you to be naked in my home." He leaned in closer. "Eventually it won't faze you to be naked in public."

I shuddered. That would never happen.

"I'm going to make breakfast now. I want you to shower. Take some time for yourself in the bathroom. Shave, but leave your pussy for me." He reached out with one hand and lifted my chin higher. "You'll find what you need in the bathroom." He leaned forward and kissed my forehead. And then he stood and left the room, shutting the door behind him.

Chapter Eleven

For a second I remained frozen in my spot. Slowly I slumped down, sitting on my heels and then releasing my hands from behind me and thrusting them forward to rock into them. I remained on all fours staring at the floor, unsure I would be able to hold myself upright or walk.

I was overwhelmed.

And horny.

I needed to come. I had needed the release since the moment I rubbed myself against the mattress.

The house was too big for me to hear Riley working in the kitchen. Silence surrounded me. How much time would he give me?

The Game

I finally lifted one foot and braced to pull myself to standing. My legs shook. I glanced down at my body, not recognizing myself. My breasts seemed larger. The bare skin at my pussy was foreign to me. Raw in a way that left me exposed—which was the intention.

I managed to make my way into the adjoining bathroom. A row of items sat on the counter clearly intended for my use. I scanned them. New toothbrush, deodorant, shampoo, conditioner, body wash. Even makeup remover.

How often did he have women stay the night? I shook the thought from my head. I needed to leave the past in the past. Just because he had women submitting to him before me shouldn't make me jealous. Of course he had other women in his life before me. He was ten years older than me.

I used the toilet and then flipped on the shower. While the water warmed, I grabbed the pile of items from the sink. He even had shower gel. I climbed in and set the girly things next to his own products. It seemed so intimate.

My shower was fast and meticulous. I wasn't sure how he felt about me dawdling, but I didn't want to find out by having him bust into the room while I was shaving my legs. I might cut a slit all the way up one side.

When I finished, I wrapped myself in one of the enormous thick towels and tried to control my breathing. I felt like I'd been for a run this morning instead of spending just ten minutes kneeling on the floor and then another ten standing in the shower.

After patting my hair until it was damp, I hung the towel on a hook behind the door and spun around. What was I supposed to wear? Fear seized my stomach at the possibility he intended for me to remain naked all weekend.

And then I spotted a silk pile I hadn't noticed sitting on the other side of the vanity. I padded toward the item and lifted it—a pale pink robe. Dainty with barely enough material to cover my ass. I slipped it on, feeling decidedly sexy the second it touched my skin.

I pushed my weird twinge of nausea back at the thought that another woman had been here and worn this robe before. I even lifted the edge of the silk to my nose and inhaled the scent. It smelled new. Who had brand new women's robes lying around?

A Dom.

Did he have a dozen of them in different sizes for his various conquests?

The Game

    I grabbed a comb from the counter and worked through my tangles a bit rougher than necessary. After applying facial lotion, I stared at myself in the mirror. I had no interest in putting on makeup. And besides, there was nothing like that in plain view. I could have dug in the drawers, but I was afraid of what I might find.

    If Riley wanted a piece of the real me, he was going to have to get used to the me without makeup. I wasn't the type to lie around on a Saturday in mascara and eye liner. Outside the house, I had always worn a meticulous combination, but at home, I didn't bother. Did that make me feel vulnerable in front of this man I barely knew? Maybe.

    Taking a deep breath, I exited the bathroom and headed down the hall toward the sound of soft music and the smell of bacon and coffee.

    I rounded the corner to the kitchen feeling cautiously shy.

    Riley spotted me and smiled. "Feel better?" His gaze roamed up and down my frame, hunger obvious in his eyes.

    "Yes."

    He lifted a brow. That was his way of letting me know I needed to rephrase.

"Yes, Sir."

He nodded to the island behind him. "Take a seat." He watched me as I shuffled across the room. His gaze bore into my back before I turned to climb onto one of the many stools around the island. I fought the urge to meet his penetrating gaze.

I held the front of the robe closed when it wanted to slide open. The belt was thin and slick. It wouldn't stay tight. Even in a knot, it would slip free. The more daunting part was the length, however. I sat on my bare ass. The hem of the robe wasn't long enough to tuck under me.

A glass of juice sat at my spot, and I reached for it and quickly drained the contents. Fresh squeezed orange juice. Heavenly. I was suddenly ravenous. I hadn't eaten since the quick microwave dinner I'd prepared before Amy and Cade arrived the previous night.

Riley turned around and handed me a cup of coffee. "Sugar? Cream?"

"Yes. Please, Sir." The word was still foreign on my tongue. I wasn't sure how I felt about calling him *Sir*. It humbled me.

I supposed that was the point. "If I'm the submissive, shouldn't I be the one preparing the meal

The Game

while you sit around with your feet up or something?"

Riley chuckled as he turned around again and set a plate in front of me. The steaming pile of scrambled eggs, bacon, and toast made my stomach growl.

"You aren't a domestic slave, baby."

"What am I?" I was truly curious. I reached for my fork and then hesitated, unsure if I was supposed to wait for permission to eat.

"Eat, Cheyenne. Go ahead." He turned around and grabbed another plate, filling it with food while I took my first bite.

When he returned, he settled on the stool next to mine and grabbed a napkin. "This is about sex, baby."

I gulped back my bite, trying not to choke.

He smiled at me and reached for my chin to hold my face steady. "I enjoy the thrill of controlling you for the purpose of making you so horny you can't think. And likewise my cock gets harder than a rock when you obey me. It doesn't work for everyone. And it's rare for two people to be on the same page enough to mesh.

"I think you have what it takes."

I stared at him. Was I truly that weak? So malleable that I was aroused by letting a man order me around?

"I can tell by the look on your face that you're misguided. It takes an incredibly strong person to submit to another. Not the opposite."

"How do you figure?" I had read that. I just didn't understand it.

"I'm not taking anything from you, Cheyenne. You have to give it."

I nodded. Amy had mentioned that.

"I'm never going to force you to do anything, Cheyenne. The decision is yours. I can demand you to do my bidding. I can even discipline you when you don't obey me, but it's all a shifting of power. It's only as real as you make it. If you choose to walk away or defy me, I am powerless to stop you."

That made sense.

He pointed at my plate. "Eat before it gets cold." He took a bite of his food.

I lifted my fork, but my mind ran in ten thousand directions. I wasn't sure I could swallow.

Between bites, Riley continued to speak. "I know you're nervous, but think of it this way—you hold the cards. I'm the vulnerable party."

I jerked my face up.

He continued. "Think about it. I'm putting

The Game

myself out there. Especially with you because you've never been in the lifestyle. You're so new you can't possibly understand the feelings you're experiencing." He shoveled another enormous bite into his mouth and chewed while I watched.

"Finish your breakfast, and then we'll talk. I don't want you to be hungry."

I turned my gaze back to my plate and concentrated on lifting the fork, sliding the eggs into my mouth, chewing, swallowing. Normal things I didn't usually think about that were almost insurmountable this morning.

When I finished, I found Riley had also cleaned his plate. He took my dishes from in front of me and deposited them in the sink. "Come."

I eased down from the stool and followed him to the living room, pulling the robe tighter around my middle. With every step, the front slid open to expose my sex. I took small steps and found Riley rolling his eyes as I approached. "I've seen you naked, baby. Why the modesty?"

"I— I don't know." That wasn't a lie. For some reason in the light of day I was self-conscious.

Riley reached out a hand and pulled me down to

sit next to him on the couch.

    My butt hit the soft cool leather, making me squirm. The front of the robe slid open at my waist even though I had a tight grip on it between my breasts.

    Riley fingered the edge of the silk at my shoulder. "I thought this would make you feel a little more relaxed, but I think as sexy as it is, it's working against me. Stop fidgeting or I'll remove it."

    I tried to relax.

    He reached for my fingers and peeled them from the robe. He wrapped my small hand in his and set it at my side. Turning so that his back rested against the arm of the couch, he spoke again. "Spin toward me. Cross your legs under you. I want you to face me."

    I carefully turned in his direction, tucked my feet up, and assumed the position he requested. My pussy was exposed this way. The robe separated at the center, barely covering my nipples and doing nothing to conceal my sex. I forced myself to lift my gaze to his.

    "As I was explaining, you hold the power here. One word and my assumed position is done."

    I thought about his proclamation. He was right. I hadn't thought about it. He was asking me to give over my control, but he hadn't done anything that would force me to do so. "I see."

"It's a give and take. For this to work—and I'm so fucking hopeful it will—we have to have continuous open dialogue about what each of us wants and needs. It's a discussion that will never end. We have to check in with each other daily to make sure we're both still happy with the arrangement and renegotiate the terms.

"I know it feels like a dictatorship to you, but it's not. At least not the way you're thinking. Do I want to totally dominate you and have you allow me to guide your every move inside the house? Hell yes. But not in a way that makes you deflated. It needs to be done with the perfect balance created when you give me exactly what you're able to give and I take not one ounce more."

So much information. I was having trouble keeping up.

"If you agree to stay with me, we'll negotiate every conceivable point. For the purpose of indoctrinating you to the lifestyle, I'm asking you to concede everything just for this weekend. In return, I'll give you a taste of as many aspects of BDSM as I can stuff into forty-eight hours.

"Bondage." He wrapped his hands around my wrists and squeezed them briefly, a smile playing at the corners of his mouth.

I gasped, shocked by his playfulness.

He tugged my wrists forward, lifted my butt off the couch. He released one arm and reached around behind me to swat my ass before I had any clue what he was going to do. "Discipline." He leaned forward, lowering me back onto my butt.

"Sir..." I had no idea how to finish that statement.

He set his hand on the back of my head and pressed forward so that my chin dipped. His lips hit my ear, and he whispered, "Submission."

A fresh wave of arousal sent a shiver down my spine.

He leaned back and lifted my chin once more to meet my gaze. "Afterward, you'll need a few days alone to think about everything and make sure this is what you want. I'll be at your mercy, waiting for you to decide." He took my hand in his and gently brushed his thumb over the backs of my knuckles. "I've dreamed of this for six months, never daring to hope it could become reality.

"That night I met you, the attraction was instant. You had no clue about my lifestyle. Amy specifically told me and Parker she hadn't shared what she had with Cade. Not to you or Meagan.

The Game

"I had to respect that. It wasn't mine to share. And I also couldn't imagine leading you down this path blindly. You were so sweet and innocent." He lowered his head for a moment. "I've kicked myself in the ass so many times over the last six months thinking about how I must've made you feel when I left you."

"It wasn't pretty."

He cringed. "I'm so sorry. It was cowardly. I was an ass."

"I can also see why you did it. And in hindsight, it's kind of endearing to think you were so attracted to me that you let me go."

He grinned. "Don't give me any points. What I really wanted to do that night was take you out back, press you against the nearest wall, shove my knee between your legs, and force you to orgasm. It wasn't altruistic."

"Forcing me to orgasm isn't altruistic? Listen to yourself."

He chuckled. "Yeah. Okay. That came out wrong."

"What about you? It seems all your interest lies in my satisfaction. You even said this was all about sex."

"It is. In the sense that my goal is to drive you insane with need and ensure you stay that way most of the time." He leaned forward, his face inches from mine. "I want to know your pussy is always wet for me, your legs always quivering with need, your nipples stiff points, your breasts heavy with the pressure of desire.

"I want to know I do that to you, that I control your responses. It makes me so fucking hard, I could come in my pants."

I didn't move. He did that to me.

"I'm shaking as I watch your reactions to my words, my actions, my commands. You're like a lottery ticket I just won unexpectedly. The winnings are right in the palms of my hands, and I don't even know what to do with my windfall but hand it back to you."

I licked my lips, my mouth suddenly very dry. "I keep thinking it's like a game."

"In a way it is." Riley lunged forward. He pressed my shoulders back so I fell against the supple leather of the couch. His hands landed on my thighs next and pushed them farther open. He inhaled deeply. "You're glistening. Tell me, Cheyenne, is this your normal reaction to a man? Or is it me?"

"It's you," I whispered.

He jerked his gaze to meet mine.

I shivered under the anticipation of the deep lust I saw tightening his face. "It's you, Sir. You do this to me.

No one else has ever come close."

His thumbs pulled my lower lips apart. He swiped them through my soaked entrance and dragged the wetness over my clit.

Before I could fully process how fast his hands moved, they were on my waist and traveling up to separate the panels of my robe and expose my breasts. "I want to tie you to my bed, blindfold you, and torment your sweet body until you beg me to let you come."

"Will you fuck me?" My voice was unrecognizable and weak.

He reached for my nipples and grasped them with his fingers, not answering my question.

I grabbed his arms with both hands. "Riley, look at me."

He lifted his gaze.

I saw the vulnerability in his eyes. He was truly afraid he would be lost if he let himself finish the deed.

I had news for him. "I'll consent to everything you demand of me for the next two days on one condition."

"What's that?" he muttered slowly, clearly dreading the answer.

"You have to fuck me. Make love to me. Have sex with me. Do it any way you want, but don't leave me like you have for the first twelve hours.

"I know you've made me come several times. And I get that you're the master at doling out orgasms at your will. You've proven that. And you're welcome to continue to prove it. I love it. But no matter how many times I come, you leave me unfulfilled when you deny me your cock."

He swallowed visibly and dipped his head for a moment. He cupped my breasts and stared at them. "Your chest is fucking perfect," he commented absently.

I waited.

"Your entire body is a work of art, actually." He released my breasts and took my wrists in his hands. "It's true your skin is tender. I'm worried about marking it with bondage."

I inhaled sharply at his indirect mention of his ex-fiancée. I didn't need the reminder. She didn't belong in our lives. And she wasn't welcome. Besides, he was avoiding my request.

"I'm not as fragile as I look, Riley. And you're ignoring my condition."

"I'm not ignoring it. I'm mulling it over in my brain." He lifted my wrists over my head, stretching my arms high and leaning over my face. He closed his eyes and dipped his forehead to meet mine.

We breathed in tandem for several seconds. Finally, he lifted his eyelids and spoke. "I'm ruined anyway. No woman will ever measure up to you. I'm kidding myself if I think keeping my cock out of your pussy will change anything. If you walked out the door right this second, you'd take my heart with you. I'd never be the same. In fact, I might even regret not taking you completely."

"So, yes?"

He nodded. "However, I want to point out this is the last time you're going to plea bargain this weekend. No more topping from the bottom."

"What does that mean?"

"It means you're trying to control me from the submissive position while making it seem like I made the choices. I'm not immune. Don't make a habit of it."

"You'll make love to me?"

"I promise you my cock will enter you when and how I see fit before the day is over."

I let my body relax, relieved to feel like I'd won the first round somehow. And I was clear on the notion that it wasn't the last round I would win. There would be many. He called them negotiations. My eyes were wide open. Negotiating with Riley would be my pleasure. I would concede nearly anything to him in the end. I already trusted him with my body. I knew he wouldn't hurt me. At least not physically.

Emotionally he had the power to destroy me. But I'd known that since the first minute we met. It hadn't changed. I'd been a shell ever since he'd walked away. I had dated no one. No man who approached me came anywhere close to making me feel the way I felt that one evening with Riley.

I'd begun to worry I was doomed.

What if I never found anyone who made me feel that way?

And then there he was, larger than life in my office building, taking my breath away as if not a single minute had passed since our last meeting. He'd made my heart race, my pussy wet, and my stomach clench with need so fast I wanted to kick myself.

Like he said, the final act of penetration wasn't going to influence how I would feel if this didn't work out. And no matter what, I was beyond caring. I wanted him inside me bad enough to take the risk to my heart.

Riley Moreno was mine. He would concede anything to me. And that knowledge caused me to give

The Game

everything to him. "Yes, Sir." I lowered my gaze and made the conscious decision to take every single second of this weekend and make it special. It was a gift. No matter the outcome, this would be the most memorable, precious two days of my life.

Chapter Twelve

Riley led me back to his bedroom.

I thought he was going to put me out of my misery finally, but he surprised me by handing me his cell phone. Amy's name was on the screen. "Call her. I'll give you as long as you need." He left me there, staring at the phone.

I jumped when the door shut with a snick. My hands shook as I pushed the button to begin the call.

Amy answered on the first ring. "Riley?" Her voice sounded anxious.

"It's me. I don't have my phone. Hell, I don't have anything. You convinced me not to take my purse last night."

The Game

She giggled. "Sorry. Are you okay?"

"So far."

"Cheyenne?"

"I'm good." I relaxed onto the bed, lying back while cradling the phone to my ear and tugging absurdly at the front of my robe.

"You sound tired. Is he going to take you home? Do you want me to come get you?"

"No. I've agreed to stay the weekend."

"Really? Are you okay with that?"

"Yes. I mean, I hope so. He wanted me to call you and check in."

"I'm glad. Listen, Cheyenne, I know you must feel like the world as you knew it just flipped upside down or turned on its axis or something, but Riley's a good guy. One of the best. I guarantee he won't hurt you. You're safe."

I didn't feel one bit safe. If she wanted to discuss my physical safety, I was certain she was correct. He'd made that clear. My emotional safety was another issue entirely, however, and I feared it was in jeopardy. "I'll be okay," I lied.

"You can call me or Cade any time. We'll come get you."

"I know."

"I'm going to call again this afternoon and make sure you're still okay. Just..."

"Just what?"

"Guard your heart, hon. I know you. You haven't let anyone in for a long time. I'm worried you'll fall hard and fast."

"Too late, Amy."

She blew out a breath. "Okay. Well, I'm here for you. And I love you."

"Love you too. Thanks, Amy. I'll talk to you later." I ended the call and set the phone on the nightstand. Instead of going in search of Riley, I lay back down and curled onto my side. I could use a few more minutes to think. Weeding through the thoughts racing around in my head would do me some good.

The next thing I knew, someone was touching my arm.

I opened my eyes to find Riley settling himself on the edge of the bed. "You fell asleep, baby." He smiled at me.

I rolled from my side to my back, noticing I was covered with the sheet. I was aware of the silk robe still around me, but it was wide open under the bed linens.

"How long was I out?"

"A few hours. I didn't want to interrupt your call, but after a while I got concerned and found you passed out. You needed the rest. We were up late, and you've been bombarded with information."

"Thanks." I lowered my gaze from his face to his bare chest. A scattering of blond hair covered his rich tanned skin. His pecs were rock solid and stunning. Lower still I looked. He wore jeans—worn and soft. The top button was open, but I couldn't see anything beneath the flap.

He cupped my face and leaned down to kiss me. His lips opened, and his tongue slid along the crease of my mouth. He ended the kiss too soon but then surprised me by nibbling a bath across my cheek to my ear. I came fully awake when he sucked the lobe in and then blew on it gently. "I love kissing you."

Continuing to kiss my neck and shoulders, he climbed over me, straddling me, tugging the sheet down my body as he inched backward. My robe was wide open, hiding nothing. It had become tangled loosely around me as I slept.

My nipples jumped to attention as the cooler air of the room hit them. I shivered.

Riley flicked his tongue over one bud and then suckled the stiff tip between his lips. "Mmm. I love how soft your skin is." He cupped my breast and brought it to his mouth again.

Suddenly he leaned back, tucking his arm under me and hauling me off the bed several inches. With his free hand, he tugged the robe out from under me and jerked it free. Two seconds later, he had my arms over my head and was wrapping the robe around my wrists.

I struggled to free my hands from the tangled mess.

Riley pressed on my arms and met my gaze. "Stay still, baby. Leave it."

I gasped as he leaned over my body farther and fiddled above my head, drawing my arms higher. I realized he was looping the robe through the slats in the headboard and tying the ends.

I tried to remember to breathe as my entire body came alive. It unnerved me to realize how aroused I instantly became. I'd never considered bondage a day in my life. I squeezed my legs together and bit into my lip, fighting a moan.

When he sat back and met my gaze, I gave the bonds a tug. My heart beat rapidly. I fidgeted under his

The Game

scrutiny as he lightly traced a finger down my face, my neck, my breast. "It's not so tight you can't escape. Just relax. Let me make your body hum."

"Yes, Sir." My voice was so low I barely heard it.

He eased himself farther down my body, nudged my knees apart, and settled between them. With both hands, he parted my folds. "So wet." He tapped the entrance to my pussy, making me flinch.

I craved more. Anything he would give me. A tight knot formed low in my belly, threatening to explode.

Riley's fingers grazed over my lower lips and up across the delicate skin surrounding my clit. "Your skin is still so smooth. You won't need to shave every day."

Hell, he'd shaved me just last night. It hadn't been twelve hours.

"Let me blindfold you?" He was asking a question—giving me the option to refuse. When I hesitated, he continued. "Every other sensation heightens when you can't see. Try it. You won't be disappointed."

"I'm so close to exploding, Riley. I ache. I don't know if I can take more."

He stroked my cheek. "You can. Let me show you my world."

I nodded. There was very little he could request of

me I would deny him. I could think of nothing.

Riley reached across me and opened the drawer on the bedside table. I suddenly wished I had explored the contents myself earlier. The idea hadn't occurred to me. As he sat back, holding up a black blindfold—like the kind people use to sleep on a plane—I held my breath.

He lowered it slowly over my face and tightened it behind my head.

Instantly the darkness heightened my senses. My chest rose and fell with every deep breath. He leaned over toward the mystery drawer again and then returned. What was he holding now?

Something delicate touched my skin at my collar bone. I shivered at the contact, my knees closing the few inches available to grip Riley's thighs between them.

He ignored my legs and continued to dance whatever he held across my skin. A feather? When the tip hit my nipple, I nearly jumped out of my skin, thrusting my chest toward him.

"So responsive. I want to train your body to follow my commands."

Wasn't that already the case?

His finger tugged on the lip I hadn't realized I was biting. "Don't bite so hard. You're about to draw blood.

The Game

It makes my cock hard when you nibble, but don't hurt yourself."

I let my lip pop out, my mouth hanging open.

The feather continued to trail around my torso, landing indiscriminately on my nipples, my belly button, the top of my mound.

"Your tits are exquisite. So round and perfect. The tips are a gorgeous shade of pink. I want to suck them. I'll be thinking about them when I'm at work Monday, trying to keep my cock down as I picture them jutting out, begging for attention."

My belly dipped, hollowing as he spoke. Every nerve ending in my body demanded he fuck me. I said nothing.

The feather disappeared, and I heard a small pop. Seconds later a low buzz filled the air.

Riley scooted down farther between my legs.

"Riley…" My senses were indeed heightened. I hated not being able to see. What was he doing?

"Shh. Baby, just feel." His hand landed on my lower belly, his fingers pulling on my skin to expose my clit.

I writhed. I needed him so badly, but if he touched me with a vibrator, I would crash over the edge instantly.

He pressed firmly on my stomach, holding me down. "You're so high right now. I want you to come. Get the first one out of the way so you can relax a little."

The first one? Relax? Was he kidding?

He was *not*.

The blunt end of some sort of vibrator landed at the base of my clit and pressed.

I screamed. My skin was so sensitive. Instantly I came, short jabbing pulses of my clit that caused my entire body to shake.

"That's it, baby. Let it go." He held the vibrator steady over my clit, pressing harder until I gasped.

"Too much." I bucked against him futilely.

Riley eased the vibrator away from my skin and replaced it with gentle strokes of his thumb.

The tight nub was so sensitive I winced.

The vibrations ceased. Thank God.

His touch did not. "So pink and swollen. Gorgeous."

I gasped for breath. The orgasm hadn't diminished my need. If anything, I was more aroused than ever. I gripped the ball of silk at my hands, holding on as if I might fall.

The Game

Riley pressed my knees higher and wider. He eased down until he must have been on his stomach between my legs, tossing an arm over my lower belly to anchor me. His fingers at my entrance brought me back to fully charged before he entered me.

In agonizingly slow motion, he slid one finger inside me and curled it up to graze over my G-spot.

I moaned. The torture was delicious. Frighteningly so. What was happening to me that I found being tied to the bed and forced to come so arousing?

A second finger joined the first, reaching deeper, scissoring inside me, stretching me.

"So tight. Jesus." And then his hand disappeared and something else nudged the entrance, probably the same vibrator he'd used on my clit. He spread my lips wider and then eased the phallus into my channel.

I moaned as he filled me. Too full.

Slowly he pressed into me.

I dug my heels into the bed, bucking to no avail.

Strange sounds escaped my lips, gasps that combined with whimpering moans. I panted as the vibrator slid all the way home.

"Cheyenne, your pussy's so tight. You're going to make me come instantly when I enter you."

If he would just fucking enter me…

Sweat beaded on my face from the intensity of the restraint and the attention to every nerve surrounding my sex—inside and out.

I tipped my head back, my mouth falling open as I got closer to the edge of a second orgasm.

And then he stopped. The vibrator disappeared, slipping from my sheath and leaving me bereft.

Like a drowning victim, I gasped as though coming up for air and finally hitting the surface. "Riley." I screamed his name.

My ears were ringing, but the distinct sound of a zipper reached my ears through the insanity. His jeans. Thank God.

The rustle of material made me lick my lips. And then a ripping sound. A Condom. Blessed angels.

He was on top of me instantly, his mouth capturing mine so fast, I was stunned. His hand cupped my face on one side as he devoured me.

His body hovered over me, making only the slightest contact against my nipples and my thighs. He set his forehead against mine as he broke the kiss. His breathing was labored. Heavy. Deep. "Don't move an inch, baby. If you do, I'll shoot off before I'm fully seated."

I nodded. "Yes, Sir." My throat was dry. My lips only moistened from contact with his.

Finally, his cock was at my entrance. His hand stiffened at my throat, indicative of what his entire body must have been doing. He pushed forward slowly and retreated. "Jesus." His breath whooshed from his lungs against my face. "So fucking tight."

My pussy gripped at his cock as he slid into me again, slightly farther this time. I wanted to lift my hips toward him, but he'd asked me to remain still. I willed myself to obey those words. For him. Because he needed this.

I didn't personally care if he came too fast. I suspected it wouldn't stop him from starting again immediately. He was that virile.

"Knees high and wide, baby."

I lifted my limp legs from the bed, drew my knees up, and splayed them wider.

Riley slammed home.

I screamed.

He held steady as I fought for oxygen, his fingers stroking my cheek. "You okay?"

I nodded. My mouth wouldn't close, and I

couldn't find any words.

"Did I hurt you?" I heard the concern in his voice.

I shook my head and stroked my tongue over my bottom lip. "No. God no. Riley. Move. Damn you." I squirmed against him, thrusting my pussy upward.

He chuckled for just a moment, and then stopped. His other hand came up to cup my face, trapping my head on both sides.

Finally, he moved, pulling out and thrusting back in on a groan.

Again.

So full. So much better than the vibrator.

Stars swam in the darkness around my eyes. All I knew was pure bliss. Heaven. The delicious feeling of having this perfect man inside me, pressing in and out, over and over. Filling me so expertly.

His breath on my face told me of his struggle. He was so close to the edge—sharp gasps that he tried to stifle. He picked up speed as his lips took mine possessively. His tongue plunged into my mouth in rhythm with his cock in my pussy.

I was overwhelmed with sensation. Every nerve ending tingled as I reached closer to the edge.

"Come, baby."

The Game

I stiffened. It didn't work that way. I couldn't come on command. Could I?

"Come. Cheyenne, come around my cock before I do."

Yes.

I tipped over that illusive edge so fast it didn't seem as though I had any control over myself. Riley controlled me. His words forced me to orgasm.

I shuddered as my entire body participated in the act, my channel gripping at his cock. My legs shook as Riley sped up and pressed harder, deeper, faster. Two last thrusts and he held himself deep within me.

His body went rigid as he emptied himself into me.

My heart stopped.

Among our gasps for breath, our sweaty bodies, my tangled restraints—I was his. No man would ever compete with Riley Moreno.

I would never want anyone to try.

Chapter Thirteen

I was so exhausted Monday morning when the alarm went off, I groaned as I slapped at my clock. I flopped onto my back and blinked at the ceiling.

My entire life as I'd known it until Friday night had been turned upside down. I wiggled my hand down my belly and cupped my pussy before jerking it away as Riley's demands about touching myself filtered in.

The delicious tingle of sex was so fresh I could still feel Riley's cock inside me. I ached in places I didn't know could ache.

The man had shown me things I never knew existed. And then he'd returned me to my life last night under the command that I needed to think hard about

The Game

what he was offering.

I knew it pained him. I also knew he was right. I needed to do some soul-searching. And there was no way I could do that under his eye.

But first, I had to get to work.

I was in the middle of a project that needed my undivided attention. After one year with Talent Marketing Group, I was on the radar of some of my superiors. I wanted to impress the hell out of them and work toward a promotion.

I loved my job. And for that I was grateful. So many of my peers groaned and complained about their work. Every day at my job was exciting and unexpected.

As a member of the advertising department, it was my job to present the client with multiple options to lure cell phone users to switch to their company—Link. This current project was winding down. I'd been on it a month. My team had met with management at Link multiple times. Now I just needed to finalize my proposal and present it to my boss.

I hurried through my morning routine and walked into the office a half hour early.

As I stowed my purse in my desk drawer, Stacy leaned around the divider between us. "Did you hear about the new director?"

"No." I knew the owners had been interviewing people for months, but I hadn't heard someone had been hired.

"I saw her when I came in. She looks formidable."

I cocked my head. "How so?"

Stacy lowered her voice to a whisper. "She's tall, model skinny. Her hair is pulled back in a bun that makes my head hurt looking at it. I didn't see her smile, but I did hear her reprimand someone in the break room. I shivered. First day on the job? That's kinda weird."

I shrugged. "Maybe she's trying to establish herself as alpha."

Stacy giggled. "If by that you mean tyrant, I think you're onto something."

A deep voice at the end of our row made us both look up. Jerald Harkins, the temporary director of my department, cleared his throat and spoke louder. "As you all probably have heard by now, a new member is joining the team. I'd like everyone to gather in the conference room at nine sharp so she can introduce herself. Please pass the word to those who haven't yet arrived."

By the time I got my computer up and running and my shit organized, it was time to head to the conference room. I squeezed in behind Stacy and flattened myself against the back wall in the crowded space.

The woman at the front was bent over the table looking at something Jerald was showing her.

A chill went down my spine a moment before she stood tall.

And the bottom of my world fell out.

Christine.

Jerald spoke, but his voice was muffled by the ringing in my ears. "This is Christine Parson. She's joining us from…"

I heard nothing else.

I couldn't blink or breathe. This couldn't be happening.

She scanned the room as Jerald made her introduction. He rambled on about her accomplishments.

When her eyes met mine, she smiled as though she wasn't the least bit shocked.

Fuck.

Whatever her game was, I started shaking and had trouble controlling the need to run from the room, the building, and the city.

My mouth grew drier with every shallow breath I managed.

Christine gave a short speech, and then Jerald ushered us out the door to return to our jobs.

It took me a moment to get my feet to move. In fact, Stacy nudged me from the side before I could even consider the possibility of walking. I wandered back to my desk silently and took my seat, grateful to have made it without falling on my face along the way.

I stared at my computer monitor, setting my hand on the mouse, but still in a daze. What the hell was I going to do?

Before I could gather a single thought, Christine herself stepped up behind me, clearing her throat and making me jump. I swiveled around to face her. Would she fire me?

She glanced at me and then Stacy and mentioned not a word about knowing me. "I'm going to be making my rounds, getting to know the staff and getting up to speed on what everyone's working on. Might as well start with you two." She turned her gaze to me. "You want to go first? My office in ten?"

I nodded, swallowing my tongue.

As she walked away, I stared after her. Should I text Riley? This was my place of work. I needed to pull my shit together and not let the woman intimidate me. I

The Game

took the ten minutes to transfer the project I was working on to a flash drive and then stood to head toward the office at the end of the hall that had remained vacant until today.

"Good luck," Stacy muttered under her breath as I passed.

Christine didn't look up when I entered. "Shut the door behind you."

My hands shook as I did her bidding and stepped up to the two chairs facing her desk, decidedly not assuming anything about sitting in one of them.

"Please, sit." She waved an arm and then met my gaze as I lowered myself. Her smile was fake and made me want to vomit. "How crazy is this? What are the chances?" She stood and shuffled around on her desk. "Sorry, I forgot your name."

"Cheyenne." I cleared my voice and spoke with more force. "Cheyenne Decard." I sat ramrod straight, my legs crossed at the ankles, my hands fisted in my lap with my jump drive clutched in one.

"Cheyenne. That's an interesting name." Her voice was syrupy. Her demeanor told me she thought I was scum with a trashy name. She smirked while she tapped her pen on the desk. "Listen, I know we didn't exactly get off on the right foot the other night. Let's call it water under the bridge and start fresh, shall we?" She smiled again, but nothing about it said she was happy or even telling the truth.

"Of course."

"Would you grab me a coffee when you leave? Black." She ducked her head and concentrated on the paper in front of her, totally dismissing me. To get her *coffee?*

I stared for a moment. Stunned. Somehow I managed to haul myself up and exit without screaming. I also headed straight to the break room and poured a mug of coffee and returned it to Christine.

Stacy arrived just as I entered the office. "Oh." She glanced at my face and then my hands, pursing her lips. Her eyes twinkled as she fought a grin. Apparently she thought it was funny I'd been relegated to errand girl.

Christine took the cup from me without looking in my direction. "Stacy is it? Come on in."

I turned around and managed to make my way back to my desk, similarly wobbly to match the way I'd felt after the brief meeting at nine. I did my best to tune out the insanity for the rest of the morning, concentrating on the campaign I was working on. It was only a few days

The Game

from being presentable. Hopefully the client would like it as much as I did.

At lunch, I ducked out of the building, headed straight for the coffee shop across the street, and called Amy. I muttered under my breath as I waited for her to pick up. "Come on. Come on. Please be available." Amy loved her job at The Rockwood Group where she tried to balance her own value as an employee against the fact that Cade owned the company. She wanted to be taken seriously as a contributing member. And she worked hard toward that aim.

"Hey," she answered on the fourth ring. "Sorry, my phone was plugged in. I had to run to grab it. What's up?"

I'd spoken to her last night, so she was caught up on my weekend with Riley. But this was unforeseen. "Christine is here."

"Fuck. Where?"

"Here. In my office. She's the new marketing manager on my floor." I leaned back in my chair and closed my eyes.

"Are you shitting me?" Her voice lowered. "Have you called Riley?"

"No. And I'm not sure it's a good idea. This is my

battle, not his."

Amy moaned. "Honey, he would flip a lid if you didn't tell him about this. It's not as if he won't find out."

"I know, but not yet. I haven't wrapped my head around it. And I'm a grown woman. This is my job. My territory. I don't want him waltzing in here all alpha and destroying what I've worked for on my own."

Amy sighed. "He would do that. Probably buy the company out from under whoever owns it before the day ended."

"Yeah. That's just wrong."

"Okay, but your idea sucks too. What are you going to do?"

"Play her game. Try to show her she can't intimidate me. Ride the storm."

"Christine is a world-class bitch. Have you forgotten what she did to me? And how she lied to Riley for years about who she really was and what her intentions were? She's a gold digger. I'm surprised she had the clout to get that job."

"Yeah, well, somehow she did, and now I have to deal with it."

Amy sighed. "Okay. Call me. Keep me informed."

"Please don't tell Cade. Not yet. Give me a few

days."

"Okay. But he's going to kick my ass if you take very long."

"I know. Thanks, Amy. I'll call you later."

"You better. I'm worried about you. That woman is pure evil. She probably knew about you and hunted you down, and she can and will do everything in her power to ruin your life."

"Excellent. Good pep talk." I tried to chuckle through the fear. She was right. How had she managed to secure this job in such a short time? Was it just to intimidate me? I wouldn't put anything past her.

"How are you going to avoid telling Riley? You aren't exactly known for your ability to lie, even by omission."

"Easy. He told me to take a few days and think about our weekend. It was intense. He's right. Even though I'm itching to have him call me and run to see him, I need to get my head on and think."

"I hope you don't regret me dragging you down this naughty path. It's been so hard for the last year to keep this to myself. But I truly didn't see you in the role. If I had known about you and Riley at the engagement party…"

"What? Would you have done anything differently?"

"At least I would have been more sensitive. I didn't know you spent the last six months so frustrated. I'm so sorry. And I hope this enlightenment is something you can embrace and run with. It's so unbelievably fulfilling. For me, anyway."

"Does Meagan know?"

"God no." Amy chuckled. "For the same reason. At first I was worried about you two judging me. It's hard to understand. Unless you jump in with both feet and experience it for yourself, it's not easy to wrap your head around."

"I can see that. I'm still struggling."

"Cheyenne, it's been three days. You should be. But let yourself feel. Rest. Eat well. Get some exercise. Take a few days to put it aside and then revisit it."

"That's what Riley said."

"He's a good guy."

"Why was he engaged to that raving lunatic for so long, then?"

Amy blew out a breath. "That's difficult to understand. Even I don't quite get the dynamic because I only met her the night of their engagement party when she chose to diss me and show her true colors. Even then, I was reluctant for Cade to call Riley and tell him how she treated me. I didn't want to be the cause of a broken engagement.

"But Cade didn't hesitate. He'd had his suspicions for years about Christine, and there was no way he was going to let his friend walk down the aisle to someone who was two-faced and a total bitch. That woman is good. She played him for years."

"And she's also submissive? Riley said she wasn't very good at it."

"Apparently it was all a lie. She did the minimum and pretended to like it." Amy hesitated. I could hear her voice catch. "Riley's been in a weird place for the last year. It's hard to trust after something like that. You were a breath of fresh air to him when you two met, but he got cold feet. He was scared to trust and scared to introduce you to BDSM if it wasn't your thing."

"He told you all that?"

"He told Cade."

I glanced at my watch. "I better get back to the office. That crazy woman will probably be timing my lunches."

"Good luck with that. Call me later."

"I will. Thanks, Amy."

"No problem."

When I got back to the office, I went straight to work. It was almost five thirty before I looked up, feeling a presence behind me.

Christine leaned against the wall of my cubicle, shocking me. It unnerved me the way she managed to sneak up like that.

"Looks interesting." She nodded at my screen.

I wanted to shout at her to get her creepy self away from me.

"I can't wait to see the entire presentation. When will it be done?"

"Thursday."

"Awesome. I'll make sure I have time to go over it with you."

I didn't want to go over anything with her ever, but it didn't seem like I would have much of a choice under the circumstances. Too bad because I loved this job and I'd built up a good rapport with people. But I didn't trust this woman. Could she manage to get me to quit? Or even get me fired?

I dreaded the idea.

"I need you to look over some copy for me. I'll

The Game

email it to you. Can you stay late?"

I opened my mouth to protest and then closed it. "Of course."

The woman was trying to goad me. I wouldn't return the favor.

I smiled at her, and she turned and walked away, her tight ass in a pencil skirt swaying back and forth. No wonder men found her sexy. I could see why Riley fell for her in the first place. And she knew it too. She walked with her head so high it almost tipped back.

Probably kept her from having to look down at the minions.

My computer pinged a few seconds after I watched her sit down behind the glass wall of her office at the end of the row. I winced as I turned around and opened the document.

Some copy? This was more like a day's work. It wasn't my job. There were other employees who were paid to proof copy. Plus, I had my own project to finish. But that didn't seem to matter to Christine. It would take me hours to get it done. It was a full brochure. No way in hell would I give her the satisfaction of finding a mistake anywhere on the pages after I combed them.

I slumped back in front of my monitor and

Becca Jameson
opened the first page.

Chapter Fourteen

When the alarm went off Tuesday morning, I was in worse shape than I had been the day before. I'd worked on the brochure until after ten o'clock. She was probably doing everything in her power to make sure I wasn't with Riley. Why did she care who Riley was dating a year after their split?

Was she trying to get him back? Not that I was concerned she would succeed. I was simply concerned she would destroy me in the effort.

I groaned as I rolled over and stared at the clock. Apparently I'd already hit the snooze button a few times. That's how out of it I was.

Like a robot, I trudged through my apartment,

bathing, dressing, primping, and eating. I didn't eat much—just toast—before I left for the office, but it was enough to get me through the commute at least. I would grab a granola bar or a protein bar when I arrived.

It was just past eight-thirty when I stepped off the elevator on the twenty-second floor of my building. It was eerily quiet. Too quiet. I glanced around as I made my way toward my desk. I was expected to be at my desk eight hours a day. For me that meant nine to six with lunch. However, it was rare that I didn't get in at least a half hour early.

And most of the staff usually trickled in that early also. So it was a shock to find the place vacant. And an even greater shock when I passed the conference room and found it jammed full of my coworkers.

My face heated. Why was there a meeting I hadn't known anything about?

I paused at the closed door and then opened it, still holding my purse and not bothering to go to my desk.

"So nice of you to join us, Cheyenne," Christine jibed.

Several people glanced my way.

"Sorry. Was there a memo about this meeting? I

didn't get it."

"Goodness. The rest of the office received it. Do you suppose just *your* email isn't functioning correctly?" Her voice was filled with attitude.

I swallowed. "Perhaps I overlooked it." Fat chance of that, but what else could I say? I reminded myself not to let this woman get to me. And I intended to keep that promise.

"Well, join in. Try to catch up." Her tone was unbelievable. Was I the only one in the room who felt the slap? "I was just showing the group what not to do when editing someone else's work."

I jerked my gaze to the screen in front of her, knowing in my gut I wasn't going to like the show.

And I was right. The brochure I had spent hours on last night was splayed open in giant blown-up proportions, and Christine was circling items up and down the page that were incorrect.

I was mortified. My face flushed deeper, my cheeks burning.

I pursed my lips and blended into the wall at my back.

As soon as she started speaking, I realized I hadn't fucked up the copy. That wasn't what happened at all. It was much worse. This wasn't the document I sent her last night before I left. Either she had another version or she'd intentionally sabotaged the one I worked on.

The word "bitch" took on a new meaning. She'd called the entire department in here simply to humiliate me. Who did that? Why was she so damn angry with me for dating a man she hadn't been with in a year?

I held my breath while she continued to flip pages and critique God-only-knew whose work.

Just when I thought she was going to keep the stab into my chest between just her and me, she dropped the gauntlet. "Cheyenne, would you care to explain how this went so poorly? Were you rushing? Do you not take your job seriously? We can't possibly send this sort of thing to press. Now I have to get someone else to do the work all over again."

I opened my mouth, fully intending to protest when I saw the gleam in her eye just daring me to contradict her. Instead I found myself stooping lower than I had ever stooped in my life. "I'm so sorry. I have no idea what went wrong. Perhaps I sent you the wrong copy." I met her halfway. I didn't spit on her in front of everyone else, nor did I admit defeat entirely.

"You're all dismissed. Cheyenne please remain to

discuss this."

Stacy met my gaze with a wrinkle in her brow that said "I'm sorry you got in the way of this crazy woman." She didn't know the half of it.

When everyone had exited, I approached Christine.

The door was still open. I wasn't sure if that was a good thing or a bad thing. "I'm truly sorry, Christine. I'll go look on my computer and see if I sent you an earlier version instead of the final."

"You do that, Cheyenne. And you need to pay closer attention to detail if you want to remain with this firm. Talent Marketing Group is not the sort of place where slackers last very long."

I burned from head to toe. I wanted to reach out and slap the smug expression off her face. My fingers shook and twitched at my sides as I curled them into balls to keep from freaking out. "Of course. I'll be more careful in the future."

"See that you are." Christine walked right past me without looking at me again.

I stared at the blank screen in front of me for several seconds. Finally, I took a deep breath and made my way back to my computer. I turned on the monitor with shaky fingers. Even Stacy didn't stick her nose around the corner to question me.

Thank God.

I wasn't in the mood for the third degree from her too.

I opened the file containing the versions of the brochure I had saved throughout the evening and scanned up and down the list until I had the last copy picked out. I opened it. It looked nothing like the one Christine had used for her little demo.

I pulled open the sent email and found that I had indeed sent Christine the correct final version.

The woman was certifiable, and I was doomed.

Fuck.

I resent the email, not even bothering to send a new one. Let her figure out for herself that I was on to her little game.

I didn't bother to get up and go make sure she opened it. What difference would it make with regard to her deadline? She had the correct copy all along.

There was nothing I could do at the moment except put my all into the project that needed completion. Blocking out anything else was mandatory. And I did it. I worked straight through lunch and didn't start to look at the clock until four thirty. I glanced several times down the row of cubicles to spot Christine's location. I didn't want to be waylaid again this evening.

That was not going to happen.

At five minutes until five, I grabbed my purse from my drawer and reached to shut down my computer.

"In a hurry, Cheyenne?" That voice. That fucking bitch. The mere tone made me cringe.

"Yes. I have to be someplace this evening." I pushed the button to power off the computer and turned around to stand. It was a lie, of course. I didn't have a single place to be other than where I currently was.

"That's too bad. I was hoping you were a team player."

I narrowed my gaze and fought the recurring urge to slap that look off her face. "Always. But I was here late last night, and I have things to do this evening."

"Last night's bit of overtime was a waste though, wouldn't you say? After all that, you messed up the document. I could have had the janitor do a better job."

I felt the flush return, but kept my gaze on hers. *Bit of overtime? That's what she calls a four-and-a-half-hour project after closing?* It wasn't as though I got paid by the hour.

"So sorry for the confusion this morning. I assume you got the redirected correct document okay after the meeting?" I worded my phrase carefully, not taking the blame for her obvious vindictive attempt to nail me to the wall. She held all the power here, and she knew it. She would fuck with me until she had the ammo to fire me. And then I would be doomed. The last thing I wanted to do was search for a job after getting fired from Talent Marketing.

"I'll be keeping a close eye on you, Cheyenne." She said my name with such distain I almost chuckled. I couldn't begin to play in the big leagues with the likes of Christine Parson. I needed to get my résumé out and fast.

But first I needed to tell Riley. I dreaded the conversation, but not as much as I would dread facing him later if I didn't tell him about this myself.

This sort of thing was exactly what I didn't need this week while I was supposed to be reflecting on our weekend and imagining myself in such an arrangement fulltime.

I hadn't spent more than a few minutes pondering my new relationship since I'd woken up Monday morning.

"I'm sure you will, Christine." I lifted my chin

The Game

high and made my way out of the office. I didn't pause to even breathe until I was in my car and pulling out of the parking garage.

I drove on autopilot to a house I'd only been to one time.

And the arms of a man I'd had the glorious chance to enjoy for an entire weekend.

It took forever to weave through rush hour traffic in Atlanta.

As I pulled up to Riley's home, I panicked. Would he be mad?

I dreaded the discussion. I hadn't even called Amy today. There was no reason for it. I didn't need a pep talk to know it was time to give up my dream of fixing this on my own.

I made my way toward the front door on leaden feet.

It took only moments for the door to open. But it wasn't Riley I faced. It was Les. Until that moment it hadn't occurred to me that Riley might not be home. He worked long hours after all. Nobody got rich leaving the office at five.

I felt decidedly inadequate in the face of this revelation, and I almost turned around and headed back to my car to make an escape.

Les opened the door wider. "Ms. Decard. So good to see you. Come in." He spoke as though I owned the place and had every right to be there. What had Riley told his staff about me? "Can I pour you a drink? You look a bit worse for wear."

"No. Thank you. Do you know what time Riley's expected?"

"I'm sorry. I don't. But I could text him for you if you'd like."

"Would you?" I was a nervous wreck. Putting this off would only make things worse. There was also the distinct possibility he would find out about my predicament before I had a chance to tell him myself.

Les reached into his pocket, pulled out his cell, and typed a quick text. "There. Done. Now how about that drink?"

I nodded. A glass of wine might calm my nerves. "Thank you, Les. White if you have it, or whatever's open will be fine." I followed Les deeper into the house and made my way to the island where I dropped my purse on the floor and climbed onto a stool.

Seconds later I had a glass of cool white wine in my hand, and I took a deep, calming drink.

The Game

"Would you like my wife to fix you something to eat?"

"Your wife?" I glanced around. I hadn't realized we weren't alone. Nor did I know that Riley had staff fulltime in his home. No one had been around over the weekend.

Les smiled hugely. "Yes. Justine. She's a fantastic cook. That's probably the main reason why Riley tolerates my sorry face each day. We're kind of a package deal."

I chuckled at the way his eyes twinkled as he spoke. He was the real deal. I loved him already. "That's okay. I've had a rough few days. I'm not quite ready to face food."

Les lifted one eyebrow. "Okay, but you let me know if you change your mind. I'm sure Riley would be pissed if he found you here and no one fed you."

"I'll handle Riley. But thank you, Les."

Now the man did chuckle, a deep belly laugh that reverberated through the kitchen and perhaps half the house.

A shudder wracked my frame. Les knew. I had no idea how much of Riley's lifestyle he was privy to, but he knew enough to find my statement humorous. And he wasn't wrong.

Chapter Fifteen

Les encouraged me to settle on the plush couch in the living room with my wine and left me to wander deeper into the house.

For several minutes I pondered my options. I had arrived here uninvited. I hadn't even called or texted Riley first. He might not appreciate me barging into his home, especially when he wasn't there.

I swallowed my fears, set my wine on the coffee table, and took a deep breath. Riley wasn't the sort of man who would be angry with my unexpected visit, but more importantly, he would be angry if I kept the fact that Christine had taken over my department a secret.

I closed my eyes and leaned my head back, trying

The Game

to slow my racing heart and gather my brain cells into something coherent before I faced him.

And that was the last thing I knew before a hand landed on my shoulder and soft words filled my ear. "Cheyenne. Baby."

Confused, I blinked, staring up at Riley.

His brow was furrowed, but he smiled as I came awake.

A delicious scent filling the house. Red sauce? Tomatoes... Garlic... Basil... Yes. My stomach growled. My eyes widened farther, and I bolted upright, knocking a soft throw blanket off my upper body to pool around my waist.

Riley sat on the coffee table, his face inches from mine. "You okay?"

I glanced around. Geez. "What time is it? I must have fallen asleep."

Riley chuckled. "You think?"

My face heated. That hadn't been my intention. Then again, I hadn't slept enough in days, especially the night before. I swallowed. My gaze scanned the room and paused when I saw a woman in the kitchen, her back to me as she leaned over several steaming pots on the stove. Justine. How had I slept through her cooking?

Riley brushed a lock of hair from my face and tucked it behind my ear. "Talk to me."

I met his gaze. I decided to just spill it. "I have a new boss."

"Yeah?" He frowned.

"Christine."

"What?" He nearly shouted as he jumped to his feet and ran his hands through his hair, making it stand in disarray. Instead of looking ridiculous, it made him even more attractive. My mouth watered, but now was not the time to drool.

"That was my reaction too."

"So you showed up at work today and found that crazy bitch in your space?" He stepped around the coffee table to pace the center of the room.

"No. Yesterday." I bit my lower lip.

Riley stopped pacing to face me. "Yesterday? Why the hell didn't you tell me then?"

"I wanted to handle it myself." That had been a bad idea. I rushed on to explain myself. "And there was hardly time. As soon as Christine got her claws in me, she put me to work until late last night. I didn't have a chance to breathe, let alone make phone calls."

Riley's mouth fell open, but he sucked in a deep

breath, seemingly deciding against his next words, and shook his head. "Tell me what happened."

"She knew I worked there." I shivered, recalling the way she'd met my gaze first thing yesterday morning, a smirk on her face.

"Shit."

"Yeah."

"I don't see how even Christine could have pulled that off. I know she's certifiable, but managing to land a job where my woman works in that short period of time is beyond the pale. She would have had to pull some major strings."

I didn't add anything. He was right. I was as perplexed as him. Besides, I was hung up on the way he called me his "woman," uncertain if I found that terminology endearing or annoying.

Nevertheless, somehow Christine had done exactly that.

"Did she do anything?"

I rolled my eyes and gave a sharp chuckle, pushing the blanket off my legs and standing. I at least wanted to add the few extra feet to my height if I was going have this discussion. "You could say that."

Riley scowled. "Tell me."

Becca Jameson

I smoothed my hand down my wrinkled blouse and adjusted it at my waist where it had come partially untucked. "She waited until the end of the day yesterday to toss a project on my desk—a project that was not part of my job description, mind you. I worked on it until after ten o'clock and then emailed the final edits back to her. She called a staff meeting for early this morning, inviting everyone but me, and then proceeded to make a spectacle of me when I came in late, pointing out what a horrible job I had done and demonstrating this fact by projecting a sabotaged version of my work for everyone to see."

"That bitch. So, that happened this morning?"

"Yes."

"And you still didn't call me."

"Can we maybe not harp on that fact?" I should have called him. "Amy warned me you would be livid if I didn't tell you."

That was the wrong thing to say. "So, you made time to call Amy, but not me." He set his hands on his hips and pressed his shoulders back, making him seem even larger than before. Formidable.

"I wanted to handle it myself," I mumbled.

I jumped when I heard the lid of a pot clang in

The Game

the kitchen and turned to find Justine still at work over the stove. She paid no attention to us, but I felt weird having this discussion in front of her.

Les wandered in at that moment and went to his wife, whispering something in her ear. She nodded and bustled around some more.

Riley cleared his throat, but before he could speak, Les beat him to it. "We'll be leaving in a moment, sir. Is there anything else you need?"

"No. Thank you, Les. And Justine, that smells fantastic. I'm sure we'll devour it."

Justine turned around, and I was granted a view of the front of her for the first time. She smiled broadly, two dimples appearing on her cheeks. She appeared to be about the same age as her husband, perhaps late fifties. Her hair was curly, short, and graying at the temples. She was just slightly overweight—the kind of weight a woman would carry after she had kids.

I loved her immediately.

"I hope I didn't wake you, dear," she said. "I tried to be quiet. You looked like you needed your nap."

I smiled. "I must have been exhausted. Never heard a thing. And considering how good it smells in here, I must have really been out." Normally there was no way I would have slept through someone cooking behind me, and this wasn't even my own home.

"I tossed that blanket over you. You were shivering."

"Thank you." I didn't love her. I adored her.

"Let's get out of here, hon. Leave these two to their evening." Les tugged on his wife's arm.

"Just let me finish up here, and we'll be out of your way." She turned back to face the stove and bustled about finishing her preparations.

"Thank you, Les. Justine. I'll see you tomorrow." Riley didn't take his gaze off me.

I shuddered, working hard to hold his gaze, not wanting to seem like a pushover.

We stayed that way until Les and Justine made their exit, the door shutting with a resounding click as though it was much louder than it should have been.

I tucked my lips into my mouth and watched as Riley padded up to me. He gently pulled me to the center of the room by my bicep and then his fingers trailed down to my hand. As he lifted it to his lips and kissed my knuckles, I tipped my head back.

"I'm sorry about Christine. If I suspected she would have interfered in your life, I would have done something about it. I can't believe she would stoop this low after all this time. I'll deal with her tomorrow."

I shook my head. "I don't want you to deal with her. I'm a big girl. I'll handle my own battles."

He frowned at me. "This isn't your battle, Cheyenne. It's mine. She's my ex, and I won't have her intimidating you. I'll handle it."

I shook my head with more force. "No. Riley, I'm serious. If you swoop into my place of work and throw your weight around, no one will respect me. I need to fix this myself with my head held high. I can do it."

Bile rose into my throat at the thought of having my new boyfriend come in and rock the boat at Talent Marketing Group. I wasn't ready for anyone in my office to know I was even seeing him, let alone have him pull strings to make my life easier.

He stared at me for several seconds before blowing out a breath. "This discussion isn't over."

I didn't move. There was nothing more to say. There was no way he would drop the subject entirely, but I felt like I had at least made my point in round one.

"I'm starving. Let's eat, and then we can talk some more."

As good as the house smelled from Justine's

cooking, my stomach was in knots. There was no way I could swallow yet. "I'm not hungry. You go ahead."

He narrowed his gaze at me and inhaled long and slow before speaking. "Submit to me then. It will help you relax. Redirect your attention to following my instructions and focus on how your body reacts to my commands."

I considered his proposition as a shiver shook my body. My heart rate increased at the idea of letting him control me in the middle of this strife.

Was it the right thing to do?

We stared at each other in a standoff. He was waiting on me. Patiently. Giving no indication one way or the other as to his thoughts.

I needed this. I needed his commands to help center me and give me something different to focus on. He could erase Christine from my day with just a word. Finally, I nodded.

In a calm, flat voice devoid of any telling signs, he stated, "Take your clothes off, Cheyenne. I want you on your knees in front of me."

I flinched, not expecting those words.

"Now, baby. Don't hesitate when I give you a directive."

He lowered himself into an armchair, crossed

THE GAME

his legs, and rubbed his chin with the fingers of his right hand nestled on the arm of the chair.

So casual.

"Cheyenne," he warned.

Shocking me, my panties grew wet. It was unreasonable. Why would I grow aroused by this man ordering me to strip for him on the tail end of such a serious discussion?

My fingers shook as I reached for the buttons on my blouse and slowly slipped each one through its hole. I was really doing this. Letting this man shift gears and take control of my every move. We had resolved nothing. He hadn't agreed to stay out of my business. Taking a one-eighty, we were switching from an argument about how to handle his ex to a full-blown D/s scene.

And it felt right. Even with my heart racing and my hands shaking, it felt like the perfect decision. I was stressed beyond measure. Why not flip things upside down and escape for a while?

Naked.

I stared at his unwavering face, the intensity in his gaze making my nipples harden. He looked like he wanted to devour me. And I was loath to admit I liked the idea. Even if we were diverting from our discussion, it was worth it if he wanted to fuck first and talk later. Maybe we could have a calmer, more rational discussion after a good fuck.

I shrugged the sleeves of my white blouse down my arms and laid it on the coffee table. Next I lowered the zipper on my navy skirt and let it fall to the floor. I swooped it up and set it next to my blouse.

Standing before this man who filled the entire room with his presence, I blew out a breath. I was down to my matching pink lace panty set.

"Take off the rest, Cheyenne."

I shouldn't have been surprised. He'd ordered me around like this all weekend—two straight days. That had only been two days ago. No part of me should have been surprised at his demands.

And yet…

I inhaled sharply and popped the front clasp on my bra, lowered it down my arms, and tossed it on my other clothes. Next, I dipped my fingers into the sides of my panties and bent down to extract them from my feet.

Now I was naked. Far more naked than just the removal of clothes. I was exposed. As if he could see into my soul.

I couldn't keep myself from crossing my arms over

my chest as goose bumps rose on my entire body.

Riley didn't bother to comment on my actions. He simply gave more commands. "On your knees, baby."

I lowered to the floor where I was, several feet from him. My thighs quivered.

"Knees wider. Shoulders back. Face the floor. Clasp your hands at your back."

I followed his instructions easily. He'd taught me all this over the weekend.

My nipples stood at attention, and I squeezed my eyes shut in an attempt to deny to myself that I was aroused. The wetness leaking from my pussy threatened to run down my spread legs.

"Good girl. When I tell you to strip, do it without hesitation, and always assume this position unless I instruct you otherwise."

"Yes, Sir." I spoke the words so softly I wasn't sure he heard them. I was stuck on him calling me a "good girl," as if I were a child. It caused an incongruent mix of emotions. I liked being praised. But did I like the words he chose?

"Now you'll listen to me."

I stiffened, jerking my attention back to his words.

"First of all, I want you to understand why I have

you in this position. I had no intentions of dominating you this week. I would have preferred you had the opportunity to take the week to think on this relationship before coming to me again. Not that I'm suggesting you should have done otherwise under the circumstances. In fact, you should have been here yesterday. Since you're here now, I need you to understand how it will be between us if you decide to submit to me permanently."

"I—"

"Don't speak. Just listen."

I closed my mouth.

He leaned forward, setting his elbows on his knees. "If you were mine, I'd insist on you submitting to me in the evenings much like this. There's no sense in pretending otherwise while you learn about my lifestyle. I know it's a lot to take in so fast, but this is the reality. This is the reason I left you sitting on that bench at Cade and Amy's engagement party six months ago.

"I'm not sure I did the right thing that night. You seem far more natural at this lifestyle than I would have expected. But perhaps I wasn't ready for a new submissive yet anyway. My breakup with Christine was too fresh."

I didn't move.

"I want you, Cheyenne. I'm not going to lie. I

The Game

haven't gotten you out of my head since the day we met. And you're so fucking sexy on your knees, it makes my cock hard just looking at you."

I swallowed and licked my lips, his words making my pussy even needier. My clit pulsed. I wasn't sure I could fully concentrate on his words in this state.

Riley didn't speak again for long moments. Finally, he continued. "What I want to do is take you over my knee and spank you. It would help ease you into a subspace and stop the shivering."

I swayed forward at his words, my body defying my brain's attempt to find his suggestion ludicrous. Instead, my breasts swelled, and I clenched my pussy. Another shudder made me squirm.

He chuckled. "You would like that."

I remembered what Amy had said about Cade no longer spanking her for punishment and winced again, wondering what Riley's view would be on the subject.

"Stand up, Cheyenne."

I lifted one foot to the center and rose without breaking my form, keeping my gaze down in hopes he would be impressed with my abilities and go easy on me. Was he going to spank me?

"Come here." He turned toward the corner of the

breakfast area and sauntered across the room.

I followed, supremely aware of the two walls of windows surrounding the table. The sun had not yet descended enough for it to be completely dark out. I could see the entire back yard as I followed him.

His back yard was amazing. He undoubtedly had a fabulous gardener who took care of the grounds. Sliding glass doors to my right led out to an enormous deck that contained a stainless-steel grill, a glass table, and several lounge chairs on the far end. Beyond that was a large yard covered in thick lush grass. Two mature trees were perfectly placed to provide shade over the majority of the yard. It was September, and they had not yet started dropping their leaves. Around the base of each tree were delicate baby roses that were currently in bloom, the red and white buds gorgeous.

"I want you to stand in the corner here." He pointed at the junction of one window with the other.

I should have known.

"Keep your hands clasped behind your back, nose to the corner, tits to the glass, feet wide."

I hesitated. What if someone saw me? I glanced at the wall around his property and realized the chances of that were slim to none. Only an intruder would see me at this hour. No way was his lawn crew going to show up this late to trim bushes or prune roses.

"Now, Cheyenne." His voice was firm. He didn't touch me either, which stung. I half-expected him to grab my arm and angle me into position. I would have preferred the contact. Even a spanking. It would have meant having his hands on me.

He knew that. He'd chosen this option intentionally.

I stepped up to the glass and did as he said, gasping softly as my nipples hit the cool glass. I wasn't uncomfortable. But I was disconcerted. Which was the point.

Was he testing me?

If that was the case, I needed to show him I had what it took if I wanted to enjoy the other aspects of his lifestyle. If anyone would have asked me two minutes ago while I kneeled before him on the floor, I would have said I was so aroused I could have come on command.

"Legs wider."

I flinched and spread my bare feet apart several more inches.

"Good girl. Don't move until I say so."

Riley left me there. In about two seconds I

understood what Amy had said about hating time outs. Being ignored was far less bearable than being spanked. I never should have told Riley I knew about this practice.

I was confused about his motive, however. He hadn't mentioned punishing me. So why was he leaving me in a corner?

I listened to the sounds behind me, confident Riley was dishing up food from the kitchen and then hearing the rustling at my back that indicated he set several things on the table. He went back and forth a few times. My mouth watered as the smells wafted closer. Something Italian and undoubtedly delicious.

I licked my lips as I heard the chair scoot out and then back up to the table. The next noises were silverware against the plate.

He was eating.

Oh. My. God.

He was going to eat and leave me in the corner. Naked. My back to him. Why had I told him I wasn't hungry? Suddenly, I was ravenous.

I rocked from one foot to the other.

"Stay still," he said through a bite of food.

Shit.

This was intense.

The Game

His gaze was on me. It was palpable.

I tightened my ass cheeks and pursed my lips to avoid moaning around the vision in my head of what his expression must be.

My stomach growled.

Riley moaned around a bite. "Man, Justine makes the best ravioli I've ever tasted."

I was starving now. And it wasn't unreasonable. I hadn't taken lunch today in an effort to get the hell out of the office as early as possible.

I stood as still as I could, hoping he would shorten my time in the corner for good behavior. I had no way of knowing if he intended to leave me here for five minutes or an hour.

The sun lowered, making me more nervous about my position than before. I couldn't see out anymore, but anyone in the yard could see me perfectly. It was unnerving.

Every nerve ending in my body was on alert. I craved contact. My nipples ached in their position pressed against the window. The desire to shift back and forth and rub them over the now heated surface made me grit my teeth to avoid acting on it. I had to squeeze my eyes shut to concentrate. My clit throbbed with the need to close my legs and apply pressure to the nub.

The thought of Riley behind me watching me caused a stream of wetness to run down my thigh. Could he see it? I clenched and unclenched my butt cheeks, but he didn't comment. Deep breaths did nothing to ease the need building in the pit of my stomach.

How could I grow so aroused be being ignored? I almost moaned. This was his plan. And it was working.

The clanking of dishes again indicated Riley had finished and was cleaning up.

I almost cried. Why was I allowing him to do this to me? I was hungry and horny and I had no idea which one was worse.

No. That wasn't true. I would choose sex over food if given the choice. And I was sure I would not be given options.

I didn't move. I wanted what Riley could give me. I wanted to feel the unbelievable need he drew out of me time and again over the weekend. Orgasms I had never thought possible. Like nothing I'd ever experienced.

And I knew in my soul no other man could pull anything like that out of me in this lifetime. That was what kept me in this position. It wasn't easy. I warred with myself over and over, half of me pleading I was insane

The Game

to allow myself to be ordered into a corner like this, the other half assuring me it would be worth it.

I had a tremendous amount of pent-up stress. Sex with Riley would erase that in a heartbeat. Sex I was going to have to wait for and accept on his timetable.

Chapter Sixteen

"Come here, baby." His voice startled me after so long, and the tone was soft and kind. He even called me "baby."

I released my hands to shove off the window. My nipples immediately jumped to attention after being flattened against the cool glass for so long. My legs were stiff from waiting. It had probably only been half an hour, but it seemed like forever.

When I inched toward Riley, I found him sitting at the table, a full plate of food in front of him as though he were about to eat when in fact I knew he'd already eaten. Which could only mean one thing.

I almost moaned at the realization the food was

for me.

"Kneel in front of me."

Again, startled, I lowered at his side and clasped my hands behind my back again. My chest rose, my nipples stiffening as they jutted toward him.

"You are *so* fucking sexy. And I'm so proud of you." He lifted my chin with one hand and met my gaze. "You're amazing." He smiled broadly, which made the last half hour almost worth it. He was right about one thing—I was now totally in a submissive frame of mind. The problems of the last two days were stuffed to the back of my head while I shifted into Riley's control.

There were clear benefits to submission.

Riley dropped my chin. "Hungry now?" He smiled.

"Yes, Sir."

He reached for the fork and stabbed a bite of ravioli. With his hand cupped under the utensil, he brought the fork to my mouth. "Open for me, baby."

My eyes widened as I realized he meant to feed me. Plump squares of ravioli glistened with fresh tomato sauce and a sprinkle of parmesan. I would swear Justine made it herself. I opened greedily and moaned around the first bite, hardly caring how ridiculous I must look kneeling on the floor and being fed by this gorgeous man. I should have been embarrassed.

Instead I was cherished.

He gave me another taste of the ravioli, a bite of salad, and then a drink of water. And then he repeated the process until all the food was gone and I was full. "Enough? Or would you like more?"

"No. Thank you, Sir. That was amazing. Tell Justine I loved it."

"You can tell her yourself. I'm sure you'll be seeing her. Perhaps more often than me."

I nodded. My heart beat faster at the implication. Did he think I would be spending more time at his home than him?

Riley carried the dishes to the sink and then tipped his head toward the hallway. "Come."

I rose to my feet and followed him. When I reached his bedroom, he pointed toward the attached bath and lifted a brow.

Grateful, I scampered to the bathroom and shut the door. Five minutes later, I had used the toilet and brushed my teeth with the toothbrush he'd designated for me over the weekend, grinning at its position in the holder next to his. I then lifted my gaze to the mirror.

The Game

I didn't recognize the woman looking back at me. She was flushed. Her hair was in disarray from napping earlier on the couch.

I combed my fingers through my tangled blonde curls and stuffed the strands behind my ears. I glanced down at my naked body and blew out a breath. This new world I found myself in was certainly unconventional, but dammit, I was horny. And that was the part I focused on.

If any other moment in my life had measured up to the way I felt when I was with Riley, I would have run from the house screaming. But the reality was, I had nothing that compared, and I wasn't about to let this opportunity pass me by.

However, I turned from the mirror and took a breath. We still needed to discuss what to do next about Riley's crazy ex-fiancée. I dreaded that. How long could we put it off?

I was surprised to find Riley naked in the master suite when I returned from the bedroom.

"Um, Riley? Sir," I amended, "shouldn't we discuss my job?"

"Nope. Later. I need to fuck you. Until then, I can't think straight. You've had my cock harder than a rock for hours, baby."

I moved toward him, my permanently wet pussy flooding again.

He pointed at the bed where he'd already turned down the comforter and sheet. "All fours in the middle."

All fours? Okay. I could do that.

I climbed onto his mattress and centered myself in the requested position.

Riley grabbed a condom from the bedside table and settled himself behind me. He nudged my legs wider and pressed into the created space. One hand landed on my waist. The other snaked around my belly and reached to stroke through my pussy. "So wet for me. Perfect." He stopped touching me too quickly, grabbed my other hip, and thrust forward, embedding himself inside me so fast, I gasped.

Shocked.

Dismayed even.

No foreplay. Almost no words.

I braced myself against his thrusts.

His hands dug into my hips as he fucked hard and fast.

I needed more. As aroused as I'd been for over an hour, I still needed some contact with my clit.

He didn't deliver. Instead, he wordlessly took what

The Game

he needed, groaning loudly as he came, buried to the hilt, his hands still gripping my waist.

And then he pulled out as quickly as he'd entered me and left me on all fours as he headed to the bathroom.

I didn't dare move. My arms and legs shook with the effort and the need, but I remained still.

"Lie on your back, baby," he whispered when he returned.

I gladly flipped over and relaxed onto my back. My eyes were wide. I didn't say a word.

"That's a good girl." He opened the drawer again, grabbed something, and closed it. Next, he took one wrist in his hand and lifted a length of rope. He wrapped one end around my wrist in a perfectly orchestrated knot and tugged it over my head to secure it to the bed.

By the time he rounded the bed and worked the other wrist in the same fashion, I was panting. And I almost balked when he took my ankle to secure it to the frame at the end of the bed.

I watched him circle to the other ankle without blinking. Whatever he had in mind, I wasn't sure I was going to like it. But at least he didn't intend to leave me hanging. Right?

Finally, he grabbed another item from the drawer

and climbed between my legs. I recognized the vibrator from the weekend. He set it down between my legs and spoke. "I'm proud of you. For someone barely introduced to the lifestyle just a few days ago, you have pleased me immensely this evening."

I smiled. Good. Now, could I please come?

He stroked a hand up my thigh, barely touching the skin so that goose bumps rose in its wake and I squirmed.

"You're so horny, aren't you?"

I nodded. It was hard to concentrate with his fingers trailing closer to my needy core.

"I'm giving you a deeper taste of the lifestyle. I know it's a lot in a short period of time, but I want you to get a complete understanding of what it means to turn yourself over to someone. To *me*."

I did. How could I not? I'd just spent the last hour naked at his bidding, standing against the windows in what essentially was a time out, and then letting this man feed me on my knees on the floor. I got it. He could wipe my head of all my problems with a simple word. It felt amazing. I'd never been so aroused. I needed to come so badly it hurt. What more did he want me to experience tonight?

The Game

With both hands now, Riley danced his fingers up my body until he reached my breasts. He tickled the undersides and then tapped lightly in a circular motion around and around, avoiding my nipples entirely. "I love these tits, baby. They're so fucking sexy. They swell when I play with them." He grazed his thumbs over the tips finally. "And your nipples are amazing when they jut out like that. They turn a deep shade of rose that makes my mouth water."

I moaned.

"Shhh," he admonished without looking at my face. He danced his fingers back down my belly and then my thighs, stroking the skin gently, maddeningly. When he reached my center, he nudged my legs wider with his knees and pulled my lower lips open with both hands.

And then he stared. "I need to shave you again."

I gulped. Now?

I hadn't shaved myself. For one, I had never done so. For another thing, he'd specifically said he wanted to do it himself. And he had. First on Friday and then on Sunday. Now it was Tuesday.

"Think you can handle it without coming?"

Why would I want to?

He chuckled and climbed off the bed. Moments

later he returned with his usual pile of implements, tucked a towel under my ass, and went to work.

He took his time, carefully dragging the razor in slow motion over every fold and crevice. I stiffened every time he grazed the edge of my clit or my inner lips, but he didn't comment. In fact, it seemed he intentionally avoided contact with the most important parts. He was all business.

When he finished and set everything aside, he met my gaze. "Do not come while I wipe away the shaving cream." He held up a wet cloth.

I nodded and bit the inside of my cheek.

The warm cloth landed on my pussy and he quickly brushed away any remnants of shaving cream.

And then the cloth was gone and I gasped for air.

"Good girl." He stroked through my folds unexpectedly, drawing my wetness out. His finger disappeared as I moaned.

And there was that term of endearment again. "Good girl." It wasn't demeaning. It was a compliment. He was proud of me.

I blinked, finding it hard to focus. "Please…"

"Baby, I've just begun."

"What?"

The Game

He smiled. His face wasn't right. It was twisted in a wicked look, his eyes dancing. "Teasing you." He leaned over me, setting his hands on both sides of my chest and meeting my gaze head on. "Orgasm denial."

"What?" My eyes widened farther. I gulped.

"I play. You don't get to come."

"No," I blurted. I wasn't even sure that was possible. And more importantly, I hated how my body reacted to the idea.

He grinned again. "Oh, yeah. And if you can do it quietly without begging, I'll let you off the hook sooner than you can expect in the future. I'm super proud of how you've endured everything I tossed your way tonight." He stroked a finger over my lower lips, causing me to open my mouth.

I didn't say anything.

"How aroused are you?"

"Very, Sir."

"See? That's the plan." He sat back on his heels and pulled my pussy open wide again, staring at my naked sex. That was enough to bring sweat to my brow. It was unnerving the way he stared.

He stroked my skin, too lightly, touching me but not touching me at the same time. His fingers moved all over, even grazing my clit. But not with enough pressure to send me over the edge.

Wetness pooled at my entrance until it ran out and eased toward my rear hole.

When he held the hood off my clit and tapped it with his other hand, I bucked my torso toward him, tipped my head back, and gritted my teeth. I needed to come worse than at any point in my life.

I tried hard not to make any noise, but small sounds escaped my lips anyway.

He released my clit and trailed through my wetness down to my perineum, rubbing the skin enough to make me whimper.

He hadn't breached my ass yet, but he had mentioned it over the weekend, and I knew it was only a matter of time.

"Shhh," he admonished again.

I pursed my lips and concentrated on his fingers working me into a frenzy. It was maddening. He knew exactly where to touch me and when to drive me crazy. He also knew precisely when to back off to keep me from coming.

He pressed one finger inside my pussy and stroked back out, gathering my wetness to swirl it around my

THE GAME

lower lips and clit. I was seconds from screaming when he finally stopped altogether.

I yanked my face to see his. He stared at me a moment and then spoke. "I have your attention?"

"Yes, Sir." My words were strangled. They sounded like they belonged to someone else.

He picked up the vibrator.

I almost came as he turned it on at the lowest setting.

He set it at the entrance to my pussy and swirled it around, not reaching inside, and avoiding my clit. "Hold on for me, baby. Let me control you."

I didn't acknowledge his words. I couldn't.

When the vibrator swirled around my clit, I stiffened. My thighs shook from the effort. Finally, he let the blunt head of the vibrator settle over my clit and thrust three fingers into my pussy. "Now, baby. Come for me."

I shattered, screaming as my body shook with the most forceful orgasm I'd ever had. My pussy gripped at his fingers as they continued to thrust in and out, dragging repeatedly across my G-spot.

He pressed the vibrator firmly against my clit and didn't let up.

One orgasm became two and then three before I tried to wiggle free, overly sensitive. "Please, Sir…" I begged.

He relented. Bless him. The vibrator disappeared, and he stroked my skin lightly as I floated all the way back to Earth.

I blinked as I regained some small sense of myself. "Beautiful, baby."

I nodded. Oh God. I was in so much trouble.

Chapter Seventeen

While I caught my breath, Riley untied my limbs and then climbed up beside me, turned me on my side, and spooned me from behind. He held himself up on one elbow and set his chin on my shoulder. As he brushed a lock of hair from my face, he murmured, "Now, let's talk about Christine."

I sighed. Who wanted to talk about their boyfriend's ex-fiancée right after awesome sexual escapades? But I knew he didn't mean it that way. I sobered. "What's there to say? That crazy woman is going to ruin my life by forcing me to resign from a job I love. It's pretty clear to me."

"She isn't."

I twisted my head to face him and narrowed my gaze. "How do you propose to stop her?" I regretted that question immediately when his smile spread.

"Baby, do not underestimate me."

I knew he had money—shit tons. I did *not*, however, want him to fling that money around to bail me out. "Riley…" We'd only been together a few days. It seemed like longer, but it wasn't long enough for him to wade into my problems.

He set a finger over my lips. "Let me handle this."

I untangled myself from his grip so fast, his eyes went wide as I sat up and twisted around to face him. So what if I was naked and my breasts were bare? "No." I shook my head. The last thing I wanted was for Riley to "handle it." "Please. This is my job. I'm in the middle of a big project. It's huge for me. I don't want to risk it getting fucked up."

"What project? When's it due?"

"Thursday. And it's a marketing proposal for Link."

"The cell phone company?"

"Yes. This is the biggest account I've handled. Hell, it's the third largest account Talent Marketing has received. I'm putting together the advertising campaign."

The Game

Riley stared at me for several seconds, not looking convinced. Finally, he licked his lips. "She'll eat you alive."

I shook my head faster. "I won't let her. It's good. Hopefully I can knock her socks off with my abilities, and she'll leave me alone."

Riley grabbed my hand and squeezed. "Thursday?"

I nodded.

"That's in two days."

"Yes. I've been on this for a month. I'll be ready. As soon as Christine sees how hard I have worked on this, I'm hoping she'll realize I'm not that bad of a human being. I know this client better than anyone in the office. My presentation is almost done. I feel good about it."

"I don't like it, baby."

"I know. But please, let me try to win her over without bringing you into it. Maybe if I make her think I don't lean on you for anything, she'll respect me."

He chuckled, a dry sound that made me flinch. And then he wrapped his larger hand all the way around mine and squeezed tighter. "I don't know how that woman got a job at Talent Marketing Group, but you're more qualified than she is to run that department."

I rolled my eyes. "I'm nowhere near qualified to

run a department, Riley. That's insane."

"I never said you were. I simply stated that you were *more* qualified than Christine. And don't undersell yourself. I'm sure you're amazing at what you do." He reached up to stroke a finger down my cheek. "She's up to something. I don't want you to get hurt in her path."

"I won't. I'm tough."

He grinned wider. "Don't I know it." He blew out a breath and continued. "I'll give you two days. If things go south between now and then, I trust you'll tell me."

I closed my eyes and nodded. If he were anyone else, I would lie my way through this mess to keep him from meddling. But I knew if I lied to Riley, he would find out, and I probably wouldn't enjoy the consequences.

* * * *

Somehow I skated through Wednesday without more than a few pursed lips and tight gazes from Christine. She peeked over my shoulder several times to observe my work, but she said nothing while I worked feverishly to finish my presentation.

I stayed later than everyone on my floor that night, preferring to have the presentation done before I went home just in case Christine considered "Thursday" to mean nine in the morning. I didn't want to take a

The Game

chance on her chastising me in front of everyone for not being ready to present when I arrived.

By eight o'clock I was finished. I saved my work to the hard drive, the cloud, and a CD. I wasn't taking any chances something would happen to my work between Wednesday evening and Thursday morning. Even a catastrophic event couldn't possibly wipe out all three venues.

I was exhausted when I got home and poured myself a glass of wine before settling on my couch to put my feet up and relax. My hands shook. I couldn't focus on anything but worrying about the next day.

When my phone rang, I smiled at the name running across the top.

Riley.

"Hey," I answered.

"How'd it go today?"

"I finished. And your ex didn't bother me, at least not verbally."

He chuckled. "Thank God I never married that bitch. And I know exactly what you mean. She can shoot daggers with her eyes."

Those were my exact thoughts. "Maybe she's done bothering me. Do you suppose she knew we fought that night at Sky and maybe even saw me leave without you?"

"Don't bet on it. Has she ever mentioned me?"

"Nope."

"Calm before the storm, baby. Call me tomorrow as soon as you finish with her."

"I will. Thanks."

"Sleep well, Cheyenne."

"You too. Bye." I hung up and resumed staring into space, taking another long drink of my wine. I needed to eat something. Arriving at work Thursday after a liquid dinner was a bad plan.

* * * *

I was up early after tossing and turning all night. I even arrived at work by eight in the morning before anyone else—except Christine Parson. She was already in her office and on the phone when I arrived.

She hung up and called my name as I walked by. "Cheyenne. Good to see you being a team player this morning. I'll expect to see your presentation in five minutes." She didn't even glance up as she spoke.

I cringed as I nodded and headed for my desk. Her syrupy voice was a bad omen. I was so glad I'd stayed late and finished the presentation since clearly I was right. Thursday meant before dawn to Christine.

The Game

After dropping my purse in my drawer, I turned on my computer and waited for it to boot up.

And waited.

It didn't come on.

How not shocking.

I fought a grin. The last thing I wanted was for that crazy woman to think she bested me. She would not.

I slid into Stacy's cubicle without detection and powered up her computer without a problem. Thank God we had exchanged log in information months ago. Twice we had needed to borrow the other's space when we had a problem. This morning she was saving my life.

Of course I still had the jump drive in my purse, but if I could get into my email and send the project directly to Christine through the cloud, all the better.

Five minutes later I was done. Sent.

I stood tall and strode to Christine's office. "I sent you the link to my presentation. Would you like me to go over it with you?"

She didn't even lift her head as she shuffled papers on her desk and feigned incredible interest in whatever she was working on. "No. That won't be necessary. I'll pull it up when I get a chance and let you know what I think later."

Becca Jameson

I blew out a long breath as I walked away, deflated. It was a presentation. One I would have gone over that day with the board. It had not a damn thing to do with Christine.

Granted, when I'd been assigned that particular marketing campaign a month ago, there had been no department head for my floor and I had answered to the top floor. But it seemed now that we had a department manager, she intended to step in and be the liaison between me and the board.

If she were any other human, like someone from this planet, I wouldn't find it out of character. But I didn't trust Christine. No way in hell that woman would have my best interests at heart.

I trembled as I slouched in my desk chair. Why on Earth did I ever for one moment think this would go smoothly? If I wasn't going to be permitted to present my campaign personally to the board, I couldn't even give the speech I had prepared.

Fuck.

Taking a deep breath, I grabbed the desk phone and dialed IT. They sent someone to my floor immediately to fix my computer. I didn't even want to know what that woman had done to sabotage it.

The Game

    I wanted to send a text to Riley and let him know the status, but the last thing I would be able to stand would be Christine catching me doing something personal on "her" time. So I refrained.

    Ten minutes later, IT had me up and running. The guy smirked and shook his head as he went by. I said nothing.

    "You're here early," Stacy said as she rounded the wall between our cubicles.

    "Yeah. I had that presentation. Oh, and my computer wouldn't start. I used yours. Saved my ass. That's why it's already on."

    "No problem." She shrugged and ducked behind her wall.

    The minutes ticked by into hours, and not a word from Christine. I spent the entire day working on my next project, trying hard not to worry myself sick.

    At five I stood, straightened my prim blue skirt suit—the one I'd intentionally worn to make a presentation that never happened—and headed for Christine's office.

    "Christine?"

    She barely lifted her face to acknowledge me. "Yes?"

"Did you have a chance to look over my presentation?"

She sat back and met my gaze finally. "Oh, right. Yes. I looked at it early this morning. It needs a lot of work, Cheyenne. I'm surprised someone of your level of education would try to turn that in as a viable option."

My face flushed. I knew I was every shade of red while she stared at me.

All I could do was blink.

"You could take another stab at it, but that would be a waste of time. I'll do it myself." She lowered her gaze back to her papers and dismissed me without a word.

I hesitated, stunned, unable to decide what to do next. Finally, I walked away, went back to my cubicle, gathered my stuff, and left. I made it all the way to my car before I broke down and cried.

I sat in the parking garage, hoping no one saw me, for a long time, unable to drive through the mess that was my face.

When my phone rang, I jumped.

Riley.

Right. He would call. It was after five and I hadn't contacted him all day.

I sniffled and answered. "Hi." My voice was low

The Game

and unrecognizable even to me.

"Cheyenne?"

"Yeah." I turned on the car, switched him to blue tooth, and backed out of the spot.

"Talk to me."

"It didn't go well."

"Why didn't you call?"

"She never even spoke to me until I confronted her at five. I didn't have anything to report before now."

"You've been crying," he stated.

"Yeah. I'm disappointed. Not going to lie."

"Come to my house. Now."

I thought for a second as I pulled out of the garage into the Atlanta traffic. He lived in Buckhead. It would be a haul at this hour. Rush hour traffic would be a mess. I knew because I'd already done the drive on Tuesday. "I think I'd rather be alone, if you don't mind."

"I do mind. Come to me, Cheyenne. That's an order. I expect you to drive straight here. Justine is making a wonderful dinner. There's always more than enough. I'll see you soon." He hung up.

The man hung up.

Dammit.

My hands shook. Did I have another option?

There was no way I would defy Riley. He wasn't the sort of man who permitted anyone to defy him. But I also didn't like that he was sort of bullying me into doing his bidding.

On the other hand, he was on my side. I could use the support.

Hell, if it weren't for him, I wouldn't be in this predicament. My life was going along just fine. Either Christine never would have known who I was and therefore wouldn't have singled me out, or—and the second option made me shudder—she never would have been working at Talent Marketing Group in the first place.

The idea that she had taken the job totally out of spite made me want to vomit. How did she manage to pull strings that were as long as those had to be to get that job in such a short amount of time after meeting me briefly at Sky? It was preposterous. And yet, I couldn't deny it was possible. Not after everything I'd been through since Monday.

Fuck. That wasn't the first time I'd seen her. She'd been at the fundraiser the week before. Somehow that bitch had figured out who I was and gotten a job as my boss between the Monday afternoon of the fundraiser and

The Game

Friday night when we conveniently saw her at Sky.

Insane. And all because I had been speaking to Riley at the fundraiser? Had she seriously taken a stab in the dark and turned me into public enemy number one from that brief meeting?

I wanted to see Riley. I needed to. If I went home to my empty apartment alone, I would fall apart. If I went to him, he would piece me back together.

I craved him like a drug. I had just seen him Tuesday night, but already I felt drawn to him like a magnet. Was it healthy?

Chapter Eighteen

It took me over an hour to work my way through the city streets to his house. When I pulled in, I was wrung out, physically and mentally. Exhausted from the stress of worrying all day, crying in the car, and then driving through traffic.

Riley came outside before I exited my car. He pulled my door open, took my hand, and led me inside. After he shut the front door, I fell apart, tears running down my face with renewed force.

Riley pressed me against the door, practically holding me up with his body. He cupped my face, tipped my head back, and kissed my forehead. "Shh, baby. I'm so sorry." He held me close.

The Game

His actions only made me feel worse. He was too sweet. I needed to have a tantrum and scream. He held me together instead. In fact, he finally swung me up into his arms and carried me through the foyer and toward the living room where he deposited me on the couch in his lap.

"You look nice," he commented, pointing to my skirt, undoubtedly trying to distract me.

I tired to smile. "Thanks."

He must have been home a while. He was already dressed in jeans and a designer T-shirt. His feet were bare. Also, we were alone. Thank God.

The house smelled fantastic. Whatever Justine had made for dinner would be amazing if I could ever bring myself to taste or swallow.

I inhaled long and slow. Spices… Beef?

"Roast." Riley smiled. "She makes the best roast I've ever eaten."

"I'm sure she does," I muttered.

He held me at arm's length and tugged my suit jacket off. Why I was still wearing it? I'd been hot since I'd left the office, but my brain hadn't been running on all four cylinders.

"What did she say?"

"She said it was awful and she would redo it herself."

He flinched. "Are you fucking kidding me?"

I shook my head. I wouldn't joke about something this important. I'd poured my soul into that project for weeks. It was excellent. I deserved to present it. And now it was never going to happen. "Shit."

"What else?"

I pressed against him and scrambled to get off his lap. I needed to pace and think. "I have to quit."

"No. You most certainly do not." He stood, looming over me.

I nodded. "I don't have any other choices. I can't work under her. She'll ruin me a little more each day."

"You can't let that bitch control you. You have to stick up for yourself. You're a strong woman. Besides, you aren't alone." He grinned. "You have me."

"You can't waltz in and make this right, Riley. It's not an option. If you throw your weight around to help me out, no one will ever consider anything I do to have any merit."

He frowned at me. "I won't let her ruin you."

"You don't have any choice."

"I have lots of choices."

The Game

"Not if you want to continue seeing me. I need you to let me handle this. If you want to be supportive and stand by my side and listen to me rant and rave, that's fine. You can't interfere. No one will take me seriously if my boyfriend fights my battles."

He smirked, one side of his mouth curling. And then he tucked his lips between his teeth, fighting a larger grin.

"What?" I cocked one hip out and dared him to make light of this.

"Boyfriend?"

Had I said that? God. Yes. I had. "Whatever," I muttered, dipping my face to hide my flush. If he thought it was a joke, I would die on the spot.

Riley stepped into my space and lifted my face with a finger under my chin. "Am I?"

"What?"

"Your boyfriend?"

"No. I mean, yes." I shook my head, freeing myself from his finger. "I don't know. Are you?"

Riley closed the inches between us and cupped my face again. He lowered his mouth to mine and kissed me gently, taking his time, teasing my mouth until I opened for him.

When I leaned into his chest and fisted his shirt with both hands, he broke the kiss. He tucked my hair behind my ear. "Does this mean you've decided to be mine?"

"Pardon?"

"My submissive. I assume if you're thinking of me as your boyfriend, you've had enough time to think about our weekend together and come to the conclusion you'd like to submit to me." He shrugged. "We haven't discussed any of the details. And I'm sure you have questions. But I've been holding my breath all week waiting for you to say something."

I gasped. He was waiting on me? "Say something? About us?"

"Of course." He leaned back, grabbing my shoulders.

I swallowed. "I'm sorry. I've been so preoccupied with my job, I haven't stopped to consider you were waiting on me. I didn't realize…"

"Hush. I'm not mad. I never said anything specific. And you aren't obligated to make any sort of decision about us right now." He squeezed my shoulders and glanced down at my body. "God, Cheyenne. I want to possess you. I want you to turn your will over to me. It

The Game

kills me that you've spent the last four days fighting this battle—which I caused by the way—alone.

"I don't want you to be alone. Ever. I know I was an ass when we first met. I deserve your hesitation. But, baby, you're exactly the woman I want in my life. You're so fresh and pure and perfect in every way. I want to come home at night and know you'll be here—willing to submit to me.

"I want to worship your body and make you scream. I want that every day. Not just on the weekends. I want to wipe your tears and listen to your heart and be there for you."

I opened my mouth, but nothing came out. I was shocked. He was serious. It was so soon.

Sure, our weekend was made of magic. I couldn't deny that. He made my body hum. Even when I wasn't with him, he made me want things I'd never considered. He'd had that effect over me for the last six months, not just the last two weeks.

Where was my head? I wasn't kidding when I said I'd spent the last four days worrying about my project and my new boss. But it was also undeniable that I had been the one to call him my *boyfriend*. He'd wrapped me around his finger and made me his on Friday night before the weekend had hardly begun. Didn't he know that?

"I'm yours, Sir." The words slipped out without my permission. They weren't untrue. What did it matter? I ducked my head in a sign of submission.

I was frazzled and confused. What my heart wanted to do right that second was submit to Riley. Let him take control. If he ruled my body, he would ease my distress. It had worked before. And it felt amazing.

Perhaps it was unconventional. It was certainly not something I'd ever in my life considered as a viable possibility. But that was before I'd met David Riley Moreno.

Before his bitch of an ex-fiancée had interrupted our drink to fill me in on the finer details of my date.

Before one of my best friend had dragged me to a fetish party and led me down a path I hadn't fully understood.

Before Riley took me under his wing and patiently taught me how to submit.

Now? Now I was a different woman with different needs. And what I needed was for the Dom to take away my problems by replacing them with his demands. It was only for the night. Tomorrow I would have to drag myself out of bed and return to the real world. But if dominance and submission provided me with this escape, I was one hundred percent willing.

He smiled at me. Without a word, he reached for the buttons on my blouse and undid them all, slowly, never letting his gaze leave mine. When he pushed the silky white material over my shoulders, I shuddered.

This was it.

Something about tonight was so much more poignant than any of our previous encounters. We were no longer experimenting, testing each other out, going for a drive. This was serious.

His brow was furrowed, his eyes narrowed.

He dropped my shirt on the coffee table and then lowered the zipper on my favorite power skirt. At least he didn't rip it off me. It was the most expensive outfit I owned.

He leaned down and tapped one leg and then the other until I stepped out of the skirt.

As I stood before him in nothing but my navy heels and my matching white bra and panty set, I pulled my shoulders back and grasped one wrist with my other hand behind my back.

It came natural tonight. I needed this. I needed to submit. I needed him to control me. Everything. From when and what I ate to when and where I slept. I needed him to fuck me or not fuck me. I needed him to make the decisions.

It calmed me. Soothed.

Riley circled around me, trailing around my belly to my back with one finger.

I fought against the urge to squirm and remained as still as possible.

"I love how sexy you are in your bra and panties, especially these unending matching lace sets you have, but I like your bare skin even better." He grabbed the clasp at my back and popped my bra loose. It fell around my arms and he nudged my hands apart for a moment to remove the lace.

He rounded to the front again and cupped my breasts with his palms, teasing the tips with his thumbs. "Yeah. So sexy. I love the way your nipples stand erect for me even more." He leaned forward and blew across them.

I jumped, but he pinched both tips sharply. "Stay still." He flattened his palm on my belly and eased it down until his fingers dipped into my panties and teased the hair growing in above my pussy.

I inhaled sharply and swayed forward when he let his middle finger dip into my folds and drag across my clit. A moan escaped my lips.

"That's my girl. I love how responsive you are. And I love that you left this for me to shave." He cupped my pussy to emphasize his words.

I swallowed at the thought of him shaving me again. I should have been used to it, but it was just so damn intimate, and he did it so reverently…

Wetness slipped from my folds to soak my panties.

Riley stepped closer and dipped his hand deeper until he reached inside me with two fingers.

I rose onto my tip toes and leaned toward him, almost unable to keep my balance.

"My girl is so wet. You like it when I shave you, don't you?"

"Yes, Sir," I managed to whisper. My stomach was a bundle of knots. I had never been more aroused. Not even during any of our encounters in the last week. I was putty. The way he mastered me slowly, deliberately, with a calm force that couldn't be denied…

It was so fucking hot, I was about to explode.

He removed his hand and stepped back to run both hands through his hair as if he'd committed an offense. "We need to discuss this. I can't continue to dominate you without negotiating. I can't believe I've been so negligent for as long as I have. It's inconsiderate."

I widened my eyes. Negotiate? Was he kidding? As long as he fucked my troubles away, anything he wanted was fine. I was in no mood to negotiate anything.

"Don't look at me like that," he stated.

"Like what?" I was confused.

"Like you don't care about making sure your needs are met and not exceeded. You must."

"I trust you." I did. Implicitly.

He shook his head. "You can't. It doesn't work like that."

"It does for me. You've rocked my world. Nothing you've done has made me want to turn and run. And as far as your character is concerned, you have Amy and Cade to vouch for you. If you were an ax murderer, one of them would have told me." I smiled, hoping to dispel his sense of doom. I wanted his hands back on me.

Riley stepped farther away. "Come. Sit at the table. Let's eat. We can talk while we eat."

"Eat?" He wanted me to do what? Chew? Swallow? I shook my head. No way could I accomplish that simple task, not with my pussy pulsing with need and my clit begging to be wrapped in his lips. I could

The Game

come standing there under his scrutiny. Eating wasn't on my short list—no matter how good the house smelled.

He chuckled, grabbed my forearm, and led me toward the table. "Yes. Eat. It's when you put food in your mouth, chew, swallow, repeat."

"I'm aware of the steps," I mumbled. "I'm just not all that interested right now. How about later?"

Riley smiled indulgently as he pulled out a chair and pointed. "Put your sweet ass in the seat, baby."

I sat, mostly because I didn't see any other option.

Riley left me there, wearing only my heels and panties, and stepped into the attached kitchen. I watched his fine ass in his perfect-fitting jeans while he swayed with each step. I wanted to look away, but I couldn't bring myself to give up the view, even if it did make my current plight that much worse.

Moments later, he returned with a huge pot. He set it in the middle of the table and dropped the pot holders to the side. And then he grabbed a bottle of wine from the corner where it had been chilling on ice. I hadn't seen it.

He poured me half a glass and did the same for himself. "I think you'll like this one. It's one of my favorites." He lifted my glass and held it to my lips, tipping it back just the right amount to provide me with the perfect sip.

I tipped my head back, leaving my hands in my lap, and let him guide the glass.

The wine was perfect. Granted, my knowledge of wines and what foods they paired with was zero. The only times I'd really had good wine were when I was with Cade and Amy. Cade was the biggest wine snob I knew until I met Riley. Perhaps thirty-something rich dudes were all wine snobs.

"Do you like it?"

"Yes, Sir. It's delicious."

"Good." He set the glass down and lifted the lid off the steaming pot.

I closed my eyes and inhaled slowly. It smelled so wonderful. Perhaps I could manage to eat a few bites after all. I silently kicked off my heels under the table.

Riley dished a portion for me and then himself. And then he took his seat. "Eat, baby. I won't always ask you to kneel and let me feed you. I enjoy doing so on occasion, but right now I want you to be at ease. Eat. Talk to me."

I shivered. How preposterous, considering I was almost naked.

The Game

"Would it help if I gave you a robe?" He pursed his lips, and I wanted to swat him.

"You would really allow that?"

"No. But I'd make an exception this one time so you can relax and talk to me. If it helps, I'll permit it."

I hesitated. He was in just as big a predicament as me as long as he had to stare at my breasts while we ate—perhaps more so. "I'll survive."

He paused a second and then walked down the hall and returned with the silk robe I'd worn the last time I was there.

I lifted my arms when he held it open and shrugged into it, tying it at the waist. I did feel better. At least maybe I could concentrate on the meal if my boobs weren't hanging out.

He nodded at my plate. "Eat." It was an order. He meant business. No messing around now. He meant for me to eat whether I wanted to or not.

I picked up my fork and stabbed into a piece of meat that nearly fell apart as I lifted it. I closed my eyes and moaned around the bite. Perhaps I could eat after all. It was that good.

We ate in silence, both of us enjoying the meal. When Riley finished, he left me a moment and returned with his laptop. He pushed his plate back and set it up. And then he met my gaze.

"I want to see your presentation."

I hesitated, swallowing the bite in my mouth. "I'm not sure about that."

"I am."

What if he hated it? What if it really was as bad as Christine insinuated?

"Can you pull it up? I'm sure you saved it to the cloud."

I exhaled slowly. "I did, but I can do better than that. I have it on a jump drive in my purse."

He smiled. "Worried?"

"With good reason," I mumbled.

"Excuse me?"

"Never mind." I stood and padded across the room in my bare feet to grab my purse. I tugged the sash of my robe tighter, grateful now he'd given it to me. If we were going to discuss work, no way did I want to be naked.

When I returned and handed him the jump drive, he pulled me into his lap as he pushed the USB connection into his computer.

I sat on his thigh, my legs between his, my hands

THE GAME

in my lap.

"What aren't you telling me?"

I rolled my eyes. Did we really have to do this? I shrugged. "Nothing. I just had some issues this morning with my computer. That's all."

"First of all, don't roll your eyes at me." He grabbed my chin, forcing me to hold his gaze. "And second of all, that doesn't sound like nothing. Did you get your computer fixed?"

"Yeah. Some guy from IT came and got it running."

"What was wrong with it?"

"I don't know, but it must have been stupid because he looked put out when he left."

"Was it plugged in?"

I snarled this time. "Yes, Master. It was plugged in. I'm not an idiot."

He chuckled. "A little snarky, aren't we? Don't get all defensive. Just asking." He turned toward the computer and pulled up my presentation.

For the next ten minutes, I chewed on my lip while he clicked through the slide show and concentrated on my work. If he hated it, I would die. Even watching him scroll through my presentation made me stand taller.

It was good. No. It was amazing. I was sure Link would love it. Christine apparently thought I was a moron. There was no way that woman could possibly do a better job. She had never even met with the client.

When he finished, he turned it off and met my gaze again.

I held my breath.

"That's brilliant, baby." His voice was soft and gentle.

I don't know why I was surprised. Until that afternoon, I'd thought it was fantastic. I only began to doubt myself after that malicious shrew got her hands on it.

"She's full of shit," he continued while loosening the belt on my robe.

I still didn't comment as his fingers slipped inside and cupped my breast.

"I'll—"

Now I interrupted. "Do nothing." I grabbed his hand to stop him from moving any farther. "Please. Do not get involved. Let me handle this."

"Baby…"

"I'm serious. You can't swoop in and save the day. If you're anything like Cade, that's exactly what's running through your head. Don't do it. You aren't involved with Talent Marketing Group. Keep it that way. I won't be able to hold my head up if you interfere. We've been through this."

"Yeah. But I didn't agree. And this is serious, Cheyenne. You can't let that woman run roughshod all over you. *I* can't conscientiously allow it. It's my fault she's bothering you in the first place." He pointed at his computer. "Your proposal is excellent. Did anyone else see it?"

"I doubt it. They would have if she hadn't taken over the department. We didn't have a department head until she came on-board Monday. Before that, the plan had been for me to present to the board. It was my big shot." *And now it's ruined.* I was furious, but not half as mad as I would be if Riley interfered.

"Let me make a few calls."

"No."

He stared at me. "She'll make your life a living hell."

"Not if I don't react. I'll go back to work tomorrow, head high, chin up, and make her like me."

"How? By bringing her coffee?"

I shuddered.

"Tell me you have not brought that bitch coffee."

I bit my lip.

Riley stiffened. "That fucking cunt."

Now I jumped.

He held me tight around the waist when I fought to get off his lap. "Stay still. We may be discussing this problem, but it's not distracting enough to keep my cock from swelling every time you move."

I froze, my face burning. "Leave this alone, Riley."

"You'll keep me apprised of what's happening?"

"Sure."

He pinched my waist with both hands.

"Ouch." I swatted at him.

"Why don't I believe you?"

He was right not to trust me on this, but I needed him to stay out of it. "I promise," I lied. I could feed him bits of information each day without him knowing every detail and call that truth, right?

"Do you know how much trouble you'll be in if I find out you kept anything from me?"

I could imagine.

He nodded to the glass corner where I had stood just days ago for half an hour while he ignored me. Naked. "You liked having your nose pressed to the

The Game

window?"

"No, Sir." There were much better ways to get aroused than standing in a corner.

"Then don't make me put you there for punishment. It's boring as hell watching you squirm. It was bad enough doing it the other night to help you submit. If I have to use that corner as a time out, I won't let you come afterward."

"Then don't punish me, Sir." It was unnerving and barbaric... And arousing. Shit. How could the idea of being punished by Riley make me horny?

Riley released my waist to push his computer and several dishes farther back on the table, freeing up the spot in front of him. He then shocked me by lifting me onto the table and settling me on my ass facing him. He spread my legs wide, angling my feet so they hung on the outsides of his thighs. "Let's talk."

I thought we were talking. The tiny excuse for a robe I wore didn't cover my ass. I still had my panties on, but they were hardly more than a swatch of lace covering my naked mound. The tails of the robe spread wide, leaving my belly exposed and separating just enough so he could see the insides of my breasts. About the only protection I was currently afforded was my nipples.

At least it was something.

"You're here. And you were here Tuesday night also. I'm going to assume you want to be here."

"I do, Sir." I couldn't think of anywhere else I'd rather be than here with this man in this oddly unconventional relationship.

"You're serious then. You're mine?"

I shivered. *His?* Sounded like he owned me. I squirmed on the table. I shouldn't like the way he worded his intentions. Why then, did the idea of being his to control make me clench my pussy?

Riley clasped my thighs and held me still.

I bowed my head. "Yes." My heart raced at the pronouncement.

"Good." He lifted my chin and met my gaze, even though my face was higher than his with me sitting on the table. "I'm so pleased. We need to negotiate a few things."

"Okay."

He lifted one eyebrow.

"Sir. Okay, Sir."

His smile melted me a little and relaxed my nerves.

"I want you on weekends. Is that a problem?"

"No. Not usually, unless I have to work."

The Game

"We'll work out those details as they come up. I also want you at least one night a week. Is Wednesday good?"

Wednesday? He wanted to specifically schedule our liaisons? That sounded kind of cold. I bit my lip and then released it.

"Do you have other obligations on Wednesdays? We can pick another night. I randomly selected the middle of the week."

"No. That's not it. It's just so…arranged. Can't we just meet up whenever it works out? Like normal people?"

"Cheyenne, I'm not like normal people. It's not the kind of relationship I want with you. I want you to submit to me. Not twenty-four-seven, but also not on a whim."

"I see."

"Do you?"

"I guess. It's just so weird."

"It feels that way because it's new to you. I get that, and I'll be patient. But it will be easier if I'm not lenient from the get go. It's not a relationship I want to ease into. Either you can and will submit to me, or you can't."

"I can."

"When you're with me, following my directives, you easily fall into the role like a natural. I've been unbelievably impressed with your compliance for someone who had very little knowledge of this lifestyle just weeks ago." He scooted his chair forward, bringing us closer together. "Think of how you feel when you turn your will over to me. Remember the weekend. Or even Tuesday night."

I did. And there was no denying every thought made me flush with arousal.

"It's sort of like hypnosis. The moment we switch into the roles of Dom and sub—" he snapped his fingers "—you immediately release the enormous ball of tension you normally carry around with you. It's obvious. And it's natural you would find that appealing and relaxing."

"Yeah, Amy said something along those lines."

"But it bothers you."

I stared at him a moment. "A little. Why would I want to turn my free will over to another person and find that invigorating?" I shuddered. "It's unnerving. It makes me wonder if I'm the strong, independent woman I thought I was. Who does that?"

Riley reached to tuck my hair behind my ear. "Baby, I know you don't get this yet, but I told you before, only a strong person can submit to another. You're the one with the power. I'm at your mercy to turn your will over to me."

"That doesn't make any sense."

"Sure it does." He smiled. "I can't do anything you haven't expressly given me permission to do. That's what negotiation is all about. If I go too far or you don't like something I've done, you use a safe word we establish and the scene is over. I would never cross that line. Any Dom who would isn't a Dom at all. They're a bully. Or an abuser."

I bit my lip again. Did that even make sense?

In a way it did. I took a deep breath. "So, you're saying you won't do anything I don't want you to do. Ever."

"Never. That's my vow to you. Normally a Dom and sub would make a sort of contract at this stage, either written or verbal. But it would be difficult for you to do that since you can't know right this second what you would and wouldn't consent to."

I widened my eyes. "There are plenty of things I would never consent to."

He chuckled. "Well, within reason. What I mean is that you don't know your limits because they've never been challenged."

"Like what?"

"Would you have imagined two weeks ago letting a man spank you or put you in a corner or tie you to the bed or insist you call him Sir?"

"Good point."

"And that extends to so many things I'll slowly introduce to you. Like anal play and more extensive bondage, to name a few."

I cringed.

"What I would prefer, in this instance, is for you to give me the liberty to push your limits when I think you're ready for the next step. If I go too fast, you say 'yellow'. If I go too far, you say 'red'."

"I can do that."

"When you're with me, I'll want you to get into the role most of the time. It's a mindset. That doesn't mean we won't talk and work out issues that come up during the day like a normal couple. It just means I want you to be respectful and follow my directives with regard to when and where you sit or stand, what you wear, what you eat. Those kinds of things."

I nodded.

"Are we in agreement?"

The Game

"I think so."

"I need you to *know* so." He stroked a finger down my cheek and let it roam lower until it trailed between my breasts and made me sit up straighter. He hooked it in the loose tie at my waist and paused. "Tell me you'll be mine."

"I'm yours, Sir." It might have sounded weird and still gave me a lot of hesitation, but to deny I was anything other than his would have been a lie. From the moment I'd met him, I was his.

With both hands, he released the sash around my waist and tugged it free. The sides of my robe fell open.

"Give me your hands."

I lifted them from my sides and held them in front of him. He wrapped the sash around my wrists and attached them to each other. It wasn't so tight I couldn't get free fairly quickly if I needed, but the symbolism made my nipples pucker anyway.

"Don't move." He stood and cleared the table of all the dishes and his computer. When he was done, he tugged me forward until my ass was on the edge of the glass table top. He eased me onto my back with a hand behind my neck to make sure I didn't hit my head.

Without my arms, I was awkward.

"Lift your hands over your head, baby. And leave

them there."

I did as he instructed, and a chill raced down my spine. The robe fell open, leaving me exposed. It wasn't as though he hadn't seen my naked chest before, but it unnerved me every time.

"You have goose bumps." He trailed a finger between my breasts and then circled each one slowly in a spiral until he tapped first one nipple and then the other lightly. "I love how your body responds to my touch." He pinched a nipple, and I bucked upward.

A whimper escaped my lips. I was already so aroused, and I still wore my panties.

This was BDSM. Powerful. Arousing.

I had consented to this. I had never felt this much in my life.

"That's my girl. Stay still." He danced his fingers down my belly, which dipped as his touch tickled. When he reached my panties, he tucked his fingers into the sides and eased them over my hips and down my legs. He held them up to his face and inhaled.

I almost died.

"Love your scent, baby." He tucked them in his pants pocket and then grabbed my thighs and spread them high and wide. He inhaled again. "So potent. I find

The Game

it hard to sit next to you and not throw you down and eat your sweet cunt." He dipped his head and did just that.

I moaned and drew my legs up higher beneath his grip.

"Mmm. Delicious."

My experience with men's faces between my legs was limited to Riley. I had no idea how other men might go about it. Hadn't ever thought about it for a second. But Riley made the activity seem divine.

He switched from a gentle administration to a full suck on my clit so fast I nearly shot off the table. Spasms threatened immediately. "Come against my mouth, baby. Give it to me. I want to taste your orgasm." He muttered all this against me, the vibrations of his words driving me higher. And then he flicked his tongue over my clit rapidly until I came.

It was almost embarrassing how fast he could play me. I never would have believed I could get off this soon if he hadn't proven it. Time and again.

As I floated back to Earth, Riley continued to stroke through my folds with his tongue. Finally, he lifted his face and replaced his mouth with his fingers. "Keep your legs wide for me, baby."

I held them open, shaking from the orgasm as a

second one crept into my consciousness.

"Call a doctor tomorrow. Get a copy of your medical records and get on the pill."

"Okay, Sir."

"I'll get my records for you too. Never play with any Dom without exchanging medical records."

"Yes, Sir."

He released me and set his palms on both sides of my chest to bring his face closer to mine. "That's going to be a moot issue, Cheyenne."

I scrunched my brow in confusion.

He grinned. "Never gonna let you go so you even have the opportunity to negotiate with another Dom."

"Oh." My legs shook. It was difficult to hold them up and open. And I arched my neck at his pronouncement. Why was it so sexy that he didn't foresee letting me go? Ever?

The Game

Chapter Nineteen

Without another word, Riley lifted me off the table and cradled me in his arms. He carried me down the hall and deposited me on his bed sideways. The robe was trapped behind my head, and he tugged it out of the way to bunch up at my hands, which were still tied and in his favorite location. He left me there without a word and returned moments later with several items in a towel.

Right. The shaving. He'd done it twice already. Why did I still get tingles up and down my spine? It was so intimate.

He tapped my ass to get me to lift and slid the towel under my butt. "When you come to me, I will shave you first." His words were soft as he began the task of lathering me and then slowly dragging the blade across my skin. "It helps put you in the mindset."

That was true. Although the orgasm he'd just given me didn't hurt either. Or that I'd been nearly naked in his home for the entire evening while he was fully clothed. Being exposed to him without reciprocation was heady. He stared at my body with reverence at all times, making me feel sexy.

He finished in silence and then wiped my sensitive skin, making me jump.

He set the towel wrapped around the other items on the bedside table. "Turn over, baby."

Awkwardly, I flipped onto my belly.

He rubbed my ass and thighs as if he were giving me a massage. "Have you ever done yoga?"

"Yes, Sir."

"Good. Draw your knees up into child's pose."

I pressed my forehead into the mattress and inched my legs forward until my hands were stretched over my head, my face buried between my biceps, and my ass in the air.

"Now spread your knees wider."

Oh God. I opened my mouth to protest, but he must have sensed my unease.

The Game

He stroked my ass again. "Baby, trust me. You have your safe words. Yellow means I'm pushing the edge. Red means I've gone over and I need to stop. Got it?"

"Yes, Sir."

"Good. Now spread your knees and allow me to control your body. I haven't steered you wrong yet. Trust me to know your boundaries."

I walked my knees out, holding my breath as the exposure overwhelmed me.

"Good girl." He rustled behind me.

I realized he was taking off his clothes. Slowly. His gaze piercing my nudity even though I couldn't see his face.

"Are you wet for me?"

"Yes, Sir." My voice was shaky.

Riley tugged me closer to the edge of the mattress and reached between my legs with one hand to stroke through my folds. He plunged two fingers into my pussy. "So wet… You're incredibly sexy like this, Cheyenne."

"Thank you, Sir."

He let me go, and a moment later I heard the rip of a condom wrapper. And then he gripped my ass cheeks and squeezed them with his palms as he nestled between my legs. His cock rubbed against my pussy as he thrust back and forth slowly. There was no way for him to get a significant amount of pressure without guiding his cock with his hand, but it was enough to torture me into wanting what he wasn't yet offering.

He pulled my butt cheeks apart over and over, molding them to his hands as his grip grew more forceful. Almost painful, but not quite.

It was difficult to concentrate on anything but the tug and release of my cheeks that left my puckered forbidden hole open to his gaze over and over as he worked. He was working up to touching me there.

I was tied in knots worrying about his intentions. But I was also aroused and curious. And I trusted him.

He took his time, easing his fingers closer to my hole in a slow progression. His cock rubbed against my pussy and clit enough to keep me on edge.

As I moaned, he released one cheek. I heard a small popping noise, and moments later a cool substance landed between my butt cheeks and oozed toward my tight hole.

Riley shifted his other hand to hold me open to his gaze with his fingers and thumb. He stroked across my puckered ass with one finger, circling the entrance over and over and then pressing gently without entering.

The Game

"That's my girl. Rock into me. Feels so good."

I pressed back, willing him to enter me by this point. He had a way of making the unimaginable seem plausible. He was patient and slow with everything he introduced me to. And it worked. I wanted him to breach me.

"One finger now, baby. Relax your muscles." He pushed his pointer slowly into my grip and then fucked it gradually in and out, never quite pulling out past the last knuckle.

"Oh God."

"Just relax." He rubbed my lower back with his other hand. "Mind over matter. There's nothing unreasonable about my finger pressing into you except what your mind is conditioned to believe. Trust me, the layer of skin between your pussy and your ass is thin. When I fill both holes at once, your head will spin."

I pursed my lips, trying not to moan any louder. I also fought the urge to rock back and forth, thrusting my ass onto his finger. It felt that good.

When he lifted his hand off my lower back, he grabbed his cock at the base and stroked it with more precision against my pussy. "I'm going to give you permission to come when you need to this time, baby. I know it's hard to hold back. The onslaught of sensations will be intense when I thrust home. But don't pull away. Let the second one build. Let me control it."

I would have acknowledged him in some way, but I was too distracted.

I gasped when he slammed into me. Luckily he held steady, buried as deep as he could reach for a moment. Indeed, the pressure of his finger against his cock was more than I could have imagined. So intense.

The second he started thrusting, I came. I lifted up on my forearms and pushed back into his every move. My pussy spasmed alongside my tight rear hole. I had no idea my ass could participate in an orgasm. But it did. And it felt amazing.

My vision fogged, and I closed my eyes and pressed my forehead into the mattress. Sound filled the room. Incoherent groaning sounds that came from me. I couldn't stop them. On the heels of the first orgasm, the second one built without warning.

Riley held my hip with his free hand and fucked me faster. He added a second finger to my ass and stroked them in a perfect rhythm against his cock.

Forget foggy. I could see stars. And I squeezed my eyes tighter, holding my breath as I concentrated on the

The Game

sensations assaulting me. My arms and legs shook. Need like I'd never experienced raced through my body. An irrational need after the orgasm I'd had earlier on the table and the one I'd just experienced a moment ago.

Nevertheless, I was so close to the biggest orgasm of my life, I almost fought against it. It frightened me in its intensity. Like a freight train barreling toward me. I couldn't get out of the path fast enough. I was stuck taking it head on.

And then it happened. Another orgasm raced through my body. It lasted longer than the first two. It consumed me. I couldn't process anything except the pleasure of the pulses washing through my pussy and ass over and over. My clit hadn't even been involved.

I startled when Riley grunted as his own orgasm peaked. I swore I could feel the pulsing of his cock as he emptied himself into the condom.

When we were both spent, I couldn't hear anything except our heavy breathing that echoed in my ears. I also couldn't move a muscle, not even to lower myself to the bed. Besides, I was still impaled by Riley's fingers and cock. Long moments went by before he eased out of me and lowered me to my side. He kissed my hip and then stepped into the master bathroom.

I sucked in oxygen, not moving an inch from where he left me.

He returned with a damp cloth, rolled me onto my back, and wiped between my legs. After he set the washcloth with the pile of shaving items, he crawled over my body, untied my wrists, and then lowered at my side to haul my back against his chest.

He kissed my shoulder. "You're amazing."

I was a goner. No man would ever be able to compete with Riley. All I could do was pray he didn't change his mind about me.

I was his.

THE GAME

Chapter Twenty

A horrible blaring noise dragged me from a deep sleep.

I groaned and buried my face deeper into my pillow, inhaling deeply.

Something wasn't right. As I blinked awake, I remembered where I was. Riley's house. Not my pillow. Not my alarm.

"Cheyenne…" Still spooned at my back, he stroked his hand down my shoulder and then cupped my breast.

"What time is it?"

"Early. I was afraid you'd be pissed if I didn't wake you up early enough to get home and get ready for work."

I dragged myself to sitting and stared at the clock. Six. Yep. That was early. But I would barely have time to get home, shower, dress, and haul my tired ass to the office before that cranky ex-fiancée of Riley's beat me there.

I didn't intend for that to happen, so I leaned over, kissed Riley on the lips, and then eased from the bed.

He followed me, not one bit concerned about his nudity as we headed down the hall. My clothes were strewn around the living room and dining area. Riley helped me gather them up and put them on. And then he took my shoulders and forced me to look at him. "Be careful driving. And call me when you have a chance."

I nodded and took a step back, but he held me tighter. "I'm not kidding, Cheyenne. I don't trust her. Keep me informed."

"I will." I forced a smile as he released me, grabbed my purse, and headed for the front door.

Just as I was about to open it, he stopped me, holding out my jump drive. "Don't forget this."

"Thanks." I tucked it in my purse and stepped out into the darkness. I sure didn't want to do this often. If I was going to stay at his place, I would need some clothes, makeup, and toiletries. Getting up before dawn to take a

The Game

walk of shame to my car was not my idea of fun.

I rushed home on deserted streets and got ready for work in record time. With a travel mug of coffee in my hand, I headed back out the door.

At eight fifteen, I was in my seat, booting up my computer, and fighting a smug smile that formed when I realized I'd beaten Miss Annoying to the office.

Game on.

****

To my surprise, Christine ignored me the entire day, never walking by my desk or making any eye contact at all.

I spent the day stressed and shaking, barely managing to pay close enough attention to my computer screen to get my next worthless project underway. Worthless because no matter what I did, it wouldn't be good enough for Christine. At lunch, I left the building alone and spent forty-five minutes surfing marketing job opportunities in the area.

It was clear I would need to find another job, though I hated the idea of letting Christine believe she'd somehow won. I could picture her smug face when I gave notice.

Nope. It wasn't an option. I worked too hard to

get where I was. I needed to stay in the game and figure out a way to get noticed in spite of Christine and her nasty need to poke and prod me.

By the end of the day, I was still trying to figure out what to do next when I got a text from Riley.

So sorry. I'm going to have to cancel on you for the weekend. Emergency in Charlotte. I'm heading up to help Parker out at Edgewater. Call me when you have a chance. I'll be in my car for the next several hours.

I stared at the phone for long moments. Emergency?

This would have been our first "normal" weekend together as a couple since declaring we were going to label ourselves as such last night. And now he was suddenly leaving town.

Get a grip… He's a business owner. He has responsibilities. Obligations.

I popped him a quick response.

No worries. Be safe. What else could I say?

And then I dialed Meagan. I hadn't seen her for weeks.

"Hey, stranger. How's the marketing world?"

"Kinda sucks, actually." I shut down my computer and grabbed my purse while I spoke quietly. As I headed

THE GAME

for the elevator, I continued. "Can you meet for drinks?"

"Sure. Sky?"

I hesitated. On the one hand, Sky was the last place I wanted to go. On the other hand, it was the one place I knew I wouldn't run into Christine. Not after the way I'd heard Riley speak on the phone about her being banned. "Sounds good. Half an hour?"

"See you then."

I hung up as the elevator opened, glancing both ways and finding myself blissfully alone.

Weird.

Christine left me in peace all day *and* she intended to allow me to waltz out the door at five without waylaying me?

I clutched the steering wheel as I drove and handed my car off to the valet when I arrived. The good thing about arriving at five thirty was beating the crowd. Later in the evening, there would be a long line outside.

"Ma'am." The bouncer at the door tipped his head and held it open for me.

When I entered, I lifted onto my tiptoes and scanned the room. Meagan was already at a table, and she waved me over. I smiled at her as I wove through the patrons getting a jump on happy hour, and then I took the seat across from her.

"You look tired," she commented.

"Been a long week."

A waitress stepped up immediately. "What can I get you?"

I noticed Meagan was already enjoying a fruity martini. Green. Apple? "I'll have one of those. Thanks."

Meagan leaned her chin on her palm. "I spoke to Amy." Her eyes danced as she grinned.

"Really? What did she have to say?" I smiled back.

"She might have mentioned that she took you to some sort of party last weekend, and you left with Cade's friend Riley."

"That might have happened."

"She might have been vague and insinuated I should get the deets from you. I'm kinda shocked you called me on a Friday night if you're in a new relationship with Riley Moreno. That man is so hot, he could melt chocolate."

I laughed. "He is." I lowered my gaze to the table and drew an imaginary picture with one finger, wondering how much to tell her. I'd been the one to call this meeting. Why hadn't I considered how much to tell her? And would Amy care?

THE GAME

"I get the feeling you two are keeping something from me. What is it? Two smokin' hot guys and all this mysterious secrecy. Are they vampires? Or wait. Werewolves?" She giggled.

"Nope. Doms." I blurted.

"Doms?"

I nodded.

"As in BDSM? Whips and chains and ropes and bondage and stuff?"

"That's the kind."

Her eyes widened. "Seriously?"

"Yes."

"I didn't know you were into that sort of thing. Hell, I didn't know Amy was either."

"I didn't know it myself. It just sort of happened."

"When?"

"Well, I met him at Amy and Cade's engagement party."

She scrunched up her face and glanced up and to the left as if filtering through her mind for details she might remember about that party. "I don't think I saw much of you at that party. I'm not sure I even met Riley."

"Yeah. That's because we spent almost the entire time talking and getting to know each other."

"So, you've been seeing him for six months and I didn't know?"

"Nope. I didn't see him again until a few weeks ago. In fact, he left me high and dry that night when he realized he was into me and didn't think I was the sort of woman who would be able to submit to him like he craved."

"Shit." Her voice rose. "My God." Did Meagan squirm? "That's fucking hot."

The waitress arrived with my drink and set it carefully in front of me.

I took a long sip from the skinny straw. "So, the next time I saw him was at a fundraiser my office was sponsoring. He was a speaker."

"Didn't you slap him across the face?"

I chuckled. "Thought about it. Instead, he hounded me for a date."

"And the rest is history? You're dating him now?"

"Well, there are a lot of holes in there, but essentially."

"What's it like?"

"What's what like?"

She waved a hand through the air as if indicating I should know what she meant. "You know… The whole…

submissive thing."

"It's different. But I'm enjoying myself." I wiggled my eyebrows.

"God. Isn't it intense?"

"Yes. Sometimes."

"And where is he now?"

"He went to Charlotte for the weekend. Some sort of emergency at Edgewater."

"Oh right. Amy called earlier and said Cade was heading to Charlotte also. Must be bad."

At least I had confirmation it was real. I had been trying to ignore the niggling thought that he made it up to avoid me, perhaps having changed his mind about us being an "us." I blew out a breath, relieved.

"I'm sure everything with those three guys is intense. It must be stressful riding the success train," she teased. "Have you met Parker?"

I nodded. "Only briefly at the engagement party. He arrived late. I was all googly-eyed over Riley by then."

Meagan sipped her drink. "He's just as hot as Riley and Cade. That I remember, but I had a date that night. I only met him in passing."

"Right. I forgot about that guy. Jeff? Did you ever go out with him again?"

"No." She shook her head. "He was so boring I almost plucked my hair out."

"Are you dating anyone now?" I asked, taking another drink through my straw.

"Nope. And I'm so busy at work, it would be difficult."

"It's September. What urgency does an accountant have in September?"

"Ha ha. We do work all year round, contrary to popular belief. And right now we're short-handed. Two people left the firm, dumping their load on the rest of us."

"And this is keeping you from dating?"

"Does Riley have a brother?"

I giggled. "No. But he has a friend."

"Parker?" She shivered. "Is he into BDSM too? I don't think I could handle that lifestyle, but thanks."

"I have no idea if he is actually."

"Well, if the three of them go all the way back to college and they're still this tight, I'm going to error on the side of caution and say that after sixteen years, he's probably into the same lifestyle."

"Seems reasonable."

Meagan sat up straighter. "Amy wants us to come stay with her for a weekend before the wedding."

The Game

"Sounds like fun. Bachelorette party?"

"Yes. I think her coworkers are throwing a shower in a few weeks. We could go and then stay for the weekend. She wants us to try on our dresses again too."

"Again?"

"I know. Crazy, right? She was the most disorganized person we knew before she met Cade. Now? She probably has her spices labeled." Meagan laughed.

"We can snoop around and check when we're there."

"Do you suppose it's Cade? You think she got all organized and tidy because of him?"

I shrugged. "No idea, but she seems happy, so whatever it is, it agrees with her."

"How's *your* job? Didn't you have a big presentation this week?"

I rolled my eyes. "Disaster. Riley's ex-fiancée moved to town and guess where she got a job?"

"*No.*"

"Yes. And worse. We ran into her, here at Sky in fact, and she's spent every second since she became my boss giving me grief."

"Shit."

"Yeah. Know anyone with a marketing opening?"

I slumped in my seat, hating the reminder that I had issues much bigger than becoming someone's submissive.

"I'll keep my ears open. God, I'm sorry. That sucks. You love that job. Do you think she moved here on purpose and took that job to harass you?"

I fiddled with the corner of the napkin under my drink. "It would seem that way. It's too much of a coincidence otherwise. But I can't imagine how she landed the job so quickly just to antagonize me."

"What did she do with your proposal?"

"Tore it to shreds and sent me back to my desk like a child."

"Shit. Amy said she was a real bitch."

"I'm not sure bitch is a harsh enough term." I took the last sip of my drink as the waitress walked up, and we ordered two more.

My liquid dinner went down too smoothly. I had enough crap going on in my life that I needed to forget.

After the third, we were like two giggling teenagers. I glanced at my watch. "I should get going. I'm exhausted. I need sleep."

"You need food."

"Not as badly as I need sleep." I hopped down from my bar stool alongside Meagan, and we made our way to the entrance.

The cool night air felt good against my heated skin.

"Ms. Decard."

I jerked my gaze to the right to find Les standing next to the building.

"Les? What are you doing here?" I spun around, wondering if Riley was somehow close by. Or hell, maybe he was inside and he'd watched me getting half-hammered all evening.

"Mr. Moreno sent me to pick you two up and take you home." He nodded at Meagan. "Ma'am."

"What? Why?"

Les cleared his throat. "He said you were drunk."

I grabbed Meagan's arm to steady myself. I was a little tipsy, but how the hell did Riley know this? "Is he here?"

"No, ma'am. He's in Charlotte."

"Is he psychic?"

Meagan giggled.

Les chuckled too. I hadn't seen him crack a smile before. "No. The manager called him and said you were here. He remembered you from a few weeks ago."

That was unnerving. Note to self: no more happy

hours at Sky. I stared at Les, a slightly blurry Les, and finally realized he was a godsend. Neither of us was sober enough to drive. We'd have to leave our cars anyway. "Excellent."

He led us to the Mercedes and opened the back door. "I'll have someone bring your cars to you in the morning."

I nodded and handed him my keys and Meagan's before I climbed in awkwardly and scooted across so Meagan could do the same.

She whispered to me as soon as the door shut. "I could get used to this kind of rich."

I wasn't sure I agreed, but in this instance, it was a blessing.

THE GAME

Chapter Twenty-One

My head was pounding when I woke up early the next morning. My mouth was so dry, my lips were stuck together.

And my cell phone was ringing on the night stand.

I slapped at it and dragged it toward my face without moving another muscle besides my arm. With one eye partway open, I saw Riley's name scrolled across the top.

I wasn't ready for Riley yet. I needed aspirin and water and a shower first. He was going to have to wait.

I dropped the phone next to me and smiled when the beep sounded, indicating he'd left a message. It took me a full twenty more minutes to gather the energy to drag myself out of bed. And when I did, I regretted it.

"Geez. It was only three apple martinis." *And no food…*

Ten minutes later, I emerged from the bathroom in my soft cotton robe, having accomplished all three tasks. Now I needed coffee. Fast.

The phone rang again as I left the room. I turned around and grabbed it, rolling my eyes as I answered. "Riley."

"Cheyenne, where have you been?"

"Right here in my apartment, in my bed, sleeping. I'm surprised you didn't know."

"How would I know that? You haven't answered any of my texts or calls."

I glanced at the phone to see there were indeed several texts from him last night, two calls last night, and one call this morning. Oops.

"Sorry. I was at Sky with Meagan, which you already know. My phone was in my purse. I never heard it ring." I glanced out the window of my apartment. I was on the fifth floor, so I don't know what I thought I might see. But I half expected to find someone rappelling down the side of the building, paused at my window, keeping tabs on my location. "Are you having me followed?"

"Of course not. Why would I do that?"

"Well, let's see, you sent Les to get me last night. That was beyond creepy."

"I didn't mean to weird you out. I just wanted you to be safe."

"Uh-huh."

"Are you mad?"

"I'm not mad. Just a little freaked out is all." I tucked the phone between my ear and my shoulder so I could get the coffee started. The instant the scent of beans hit my nose, I felt better. "Is everything okay in Charlotte?"

"Working on it. But I'm not going to be able to come home until late tomorrow night. I'm sorry our weekend got ruined."

"It's okay. I need to catch up on sleep and get ahead on my next project."

"For work?"

"Yeah."

"Cheyenne…"

"Don't say it. Whatever you were going to say, keep it to yourself. I need to handle this." I didn't have a clue how I was going to "handle it," but I didn't want

Becca Jameson

Riley to interfere.

He exhaled slow and loud enough for me to hear. "We'll readdress this next week. Can I see you Monday night?"

"Monday wasn't in our agreement," I teased as the coffee dripped into the pot too slowly for my taste.

"Baby…"

"Kidding."

"Good. I'm going to be super busy today. I'll call you when I have a chance. Might be tomorrow."

"Okay. Later then."

"Bye, Cheyenne."

I set the phone on the counter and watched as the rest of the coffee emptied into the pot. I could have made a quick single-serve cup, but I knew today was a pot of coffee kind of day…

****

On Monday morning, I had barely dropped my purse in my desk drawer when my office phone rang. I leaned across the desk and grabbed it without looking. "Ms. Decard. Would you please come upstairs to my office?"

I sat up straighter, instantly on alert. The CEO wanted to see me?

The Game

Shit. This could not be good.

"Yes. Of course. I'll be right there."

My entire body shook as I stood, straightened my skirt, and headed for the elevator. Christine was not in her office, but the lights were on. She was undoubtedly somewhere in the building.

I took deep breaths as I rode to the next floor and stepped off the elevator. Mr. Schultz's assistant smiled widely as I approached. "Go on in, Cheyenne." She pointed at the conference room. There was no evidence from her expression that she had any idea why I'd been summoned.

I pushed through the double doors and stepped into what had to be an ambush. There were four people sitting around the large table. Mr. Schultz was just one of them. Mr. Davis and Ms. Zumeski, two members of the board, were also there. And Christine.

I swallowed.

"Please, Ms. Decard, have a seat." Mr. Schultz held his palm out to indicate an empty chair.

I sat tentatively. What in the hell was about to happen here? Would they fire me? And on what grounds? If Christine had set me up, telling the board I was incompetent... I wouldn't put it past her. In fact, I couldn't figure out for the life of me why I had ever let it go this far.

"Since we're aware you were the original employee working on this project, I thought it only appropriate that you be present for Ms. Parson's presentation. I understand yours wasn't quite up to par and she took over to polish it up."

I stared at him, but made no move. What could I say? Was there any possibility Christine had come up with something so much better than mine that she'd made me look like an idiot? And had she even shared my findings with the others or simply pooh-poohed it and told them it was awful?

"Is that accurate?" Mr. Schultz asked.

Shit. I glanced at Christine, who sat prim and perfectly coiffed on the edge of her seat, smiling at me as though she'd done me a favor. "It's okay, dear. You're young. We all made mistakes as we pave our way."

I was so shocked by her demeanor I could barely breathe. I turned my gaze back to Mr. Schultz and nodded consent.

"Okay then. Let's get started." He turned toward Christine and handed her the remote so she could change the images on the projection on the far wall of the room.

The Game

"As I was saying," Christine began, standing as she spoke and heading to the front of the room, "this particular cell phone is believed to be the most innovative design of this decade. Because of that, it's imperative that Link have the perfect catchy marketing designed to show off the benefits as well as convince the public they need to run to the nearest store and trade in their old phones immediately."

Mr. Davis and Ms. Zumeski chuckled as Christine flipped to the first projection.

Mr. Schultz did not. The man sat stoically, leaning back in his chair. His legs were crossed casually, and he had one elbow on the arm of his seat, his fingers tapping his lips.

Most importantly, his gaze was on me.

I shuddered as I blinked and glanced at the screen.

Holy mother of God.

I held my breath, not hearing a word of Christine's presentation while I watched each projection whip by on the screen. My head started ringing and my mouth got so dry I couldn't swallow. My face heated to ten shades of red.

The bitch stole my work and presented it as her own.

What the hell was I supposed to do?

Mr. Davis and Ms. Zumeski nodded and chuckled appropriately in the exact spots I had intended—although I would have taken more time, been more dynamic and engaged them more frequently than Christine.

I risked another glance at Mr. Schultz, who was still watching me out of the corner of his narrowed eyes. The man looked fit to kill. I couldn't understand why he didn't just fire me when I walked in. Why make me sit through this agonizing torture if that was his intent?

Finally, Christine finished. She closed the last image and turned the lights in the room back up.

Silence reigned for about two seconds.

And then Ms. Zumeski spoke. "Clever. Love it. Good job. I'm impressed with the amount you've accomplished and how quickly. The client will salivate over this."

Mr. Davis spoke next. "I agree."

Mr. Schultz leaned forward and put his elbows on the table. "What do you think, Ms. Decard?"

I swallowed hard and licked my lips. "It was very nice." My words sounded foreign.

"I would love to see the presentation you put together. Do you have it available? We should compare."

The Game

"I—"

Christine interrupted me. "I asked Cheyenne to dispose of it. I didn't want her to embarrass herself in front of all of you."

My eyes widened. How could this be happening?

Mr. Schultz reached to the center of the table and pushed the call button on the phone. "Lauren, could you send Roland from security to the conference room, please."

"Yes, sir." His assistant's voice sounded shaky, not at all like the chipper woman I'd greeted half an hour ago.

Now I was certain I would be fired. And why not? Apparently, not only did I do a horrible job wasting company time to put together a presentation that wasn't worthy of being seen, but I had also destroyed the evidence of my hard work. Incredible. I was so tongue tied, I couldn't even defend myself.

I glanced at Christine, who stood in the same spot, smiling smugly as though she'd won a marathon and trampled everyone in her path to get there.

Technically, she had.

And on top of that, Riley was going to kill me when he found out. He had wanted to intervene. Had insisted. And I'd turned him down repeatedly. When he found out his ex-fiancée ruined me out of spite, there was no telling what he would do in retaliation.

Mr. Schultz stood. "Sit down, Christine."

I flinched. He called her by her first name.

And he did not sound pleased.

He rounded to the head of the table and leaned against it, towering over all of us. "See, the funny thing is, I've already seen that presentation." He pointed to the screen behind him as though it were physically there. "This project you claim to have spent the entire weekend putting together was in my inbox on Friday morning with Ms. Decard's name on it."

Christine gasped. "Did I say I worked on *this* project over the weekend?" She chuckled nervously. "I must have misspoken. This one was ready last Thursday. I was working on the next project over the weekend." She waved a hand through the air as though brushing away the misunderstanding. "I used the base Cheyenne started to spruce it up and make it much better. I must have forgotten to change the name on it."

"Uh-huh." Mr. Schultz faced her head on. "And where did you send it from?"

She hesitated and glanced around, nervously licking her lips. "I don't recall precisely, sir."

"I see." He stood straighter and crossed his arms over his chest as the door opened and Roland stepped inside. Mr. Schultz ignored him and continued, "Ms. Parson, I didn't want to hire you. You're not qualified to do this job, your résumé is abysmal, and frankly, you don't have a single recommendation that gives anything you've done in recent years any weight."

Roland shuffled just inside the door.

Mr. Schultz dropped his arms to his sides and kept going. "I gave you this job as a favor to your father. The man apparently either loves you unconditionally, or he wanted to get you as far away from Virginia as possible. Either way, my friendship does not extend this far. You've made a fool out of yourself. Gather your belongings and vacate this building immediately." He turned toward Roland. "Please escort this woman out of our offices."

Roland nodded. "Yes, sir."

Christine jumped to her feet, stammering, "Mr. Schultz—"

He lifted a hand and stopped her. "Get out."

Without a glance in my direction, she straightened her suit jacket and strutted from the room with her head held high.

The door swung shut with a resounding thud,

leaving me staring at the three board members, two of whom were so shocked they hadn't said a word.

Ms. Zumeski spoke first. "Is this true? Why didn't you say anything?"

My knee bounced under the table, and I grabbed it with a hand to steady my nerves. "I was trying to handle it. I had no idea she'd stolen my work until I came in here this morning."

"Why did you let her present the entire thing as if it were her own?" Mr. Schultz asked.

I didn't want him to know about my relationship with Riley or Christine's history. It wasn't professional.

He shook his head and changed directions. "Who sent me this presentation, Ms. Decard?"

I hesitated.

"Whoever sent it has a very sophisticated system that was able to encrypt the sender so I would have no idea where it came from. That was my first clue something was out of whack. My second clue was when you didn't come forward Friday to present it after sending it to me. You never knew I had it."

"True."

"So, you gave it to someone else."

My ears burned. I was so angry with Riley, I

couldn't think. Damn him. I didn't care that he'd just saved my ass and my job. I specifically told him not to interfere, and he'd done so behind my back anyway. He'd copied my jump drive into his computer and sent my work over Christine's head early Friday morning after I'd left his bed.

"Cheyenne?" Ms. Zumeski prompted.

"I did show it to someone else. I'd rather not say who."

Mr. Schultz jumped on that. "Please tell me it isn't a competitor."

I shook my head. "No. Nothing like that. Just my meddling boyfriend." Surely I could say that much without digging any deeper.

Mr. Schultz leaned back and laughed, shocking me. "Your boyfriend? Did you mention you thought Christine would steal it out from under you before you had a chance to present it?" He continued to chuckle. "He must be a computer whiz. Perhaps I should hire him too."

"I might have told him I was concerned about Ms. Parson." I chewed my lower lip.

"Well, you owe him. He saved your hide today."

I wasn't convinced Riley had saved anything. What I knew for a fact was he'd just started World War

III. I had little doubt Christine would have already keyed my car and dumped tar over my computer on her way out if no one was watching. I wouldn't be able to go anywhere or do anything without looking over my shoulder.

"Anyway," Mr. Schultz was still smiling and shaking his head, "I got a call this morning requesting a bid from the largest customer we've ever had. I'd like you to take a stab at it. If you can replicate the kind of work you did on the cell phone piece, we just might win the bid."

I froze. I knew exactly what company he was about to name, and I was fuming. I'd been freaked out for the last five minutes, pissed as hell at Riley. Now I was so far past angry, I'd moved into murderous. I opened my mouth, and with a shakier voice than before, uttered, "Mr. Schultz, I'm really not qualified for a project of that magnitude. You should give it to Stacy. She's been here much longer than me, and she has brilliant ideas."

"I haven't even told you what it is yet." He frowned, sobering in confusion as the other two board members gathered their papers and stared at me wide-eyed also.

"Nevertheless…" I turned and fled the room, nearly racing to get out of there. I had made a total fool

The Game

of myself, but there was no way in hell I was going to stand there and grin and promise to present a marketing campaign to Alexander Technologies. Every inch of my skin crawled with the desire to run from the building, hell Atlanta even, and gasp for oxygen. I couldn't breathe.

Chapter Twenty-Two

When I got back to my desk, Stacy took one look at me and jumped to her feet. "What happened?"

I shook my head and grabbed my purse from the bottom drawer. "Nothing. No big deal. I just don't feel well. I'm going to take the rest of the day off." Before she could comment, I fled my cubicle and scurried toward the elevator, happy when it arrived seconds after I pressed the button.

By the time I got to my car, I had been holding my breath and my emotions for so long I was a mess. And I kept a narrow hold on them to start the car and pull out of the garage too. In fact, I made it all the way home before I fell completely apart.

The Game

  The crazy thing was my job had very little to do with my anxiety. I was steaming angry with Riley. So much so, I didn't think I could speak to him even to yell at him. I tossed my purse on my couch and yanked off my jacket as I stepped through my apartment. When I got to my room, I kicked off my shoes and went to work on the buttons on my blouse. My fingers shook so badly I had to work hard to get each disk through its hole.

  By the time I was able to jerk my arms free, I was so frustrated, I nearly ripped the material. Next went my skirt. And then I opened a drawer and grabbed my favorite jogging clothes. I tugged my spandex pants on, donned a sports bra, and slipped into a T-shirt. In minutes, I had my running shoes on and I was back out the door, leaving my phone inside my purse on the couch.

  The air outside was chilly. I relished it.

  Tears ran down my face, but I brushed them away and ran toward the park by my apartment building. The park was filled with moms and toddlers. I was glad I didn't have to greet many people pleasantly on the path. I was in my own world.

  My confused, angry, torn-up world.

  I ran harder than usual, covering more ground. My mind raced. Somehow my entire life had turned upside down in just weeks. I'd been a regular working woman making my way like every other post-graduate in their mid-twenties. I had a job I loved, and…

Well, I had a job I loved.

Now? Now I had a Dom. A man who thought he knew what was best for me. A man who had a history that included a bitch of an ex who had decided to ruin my life and stomp on the pieces.

And I had no doubt she would succeed. This wasn't over. The fact that Riley had interfered and saved my job only meant that crazy woman was right this minute out planning my complete demise. To think otherwise was ludicrous.

Nope. I had nothing to say to Riley. He could go fuck himself. I wasn't about to speak to him about this issue or any other. I was done with Riley. He'd gone too far. And damn him for not even *telling* me he'd sent my presentation to my boss. That had been four days ago. He'd had all the opportunity in the world to fill me in. I would have looked much less idiotic if I'd known.

I ran faster. I was gasping for oxygen, but I didn't care. I just wanted to wear myself out and then find someplace to wallow in self-pity.

When I finally stopped running, I bent at the

The Game

waist and heaved air into my lungs. My muscles ached. I was depleted. It took several minutes before I righted myself and walked slowly back to my apartment. The burn was delicious. But the pain hadn't subsided.

Back at home, I shrugged out of my clothes for the second time, dropped them in the hamper, and stepped into the shower. I didn't care that the water was cold because I hadn't given it time to heat up first. I only cared that it stung where it hit my skin, punishing me for my stupidity.

Why had I ever agreed to go out with that controlling man in the first place? *Because he steamrolled you, that's why.* He hadn't taken no for an answer. He'd insisted. His persistence had made me cave. The way he'd looked at me…as if I was the only person in a room…

No way. Surely I imagined all that because he was so damn attractive and smelled so fantastic.

I'd been fine. Six months without him had nearly wiped him from my memory.

Sure. Right. And I never masturbated to his image at night. Nope. Never. I had been going along with no recollection of meeting him that night at Amy's engagement party. *Just keep telling yourself that.*

Stupid.

I squirted shampoo into my hand—enough for six people—and scrubbed my head as though I had lice. My scalp was going to hurt later. Maybe I could wash Riley out of my system.

I grabbed the bar of soap next and rubbed my body until it turned pink. The water had gotten too hot. As I worked furiously, tears leaked from my eyes and ran down my face.

By the time I was finished, I was so exhausted I couldn't hold myself up any longer. I leaned against the cold tile wall and slid down until I sat on the floor of the shower, letting the tears fall.

I sobbed. Loudly. Loud enough that someone would have heard me if the shower hadn't muffled my mini-breakdown.

I set my forehead against my knees and cried for so long the water got cold. I didn't care.

Finally, I lifted my head when I had no more tears left and leaned it against the wall behind me. I needed a plan. I needed to think.

I needed to get the hell out of my apartment and go stay somewhere else tonight. For a few days actually. At least until I could figure out what to do next. I didn't trust Riley not to come banging on my door at any time.

The Game

And I sure didn't trust Christine not to come with a gun or worse.

The woman was whacked. It would be easier if she just killed me and put me out of my misery than stalk me and make my life a living hell for the next ten years.

Damn my interfering boyfriend.

I struggled to my feet on shaky legs, flipped off the water, and stepped out of the shower. I shook from nerves, cold, and fear.

Even wrapping myself in my giant fluffy towel did not take away the chill.

I wanted to crawl into my bed, pull the covers over my head, and sleep. But that was too risky. I needed to get gone.

With renewed urgency, I dried quickly, scampered back to my bedroom, and started opening drawers.

In my favorite comfy jeans and T-shirt, I grabbed a bag and stuffed panties, bras, shirts, and more jeans inside. I hustled back to the bathroom and grabbed my toothbrush and a few other toiletries.

Minutes later, hair wet, uncombed, and hanging loose down my back, I shrugged into my tennis shoes and left the apartment. I held my breath until I was in my car, silently berating myself for ever coming to the apartment

Becca Jameson

in the first place. It was a risk.

I was driving out of the underground parking lot before I heard my phone ringing in my purse. Who knew how many calls I'd missed? I didn't care. I didn't look either. I just drove.

On auto-pilot, with no particular intentions, I drove until I realized I was heading for my parents' house in the suburbs. I relaxed my shoulders and eased my grip on the steering wheel. My mom would make me some soup. My dad would smile and nod. I could sleep in my old room.

Perfect. Just what I needed.

Home.

THE GAME

Chapter Twenty-Three

I slept hard. I slept for twelve hours. I slept without ever checking my phone. I was supposed to meet Riley Monday night. I not only couldn't face him, but I also didn't want to be tempted. So, I ignored all calls. In fact, I didn't even bother to turn the ringer off. Instead I tucked my entire purse in the back corner of my closet and buried it under the quilts my mother had stacked inside.

Childish.

When I woke, it was six o'clock in the morning. Early, but I'd gone to sleep just after six the night before. For the second time.

I'd arrived at my parents' house at lunch time.

And my mother had taken one look at my face and wrapped me in her arms. "Sweetie. Come in. Sit down. I'll make you some soup."

I smiled now at how kind she'd been as I snuggled deeper into my childhood bed and curled onto my side.

"A man?" she asked.

I couldn't deny a man was involved, so I nodded and let my tears fall again. It was a wonder I had any left.

"Sweetie… I'm so sorry. You want to talk about it?"

"No." I did not. I most assuredly did not want to tell my mother that my new boyfriend was into BDSM and I'd consented to let him order me around, which apparently extended to interfering with my job. And I sure as hell didn't want to explain the crazy woman who was even that moment plotting to take me down.

So I declined the offer to discuss, rejected the soup, and excused myself to go to my room—just as I had on several occasions in high school.

I had napped briefly and then paced my room for hours.

My mom knocked softly at five, and I came out and joined her for a silent early dinner of homemade soup and hot bread. It tasted fantastic, and I was starving by

The Game

then.

When my dad got home, he greeted me with a kiss to the forehead and didn't say a word. I was sure my mother had given him the head's up at some point during the day.

I went back to my room after my early dinner and quickly fell asleep.

Twelve hours later I should have felt refreshed. I didn't.

In fact, I had no more ideas, plans, or options than the day before.

I slipped from the bed in my oversized T-shirt and reluctantly opened my closet to grab my purse from its buried hideaway.

The battery was almost dead. I would need to charge it soon. Before checking any messages, I dialed my office manager and left her a message that I was still under the weather and would be out again today.

And then I settled back under my covers to read my texts and listen to the litany of messages left by first Riley and then both Amy and Meagan. He'd undoubtedly called Cade when he couldn't find me.

Fifteen texts. Six voice messages. Impressive.

And he truly did sound worried.

Good.

I hated that I'd upset Amy and Meagan, but it couldn't have been helped. Neither of them were on my mind while I was fretting the day before, and Amy would have told Riley where I was in a heartbeat if she thought it would help.

I grabbed my cord from my purse, plugged my phone in, and then dozed for a while. When the ringing started not more than a half hour later, I jerked awake.

Riley.

I stared at it for a moment and then opened the line but didn't say a word.

"Cheyenne?"

I still hesitated.

"Baby. Where are you?" He sounded frantic and tired. Good. "Please, just tell me where you are. I know you must be pissed, but—"

"*Pissed?*" I nearly shouted the word before I could stop myself. I lowered my voice before continuing. "Do you have no scruples?"

"Baby—"

"No," I interrupted. "Don't baby me. And you can stop calling. I'm fine. Leave me alone to work out what to do. You've turned my life inside out. I need to think."

"Cheyenne..."

"This isn't your call."

"I just want to talk. Can we meet somewhere and talk?"

"No. You should have thought of that before you broke your promise to me and made me look like a complete idiot. I was totally blindsided. That was my job, Riley. My *job*. Do you have no respect for boundaries?"

"It still is your job. Mr. Schultz is very impressed with your work. I spoke to him yesterday, and he—"

"You *what*?" I sat up, letting the blankets fall to my waist. "Riley, stop it. Stop meddling. Do *not* speak to my bosses. Do *not* speak to me. You do *not* own me. I'm my own person. This is over. Leave me alone. Move on. Let me pick up the pieces and figure out where I can move to, get a new job, a new apartment, a new life for fuck's sake. Leave. Me. Alone." I hung up.

He spoke to my boss?

Jesus.

The phone rang immediately.

I switched it to silent and flopped back onto the bed.

What a mess.

Was Riley so stupid he thought it was no big

deal that he'd gotten in my business and essentially bought my spot at Talent Marketing Group? How was I supposed to earn the respect of my peers and my bosses if my boyfriend was some rich guy who strode in and gave my boss a project for me that was way above the level of marketing he was accustomed to?

Fuck.

And that didn't even begin to take into consideration the fucking crazy bitch he had been engaged to. If the woman would stoop so low as to steal my ideas and present them as her own, I knew she would do anything in the world to sabotage my life.

I was ruined. I couldn't go back to that job or that city. I needed to find someplace to hide before Christine hunted me down and killed me. If she had done all this to get Riley back, she could have him.

In fact, maybe it was in my best interest to find her and tell her just that. Let her know she'd won. I was leaving the city and the man. Maybe, just maybe, if I threw in the towel and gave her everything she wanted, she wouldn't stalk and haunt me for the rest of my life.

I could tell Mr. Schultz the entire project was hers in the first place and I'd stolen it because I wasn't good enough to do the same level of work. I could get her job

The Game

back that way. Then I could quit—or leave when I got fired—and move away. I would also agree to never speak to Riley again.

She won.

I didn't even give a fuck if she won. As long as I didn't have to look over my shoulder. She could have him—the controlling bastard.

I jumped from the bed and crossed the hall to get to the bathroom. With renewed energy, I showered and got dressed. It was time to pull my shit together. I had a plan.

Granted, it was a shabby, weak one that might backfire on me, but at least it was a plan.

When I got back to my bedroom, I called Amy. I knew she would be more worried than Riley. And she was one of my best friends.

Meagan would sleep at least. Amy would have stayed up tossing and turning all night. Though I was surprised neither of them thought to call my parents' home.

"Cheyenne," Amy nearly yelled as soon as she answered. "Where are you?"

"Come on. Where do you think I am? And don't say it out loud. I'm sure Cade is wrapped around you."

She hesitated. "Okay. You're right. I should have thought of that. Duh. I just figured you were out late thinking. It didn't occur to me you might have packed a bag."

"Well I did. And I'm going to go home and pack a bigger one now."

"Why? Honey, I'm sure you can figure this all out."

"Are you insane? You should know better than anyone what Christine Parson is capable of. Don't even try to pretend that woman couldn't stomp my lights out and buckle with laughter while she watched me die a slow death."

Amy sucked in a sharp breath.

"See?"

"Yeah. You're right. But why not let Riley handle it? Cade could head down there and help out. Hell, Parker hates that bitch too. He'd jump in also."

"Nope. Riley made this mess. I don't want to see what his cleanups look like."

"He didn't mean to. He was just trying to help."

"Like hell. If this is the way you live under Cade's thumb, I don't want anything to do with it. We had a deal. He wasn't supposed to interfere. I was working it out myself."

"How? How were you handling it?"

I chewed my bottom lip. "I was thinking."

"You didn't have a plan. You were about to get fired, weren't you?"

"Who would know? My damn knight in shining armor floated in and changed history."

"Riley just wants what's best for you."

"Riley had his own agenda, and it didn't include him thinking through the repercussions."

"Maybe his reaction was knee-jerk. But, honey, he's head over heels for you."

"And you would know this how?" I hated asking that question the second it left my lips. I didn't want to hear the answer.

"He told me. I mean, he told Cade. But I could hear him shouting through the phone."

"I'm sure he's just pissed he didn't have complete control of my every action. It unnerved him that I wasn't at his feet bowing down in submission. I'm sure he hated not knowing where I was."

"Cheyenne, that's not true. Riley isn't like that."

"No? Then explain why he stepped into my business when I specifically asked him not to."

"He didn't think your idea was a good one?" she hedged. "Honey, he knows how Christine operates. You just met her."

"Really? If he's so sharp about all things Christine, why the hell did he spend ten years with that conniving bitch and why on Earth does he think she won't hunt me down with her claws out now that he got her fired?"

"Well… I'm not sure about her claws on this one, but I do know she can fake nice like you cannot believe. And she managed to fake like she was someone else completely during their entire relationship. It wasn't until the woman pulled out her fangs and nearly bled me to death at their engagement party that he was able to see her true colors. She didn't show them."

"Then he's a bigger fool than I thought."

"Cheyenne…"

"No. Amy. I'm right on this. I know I am. Please don't tell Riley, or Cade for that matter, where I am. I won't stay here long anyway. And I don't want anyone I love in the cross fire of ugly." I hoped she realized what I meant by that. The last thing I wanted was a knockdown drag out with either Riley or Christine in my parents' front yard.

"Okay," she drawled. "But please stay in touch

THE GAME

and keep me up to date. I don't like this."

"Thank you, Amy. I'm a smart girl. You know me. I'll survive."

"Yeah. Bye."

I ended the call and tossed the phone on the bed. I had things to do. Sitting around my parents' home feeling sorry for myself wasn't going to make the world spin more upright on its axis.

Chapter Twenty-Four

I drove the hour back to my apartment with a firm plan. I needed to change first and then head to my office and smooth things over with Mr. Schultz. After that, I would find a way to track down Christine and concede defeat. And finally, I would pack up my shit, put it in storage, and head for Nashville. I could look for a job there and have at least one friend in town I could meet on the sly without getting caught.

I was feeling almost energized and human when I stepped from the elevator to my fifth floor apartment.

And then my shoulders slumped. Of course. Why did I think it would be so simple?

That woman had wasted no time at all.

THE GAME

My shoulders slumped as I lowered my bag to my hand and nearly dropped it. My steps faltered, and I slowed my progression toward my front door as if I could somehow make the insanity in front of me disappear if I made time stop.

"*Cheyenne*," my neighbor yelled. The older woman clasped her hands over her mouth and looked as though she were about to cry. She was in her nightgown and matronly robe, her feet in slippers. "Oh God, I thought maybe you'd been abducted. I'm so glad you're okay." She wrapped her arms around me in a tight hug as I stared past her at the unbelievable scene that was the entrance to my apartment.

Two police officers had turned to look at me as my neighbor yelled my name.

"Are you the renter?"

"Yes," I managed to squeak. From what I could see of the entrance to my place, I didn't even want to go inside.

The officer turned fully in my direction and met my gaze. "I'm sorry, ma'am. It looks like you've been robbed."

I sincerely doubted that was the case, but it also appeared I would never know. Sorting through the mess I could now see through the entrance could be so enormous that it wouldn't be worth it. Hopefully I could get inside one day and find my photographs and my grandmother's jewelry. Other than that, the place looked like a total loss.

"Do you know anyone who would do this to you? An ex or something?"

I let out a wry chuckle. Did I ever.

"Ma'am?"

I sobered and looked him in the eye and lied through my teeth. "No one."

His shoulders slumped this time. He'd been expecting me to give him a name. And I'd refused.

"Do you have an estranged boyfriend?"

"No."

"Old roommate that wants her stuff back?"

"No."

"You can't think of a single person who would break into your apartment and shred every single thing they could get their hands on?"

"No, sir. Sorry. I can't imagine who would do this to me." I bit my lip and tried to drag tears to the surface. Ironically I couldn't. I had probably used them all up yesterday. Today? Nothing would faze me.

I was numb.

THE GAME

"We're going to need you to inventory your belongings…" he looked over his shoulder and shuddered, "…somehow and let us know what's missing."

"Okay," I lied again.

What was wrong with me? I didn't recognize myself. Last month I'd been a normal human being who would never have lied to her boss or the police. But now I was a woman fearing for her future safety. If it took lying to ensure I escaped this shitstorm alive, I would do it.

Sending the cops on a chase to hunt down Christine would only make matters worse. The woman would come back with bigger guns.

I didn't want to waste another minute in this disaster. I didn't even want to go inside. The fluff from every single chair, couch, and mattress I owned spilled out the door to coat the hallway in white snow.

I was out of there. I turned without a word and left.

"Ma'am?"

I ignored the officer. It didn't matter to me a single bit what they did or didn't do. They could file a report or not. They could leave the place standing open for anyone and everyone to enter if they wanted. Even a robber wouldn't attempt to steal anything from me today.

****

It was noon when I pulled into my usual spot in my office garage. I still wore my faded ripped jeans and tight purple Bruce Springsteen T-shirt. I had on my most comfortable tennis shoes and no makeup. I also hadn't touched my hair with a comb since I'd showered that morning. It hung in long curls down my back, probably looking like a rat's nest.

I didn't give a fuck. Someone might say I was having a nervous breakdown, but I was completely in tune with my faculties. The ransacked apartment was just a small glitch that prevented me from making myself more presentable to the office staff. Who cared really?

I wasn't here to impress anyone. Quite the opposite. I was here to lie through my teeth and plead Christine's case. And then I was never going to see anyone I worked with again.

I didn't even stop on my usual floor. I took the elevator to the twenty-third floor where the upper management offices were located.

When I stepped out of the elevator, I held my head high and strode past Mr. Schultz's assistant, Lauren, without a word.

"Cheyenne?"

THE GAME

I ignored her, noticing most of the members of the board were in the conference room where I'd left them yesterday. In a brief moment of hysteria, I had the sensation they hadn't moved since then. I almost giggled.

I opened the door without knocking and stopped dead in my tracks.

Son of a bitch.

Riley.

He turned to face me as I entered, and his face lit up. "Cheyenne." The next instant, his face fell into a look of concern as he glanced up and down my frame. After all, I wasn't dressed for the office.

"What are you doing here?" I asked.

"Meeting with your board. They have some great ideas for my campaign…" His voice trailed off. Undoubtedly because I stared at him with a pasted smile that was not my own.

"How nice for you. I'm sure Christine Parson would be an excellent choice to work on whatever project you have in mind." I turned toward Mr. Schultz and continued, "I'm so sorry about yesterday, sir. I was too tongue-tied to properly address the situation. The reality is that none of that marketing plan was ever my own doing—"

"Cheyenne," Riley gasped behind me. He grabbed my bicep with one hand and pulled me, trying to get me to face him.

But my eyes were on Mr. Schultz, who stared at me in confusion.

The rest of the room fell into a hush.

Mr. Schultz cleared his throat, but I didn't let him interject.

"It was silly, really. I have no idea why I thought I could get away with it. She's much sharper than me and far more educated and intelligent. And she has an array of experience I can't compete with. It was insane that I thought for one moment I could compete with her or steal her ideas." I even batted my eyes in a lame attempt to be believed.

"Cheyenne?" Riley stepped in front of me, blocking my connection with Mr. Schultz. "What the hell is wrong with you?"

"Nothing. I'm just 'fessing up to my deception. It was rude of me to ruin another woman's career to advance my own."

"Is she blackmailing you, Cheyenne?" Mr. Schultz asked.

I was taken aback. "What? No." I waved a hand

The Game

through the air, blowing off his suggestion.

"Do you have any idea what happened here last night?" he asked, leaning around Riley to meet my gaze.

"No..." My voice trailed off. What was going on?

"Did you not stop at the lower floor?"

"No. I came straight here. What's this about?"

Riley tilted his head closer to mine, narrowing his eyes. "Cheyenne, the place is trashed. Christine broke in last night and turned the lower floor into a hurricane."

"What? Are you sure? Maybe it was someone else. It could have been anyone." Though I knew that wasn't true. If the twenty-second floor looked anything like my apartment... I shuddered.

"Cheyenne, her prints are everywhere. She started with your cubicle and moved outward."

"Prints?" Did that mean they were all over my apartment too?

"Yes. The police have been combing the place since early this morning. They've already definitively identified her hands on nearly everything. She didn't even bother to wear gloves."

Yep, her prints would be all over my apartment. And my plan to reinstate her was ruined. If only she hadn't flipped out with such haste... I could have saved her and thrown myself under the bus. Now? Now she was just fucked.

"How could you identify her? Surely she doesn't have a record."

"She didn't need one. We compared her prints to her office phone. She's been the only person in there in over a week," Mr. Schultz added.

I nodded, feeling a bit like an idiot. And then I turned toward the door, thinking to leave.

Riley grabbed my wrist this time, his hand slipping down to hold mine tightly as he tugged me back to his side. He wrapped his arms around me and pulled me closer. He even kissed the top of my head. "Baby…"

Could this get any worse? I struggled against him, trying to save my dignity and get the hell out of there.

But he held firm.

In fact, everyone else in the room slipped out, and it occurred to me that Mr. Schultz had been informed as to just who my "boyfriend" was and figured out Riley had sent the presentation. I could feel them all leaving, even though I had shut my eyes tightly and buried my face in Riley's starched dress shirt.

The door shut with a soft snick, and then Riley released his grip enough to hold me at arm's length. His expression was full of concern. "What the hell is going on?"

If his voice hadn't been so soft and gentle, I would have thought he was mad at me. Instead, he was genuinely concerned.

I took a deep breath. "She trashed my apartment last night too." I don't know why I thought it necessary to declare that fact, but I did it anyway. Probably to avoid the real issues.

"What?" He stiffened. "That fucking cunt."

I shuddered at his sharp words. Though I don't know why. He was only stating facts.

"Did she take anything?"

At that question, I started laughing. Like a maniac. Uncontrolled guffaws that included snorting and tears. Was he serious? "Have you been to the twenty-second floor?"

"No. Why?"

"Well, I just came from my apartment. I can only imagine the damage here if it's anything like that." I wiped tears from the corner of my eyes. Perhaps I was having a nervous breakdown.

"That bad?" A wry smile caused one corner of his mouth to lift.

"Let's just say I'll probably never know if anything's missing."

He reached up and tugged something through my hair and then held it in front of my face. "Mattress?"

I nodded. I hadn't realized I'd gotten cotton fluff on me. I'd never even entered the apartment.

"We need to let the police know about your apartment so they can coordinate with each other and link the two scenes. If she left prints at your place too, she'll go down for sure."

"Right." I hadn't thought about that. I hadn't thought about anything really. My brain was still a cloudy mess in fight or flight mode.

"Sit." He angled me toward a chair and helped lower me into the smooth leather. "Don't move. I'll be right back."

I nodded. I knew he was going to speak to the officer in charge. It made sense.

He left the door open a crack, and a few minutes later Lauren came in and set a cup of coffee in front of me. Cream and sugar. How did she know how I liked my coffee? She smiled tightly, her eyes expressing her sorrow.

I jerked. I needed to get out of there. Before Riley came back. He was so domineering he would talk me out

The Game

of it. And this wasn't over. Not for me at least. I had no intention letting him steamroll me.

He lied to me. I couldn't trust him. And his ex was still out there somewhere with every intention of making my life miserable.

I ignored Lauren's coffee and jumped to my feet to barrel past her without a word. I didn't even take the elevator. I headed straight for the stairs, hitting the top one and taking them two at a time before the heavy metal door even slammed shut behind me.

I didn't want to risk the elevator opening to reveal Riley inside. I ran down several flights and then took a deep breath and calmly exited the stairwell to pick up the elevator on the nineteenth floor. Luckily that level was all office space and no one saw me exit the stairwell in my state of complete disarray.

I looked like someone who had entered the building to escape a rainstorm and then partially dried off in the last half hour, leaving my hair in wet tangled clumps and my clothes wrinkled and plastered to my skin.

I ran toward my car when the doors slid open and exited the garage as if I were being chased.

Riley either didn't know I'd left yet, or he wasn't fast enough to catch up.

Either way, I was relieved. I would call Mr. Schultz later and explain my insanity, but at this point the man would be crazy to keep me on as an employee of Talent Marketing Group after I'd acted like a lunatic several times.

My tires screeched on the smooth concrete garage floor as I pulled out into the afternoon traffic.

Deep breaths helped me gather my wits.

Chapter Twenty-Five

The grip I had on the steering wheel was so tight my fingers ached. I had no idea where to go next. My apartment was trashed, my parents would be out of their minds with concern if I returned there, and my only local best friend would be at work.

I wished I could talk to Amy. She would be at work too, but at least her mind would be clearer than mine, and she could help me calm down and figure out what to do.

I made several turns and headed out of the center of downtown in search of a place to pull over. I chose a fast-food parking lot and pulled into a vacant section in the back corner.

My phone rang as I reached for my purse, startling me. I glanced at the caller ID. Riley. Of course. I declined his call and made my call to Amy.

She picked up on the first ring. "Cheyenne. I've been so worried about you. What's going on?"

I leaned my head back against my seat and closed my eyes. "My apartment was trashed, and apparently so was my office."

"I heard. Are you okay?"

"You heard already?" Jesus.

"Yeah. Riley called when you left your office."

"Could he possibly meddle any more than he has?" My high blood pressure kept shooting higher.

"Cheyenne, listen to me. You need to go to Riley's house. Let him explain."

"Are you crazy? I didn't call you to give me that kind of advice. Amy, I need you to be supportive. If you can't, I'll hang up now."

"Cheyenne, please. I'm not trying to be a bitch here."

"You are if you're on his side."

"There are no sides, Cheyenne. I just want to help."

"Well, the sort of help I need is cry-on-your-shoulder help. Not go-talk-to-the-lying-bastard help."

She giggled.

"*Amy,*" I shot back. This wasn't funny at all.

"Sorry." She tried to sober, but I could picture her bottom lip between her teeth as she fought another laugh. "Cheyenne, if you don't listen to reason, Christine wins."

"I don't give a fuck if Christine wins, Amy. That's the whole point. She can have him. She can have the job at Talent Marketing Group. I just want to be left alone."

"I know you do, hon, but it doesn't work like that with Christine. And you can't seriously tell me you'd let that bitch win and walk away. I thought you had more spunk than that."

"That was before my life was ruined. I don't give a fuck anymore. I just want to leave town and reinvent myself somewhere where neither of them can find me and I don't have to look over my shoulder to make sure I'm not about to get stabbed. I've had enough of conniving rich people."

"Riley isn't like that." She sighed.

I was losing my patience with her lack of support. "Riley lied to me."

"He was only trying to protect you."

"I didn't ask for protection. I asked him

specifically to stay out of it."

"Cheyenne."

"What?" I screamed.

"Please do me this one favor. Before you go off half-cocked, stop at his house and let him tell his side of the story. That's all I'm asking. Surely you can do that one thing. Do it for me. Do it for you."

I stared out the windshield at the bushes that ran along the back of the parking lot. I wasn't sure I could do what Amy wanted. And I definitely couldn't see the purpose.

However, I also didn't have an immediate plan. I would need to go back to my apartment at some point and clean up the mess so I could gather whatever was salvageable and take it with me. That wasn't going to happen today. Which meant I needed someplace to stay. Meagan's was the logical choice.

"Cheyenne?"

"Yeah. I'm here."

"Drive to Riley's."

I let my eyes flutter closed again. "Okay."

"You will?" Her voice perked up.

"Sure." What could it hurt? At least I would have closure when it was over. And I would need to find a

The Game

way to get along with the man for the rest of my life if our lives were going to be so intertwined with Amy's and Cade's.

I ended the call with Amy and backed out of the spot.

With extreme hesitation, I headed to Riley's. Why was the man going to be home in the middle of a Tuesday anyway? And why was he at my office earlier?

There were several cars out front when I pulled up and turned off the engine.

I climbed from my car on wobbly legs, too exhausted for this forced confrontation that would surely end with both of us angrier than we already were.

Riley opened the front door and hurried in my direction before I got halfway up the front walk.

"Cheyenne," he whispered as he approached, slowing his gate and not touching me. His brow was furrowed. He looked like he hadn't slept in days. I hadn't noticed that at my office.

I stopped walking. "Amy insisted we make amends."

He smiled, his eyes lighting up. "You'll do what Amy asks, but not me?"

My ears flamed red as I opened my mouth to

counter that insanity. "Pardon? How dare you. I've done all sorts of shit for you, most of which isn't mentionable in public. It's you who won't do as I ask."

"Touché." He reached for my bicep and gently nudged me forward. "Come inside. There are some people here you need to meet."

Was he kidding? I was in no mood to meet anyone. Hell, I never wanted to be introduced to any of his friends again in this lifetime, but certainly not today.

Riley's shoulders slumped. "Please, Cheyenne. Cut me some slack here. I'm trying to come clean."

"With guests?"

"It's not like I'm throwing a party in there, baby. This is important."

I narrowed my gaze. I looked like a homeless woman at this point. And why should I care? If he wanted to introduce me to people at this juncture, it would only make him look like he'd lost his marbles for ever dating me in the first place.

"Fine." I nodded toward the house and followed him inside, shaking off the slight touch he had on my arm.

After he closed the door behind me, he set a hand on my back and led me toward his spacious family room. I'd stood naked in that room several times, and just thinking about that made me shudder.

Riley didn't comment.

Two men stood from where they sat on the couch. Both turned toward me and smiled. One was Riley's age with gorgeous dark hair that curled slightly on the ends and green eyes that made women melt at his feet. I remembered him. This was Parker Darwin, the third friend of Riley and Cade who lived in Charlotte, North Carolina.

The other man was significantly older, old enough to be their father. His hair was gray and he was balding on top, but he was clearly sophisticated and wealthy. His suit jacket was draped over the back of the couch carefully. His white shirt was perfectly starched, and he smoothed a hand down his designer tie as he smiled at me. "You must be Cheyenne."

I was skeptical. Who was this guy, and why was he in Riley's house? I felt like I was at an intervention. If he was some sort of BDSM mentor or something, I would not only run from the house, I would also shoot Riley in the head the next chance I got.

Riley pressed me forward, his hand still at the small of my back. "Cheyenne Decard," he addressed the older gentleman first and then turned toward Parker. "And you've met Parker Darwin before, right?"

I nodded toward Parker.

"And this is Harold Parson."

Parson? As in Christine Parson?

"Christine's father."

"Sorry to meet on such a stressful day," the man said as he stepped closer and reached to shake my hand. "I'm also sorry for what my daughter has put you through."

What? I took his hand and let him shake mine, but I didn't put much energy into the grip.

"Let's sit." Riley nodded at the couch where Harold and Parker had been sitting when we walked in. He grabbed my hand and tugged me toward the love seat at an angle from the couch, gripping me firmly enough to keep me from withdrawing.

I perched on the edge of the cushion, careful to avoid any contact with Riley. In fact, I scooted away from him several inches when I regained control of my hand. I crossed my legs and sat up straight, my hands on my top knee. "What's this about?"

Mr. Parson spoke again. "It seems my daughter has caused quite a disturbance here."

The Game

"That's an understatement," Riley muttered.

"I want you all to know that you have my cooperation with regard to locating her and turning her over to the police."

What was this man up to?

"Perhaps I shouldn't have been so obtuse when it came to Christine, but she is my daughter, and I fear I gave her the benefit of the doubt one time too many."

Riley leaned forward. I could feel him staring at the side of my head. "Harold is one of our lawyers. His firm represents Edgewater Inc. in Charlotte. He has worked for us for many years."

I turned to look at Riley head on, giving him a why-should-I-give-a-fuck stare.

Riley blew out a breath.

Parker took over, and I turned my gaze willingly to face him. "Six years ago, when we were all in good standing and Riley and Christine were an item that seemed inseparable, we hired her father to represent Edgewater. He owns a law office in Charlotte and another in Roanoke, Virginia. His firm represents many large clients in both states."

Ah, so this was a rich guy. Richer perhaps than Riley and his friends.

"I haven't seen Harold since Christine and I broke things off last year, but he's been working with Parker."

Mr. Parson cleared his throat. "My daughter weaves a very different tale than the one I've gathered from Riley over the past few days." He smiled politely and continued. "She led me to believe Riley had dumped her for no reason other than the fact that someone had spread lies about her and he believed them.

"She has spent the better part of the last year conniving to earn him back and get him to see reason. I chose to stay out of it and let her figure things out for herself. I should have spoken to Riley a year ago, but I was a bit miffed he'd broken things off with my daughter, and I didn't want to risk destroying the business relationship we'd established."

Undoubtedly because it was a lucrative arrangement. The man's actions couldn't be wholly altruistic.

"Frankly, I should have contacted you myself, Harold. I take full responsibility for that." Riley ran a hand through his disheveled hair and continued. "I didn't have anything nice to say about Christine, and I didn't see the need to drag her through the coals with you, sir. So, I took the easy way out and left it alone."

THE GAME

Mr. Parson nodded. "I can understand that. Neither of us should have stepped away, especially since we still have a business arrangement that could have suffered from the misunderstanding."

Parker chuckled, shocking me in the middle of this serious come-to-Jesus moment for Riley and Mr. Parson. "Misunderstanding is an understatement. Christine is a lunatic."

I was shocked at how blunt Parker was.

Mr. Parson nodded again. "Apparently."

"What does this have to do with me?" I finally interjected. All I wanted to do was get the hell out of town. I didn't give a fuck what misunderstandings these three men needed to work out.

Mr. Parson spoke again. "Christine came to me several weeks ago and asked me to get her a job in Atlanta. It seems she thought if she moved closer to Riley, she could win him back. I personally didn't think it was a good idea. If the man wanted her around, he would have made himself known. But I called in a favor from my old friend Joseph Schultz."

I flinched.

Parker tapped his lips with one hand and blew out a breath as though exasperated. "None of us had any idea she had gotten that job or that she was moving to Atlanta. And we certainly didn't know you worked there."

"Hell," Riley added, "even I didn't know where you worked."

"Apparently Christine did. Yay me."

Mr. Parson smiled at my sarcasm. "Christine must have lost it when she realized Riley was seeing another woman and then found out where you worked. She called me the day after she saw you at that fundraiser and asked me to get her a job at Talent Marketing Group. Said she wanted to make a fresh start from the bottom rung."

I flinched at his reference to my company being the bottom rung.

Mr. Parson waved a hand in the air. "Her words. Not mine. I swear I had no idea she was planning to sabotage your job or your relationship."

I jumped from my seat. "With all due respect, sir, your daughter has ruined my life. She trashed my apartment and my work place. I can't go anywhere without looking over my shoulder. I have to move to another city to start over."

Riley stood next to me and wrapped an arm around my middle.

I jumped out of his reach and stepped backward,

The Game

holding out both hands. "I don't care what happens between you and Christine. You can get back together with her for all I care. In fact, I wish you would so she would leave me alone. I just want to get out of here and move on with my life."

His face fell. What? Was he shocked? Jesus.

"That's not what I want."

"I don't care what you want, Riley. Don't you understand? Why is it always about what you want? How about asking me what I want for a change?"

Mr. Parson stood and cleared his throat. "I'm going to let you two sort this out without an audience. I just wanted to let you know how sorry I am for perpetuating this problem, Ms. Decard. And I want all three of you to know that I'll be working with the police to locate my daughter and turn her in. I'm mortified and embarrassed beyond belief. I didn't raise her to be such a bitch."

I flinched when he called his own daughter such a derogatory name. Deserving, but still...

He nodded and turned to leave. "You've got my number, Riley, if you hear anything. I'll be in town several more days until this is wrapped up."

"I do. And thank you, sir." He followed Mr.

Parson toward the foyer.

"I'm just sorry it came to this. I hope you two can work things out." The older man spun around and waved at me.

I nodded.

Parker reached out a hand to shake mine. "Sorry about all this. Give Riley a chance. I know you're pissed, but he's a good guy, and I know he really cares about you." He smiled broadly and left me standing by the couch.

Great. Joy. I would be alone with Riley.

I crossed my arms and tapped a foot, wondering how long I needed to stay here and endure more groveling before I could escape.

The front door shut with a resounding click that left us in silence.

Riley came back into view, his hands in his pockets. He leaned against the back of the couch and stared at me. "You gonna give me a chance here?"

"No." I shook my head. "I don't see the point."

He took a deep breath and righted himself. "Cheyenne, the point is I can't imagine letting you go. I know we haven't been together long, but it feels right, and I want to explore it further."

"I guess you should have thought of that before

you lied to me."

"I never lied to you." He narrowed his gaze.

"Semantics. And you know it."

"Fine. But there was no way I was going to let that woman drive over you with a freight train just because you thought you could handle it. You had no idea what you were up against."

"And you did?"

"No. But I had far more information than you did."

"Then you should have shared more details."

"I'll admit that. I could have handled things better."

"Call the presses." I rolled my eyes.

Riley chuckled.

I was in no mood for funny.

He sobered. "She contacted me."

I raised an eyebrow.

"Friday. Said she wanted to meet."

"Did you?"

"Fuck no." He furrowed his brow in frustration. "But that only made her angrier. She threatened me."

"How?"

"She wanted to make a trade. If I would break up

with you and start seeing her again, she would leave you alone."

"Jesus."

"Yeah, so I told her I'd think about it, and then I called Parker and told him I was heading to Charlotte and he needed to arrange a meet with her father."

"You told her you'd think about it?" My voice rose with each syllable.

"Cheyenne, I was lying. Give me some credit. I needed to get my ducks in a row, and I didn't want her to come after you over the weekend. It was a bit of a cease-fire I suppose."

"And you didn't think I should know this?"

He blew out a breath. "I should have told you."

"Ya think?" I wanted to scream.

We stood staring at each other for a long time.

"I should spank you."

"You should find someone else who likes to be ordered around and spanked." Though I squirmed at the mention, pissed at my traitorous body for finding his suggestion so sexy.

He inched toward me.

I backed up.

When he stopped, he continued. "She called me

other times as well. I ignored her."

"When?"

"Ever since that night we saw her at Sky. She would call and hang up sometimes. Other times she would leave a groveling voice message. Sometimes sweet as molasses, other times threatening or demanding. I knew she was cracked."

I said nothing.

"When I found out she was suddenly your boss, I lost it. I knew she would flatten you like a pancake and brush the crumbs off her hands as she walked away. I didn't want that for you."

"And yet, it happened anyway."

"I see that." He held my gaze in a way that I found it impossible to break the stare. "The police will find her. She'll go to jail for this."

"Must be embarrassing for you."

He smirked. "Cheyenne, not in the slightest. I feel like an idiot for maintaining a relationship with her for so many years and ignoring the signs that she was only in it for the money. But other than that, I can hold my head high. At least I didn't marry her." He shuddered.

"Yay for you. Can I go now?"

"No." He stepped closer.

"Riley, we're done here. Let me leave."

"No. We aren't done, and I don't want you to leave. Ever."

"Ever? That's crazy. I can't trust you, and I have about a thousand problems to solve before I can leave town."

"You aren't leaving town."

"You can't tell me what to do, Riley. I'm a grown woman."

"I can see that." His gaze wandered up and down my body. "And I wish you would drop your arms and stop trying to hide the details."

I wrapped them tighter around myself. "Apparently we don't always get what we want."

"When did you get so stubborn?"

"When I asked you to stay out of my problems and you sent my proposal to my boss behind my back."

He was in my space now, and I'd backed up until I had nowhere else to go. My legs were against the arm of the couch. He reached up and tucked a lock of my messy curls behind one ear. In a gentle voice, he spoke again, "What do you think would have happened if I hadn't done that?"

"Christine would have handled that account, and

we would have gone on as if it were hers, nobody the wiser."

"And you think your problems would have ended there? She would have simply assigned you another project and given you credit for it and moved on?"

I bit my lip. Probably not. "Doubtful, but I would have eventually quit and moved on."

"Letting her win."

"Yes." I stood taller and shook his fingers from my cheek as he stroked my skin. "Riley, I don't care who wins. I just want her out of my life. If I had fought her, she would have made my life miserable."

"More miserable than she actually did?" He lifted one eyebrow.

Damn him. He had a point there too.

"I don't think she ever would have stopped until she had me back and you gone. In fact, I'm sure of it."

He was probably right.

"And it wouldn't have mattered if she worked at Talent Marketing Group or not. Once she saw us together, you were on her hit list." He stepped even closer until inches separated us. His hand slid back to bury in my hair, his fingers threading into the curly mess and tugging my head back so I fully faced him. "Don't. Let.

BECCA JAMESON

Her. Win."

Is that what I was doing? I didn't see it that way. The way I saw it, I didn't want to get involved in Riley's fucked-up mess, and I sure didn't want my life ruined.

"She got under your skin."

True.

"She wants us to break things off."

"I'm sure she does."

"Do you think I would get back together with her?"

"I don't care."

"Don't you?" He leaned closer.

I licked my lips, hating the way my body was drawn to his like a magnet. My panties were wet, and I squeezed my legs together to stave off the desire brewing between them. He smelled so damn good, and the intensity in his stare was enough to make anyone go weak in the knees.

Okay. I cared. I couldn't stand the visual of Riley with Christine. It made me want to vomit. Even the thought of him being with her for so many years made my blood boil.

"No matter what you choose to do, Christine is going to jail, and I'm never going to have anything to do

THE GAME

with her. But it will piss me off if she succeeds in ruining this fantastic thing I have with you because you're afraid to take a chance on me."

"I'm not afraid," I retorted.

"Really?" He dared to kiss my nose and then gently set his lips on mine for a moment before pulling back a few inches. "Mmm. You always taste so sweet. I hated missing our weekend together. My cock was hard the entire time thinking of what I would have rather been doing with you."

"What were you doing?"

"I told you I was in Charlotte, with Harold and Parker, trying to sort things out and get a handle on this situation."

"How did her father get involved?"

"Parker called him."

"Parker?"

"Yep. I didn't have the balls to do it myself, and Parker was fed up. He called him and told him to call off his daughter and get her ass out of Georgia and back to Virginia, or we would fire his ass and find someone else to handle the account."

I gasped.

"Yeah. So, I had no choice but to get involved and

head to Charlotte Friday. I needed to grow some balls and meet with Harold myself and tell him what happened a year ago."

"And he believed you?"

"Not at first, but he was diplomatic since we're one of his largest accounts and it was clear we weren't kidding around about firing him. Especially since Cade made the trip too."

"Geez."

"Yeah." He kissed my lips again. This time I didn't draw back as quickly. God, he made me melt. I didn't want to react to him this way.

"You still lied to me."

"I didn't do it with malicious intent, baby. I did it to save your ass."

I could see that, but I still didn't like it. "Doesn't matter. I don't want you to go behind my back ever and do something I asked you not to do, not for any reason. If you disagreed with me, you should have explained yourself better instead."

"Agreed."

I released my tight grip around my middle and pushed on his chest to back him up a pace. "Give me space, Riley. Stop crowding me."

The Game

He stepped back and dropped his hand from its tangle in my hair. "Please, baby."

His face was drawn with the fear I would leave.

I stepped out from between him and the couch and paced the room, trying to figure out what to do without being completely surrounded by his overbearing warmth and scent.

Riley spun around to watch me. "I need you. We're so good together."

"You need to boss someone around," I pointed out.

"Not someone. *You.*"

"We need a renegotiation." Was I actually going to give him another shot? What was the matter with me? I was weak from being in his house, that's what. And so tired. I didn't want to argue anymore.

"I can do that. We'll renegotiate several times a week at first, baby. That's how this works."

"How *what* works, Riley?"

He waved a hand between us. "This. Our relationship."

Was this really a relationship? I stopped pacing and crossed one leg in front of the other, swaying a bit in an effort to clench my pussy. I crossed my arms under my chest again. "I don't know, Riley. I'm a bit jaded now."

"I see that. Give me another chance." He stepped tentatively closer. "You're scared. That's understandable. This is a huge commitment. If I didn't think you could do it, I wouldn't ask. If I didn't think you were submissive, I wouldn't have taken this leap in the first place. Being a Dom is who I am. It's a part of me. I can't change it. And I don't think you'd want me to."

"Actually, you didn't think I was submissive when we first met. That's precisely why you took off and didn't even have the balls to say a word to me first."

"This is true. But I regretted that almost from the moment it happened. I even convinced myself I could give up this way of life if I had you."

"Seriously?" He'd never said anything like that before.

"Yeah. And then I saw you at that fundraiser and my heart jumped in my chest. I knew I would do anything for another chance."

"How many chances do you want from me?"

His mouth lifted on one side. "Apparently, I'm a bit of a fuckup, and I might need you to extend an olive branch now and then." He was in my space again. "Forgive me. Forgive me for being a coward that first night. Forgive me for interfering in your life this week. Know that I did it with your best interest in mind, and I swear I'll never go behind your back again.

"If we ever encounter an issue in the future, I'll spread out the details better and talk it out instead of taking matters into my own hands."

I wanted his words to be true. My breasts ached, swollen from the pressure I had on them to keep my nipples from pebbling in his presence.

"Be mine."

"I don't want you to own me, Riley. I want you to love me. Unconditionally."

"I do."

My eyes widened.

Seconds ticked by.

"Forgive me?"

"Do I have a choice?"

"Yes. You always have a choice."

"Right answer." I licked my lips.

"Open yourself up, baby. Drop your arms. Spread your legs. I hate that stance you have. So closed. Cold."

Slowly I let my hands fall to my sides and uncrossed my legs. I trembled under his gaze. He had something over me that was undeniable. I could fight this.

I could leave. Run. Hide. But what would I gain?

Even if he was occasionally an asshole and meddled in my life, I would always forgive him. That's how strongly I felt about him. I was putty in his presence. I'd been kidding myself about being able to turn it off and leave town as if I could forget him and move on.

The truth was, I would have spent weeks crying my eyes out over the loss. I had no choice but to give him another shot. It would kill me not to.

THE GAME

Chapter Twenty-Six

Riley's gaze roamed up and down my body. "Thank you. I know this is hard for you. I also know it's my fault. Don't let that bitch win. Please, baby. Stay with me. Fight. Hold your head high. I'm yours."

He's mine...

He was right. I would fight for him.

He reached for me, his fingers moving slowly to stroke my cheeks and then down my chin and neck until he softly floated them over my nipples.

I arched into his touch.

"God, I love how your body responds to me."

I did too.

"I need you. I need to see you. All of you." If I

wasn't mistaken, his fingers shook as he lowered his arms. "Take off your clothes, baby."

I hesitated. It was so fast. We had a tendency to go from anger to sex in point five seconds.

He waited, though I knew he wouldn't be this patient normally.

"I want to spank you."

I swallowed, wetness flooding my panties.

"I'm not going to."

My shoulders slumped before I could stop them.

"I'm going to flog you."

Flog?

I had my fingers fisted in my T-shirt, ready to lift it over my head, but I hesitated and stared at him. "Not sure I'm ready for that."

"Talk to me. What are you afraid of?"

"Uh, pain?"

He took my hands and met my gaze, pulling me closer. "There will be no pain. Only pleasure. I promise. The flogger feels more like a massage than anything else. It soothes, relaxes you. I'll start out easy, and I won't flog you any harder than you can tolerate."

I chewed on my lower lip for a moment and then nodded. His expression was sincere. He would never hurt me.

He lifted a brow.

"Okay, Sir."

He tugged my T-shirt over my head and tossed it aside with no regard for where it landed. His fingers danced down the lace of my bra and dipped into the upper swell to stroke my nipples.

I moaned and leaned into him, grabbing his forearms for balance as I swayed too far.

"So sexy," he muttered.

My eyes fluttered shut.

"Trust me. Trust me to know what you need and what you can handle. You have safewords."

I nodded.

"What are they?"

"Red. Yellow."

He smiled.

I glanced down. "I'm a mess." I lifted my hands to my uncombed hair and remembered I also wore no makeup.

He chuckled. "I don't care. I will admit, though you are smokin' hot in jeans, I hate them. Jeans in general. They get in my way. But I do like knowing they're tight and rubbing against your pussy."

More wetness. "Stop it."

"Stop what?" he teased.

"Speaking."

"Never." His gaze lowered to my waist. "Take them off. I want to watch."

I undid the button, lowered the zipper, and then wiggled my ass back and forth to ease them over my hips. When I kicked off my tennis shoes and stepped out, he grabbed my hand to steady me. I released him to crouch down and remove my socks.

"I'll run you a bath. I bet you could use the hot water and relax a while."

He was going to let me soak in the tub? Sounded heavenly.

I followed him down the hall into the master bedroom and through to the master bath.

Riley turned on the tap and held his hand under the water until it heated. Then he pushed the stopper down and stepped back. "Get in, baby. I'll go grab you something to drink." He paused at the doorway and looked back. "When was the last time you ate?"

I nibbled my lip. "Sometime yesterday I think."

He nodded and left without a word.

Ten minutes later as I lay in the tub, covered with

warm water, he returned, carrying a tray. "Brought you several things."

I smiled at his assortment. Suddenly I was starving. I lifted a hand out of the water, but he shook his head. "Just relax."

When I lowered my hand back under the water and tipped my head back to see him better, he sat on the edge of the tub and held up a grape.

It was just a grape, but I moaned around it. The way he fed me made everything taste sharper. More flavorful. Delicious. The unexpected—not knowing what he would offer next—heightened my senses.

A piece of hard cheese followed. I closed my eyes as I savored the flavor. Expensive cheese. Not something I'd ever had before.

He offered me a pretzel next, and I almost giggled at the simplicity of the selection on his platter of a variety of fruits, cheeses, and prosciutto.

He tapped my nose. "What's so funny, imp?"

"Nothing," I mouthed around the bite.

We went on like this until everything was gone and the water in the tub was cooling off. Sometimes Riley took a bite. Mostly he fed me. And in between he offered me sips of white wine. Crisp. Dry. Perfect.

"You're shivering."

"The water got cold."

He set the tray aside and reached a hand out to help me out of the tub. When he wrapped me in a giant plush white towel, I sighed. He led me from the room. Damp tendrils of my hair hung across my shoulders.

The bedroom was bright from the sun spilling in the window to land in long rays across the floor. The comforter was pulled back to reveal the dark midnight blue sheets.

Riley eased the towel from my body. At some point he had removed his shoes, and now he tugged his shirt over his head. He stood before me in nothing but worn jeans that hugged his body low on his hips in a way that any woman would drool. "Kneel in front of the bed, Cheyenne. Hands on the mattress. Head ducked. Knees apart."

I followed his directions, my heart pounding. I glanced around, my gaze landing on the flogger I had managed to somehow miss when I entered the room. It rested on the bedside table, thick with long black leather strips. I held my breath.

"Don't panic. We'll take it slow. You'll be surprised by how good it feels to be flogged. It's like an intimate

THE GAME

massage. I know you think it will hurt, but you're wrong. You'll love it. Just relax." He set a hand on my shoulder and pointed at the side of the bed. "Eyes to the front. Chin down. Safeword red."

I gripped the sheet around the mattress with both hands, bracing myself. Would this be the time I finally needed my safeword?

Instead of swatting me with it, Riley dragged the ends across my skin, dancing them over my shoulders and then down my back. It tickled more than anything.

I relaxed marginally as he continued to shake the ends across my ass and thighs and then my calves.

"I'm going to strike you now, so softly you will hardly notice. You ready?"

"Yes, Sir."

When he lifted it away, he wasted no time before it landed on my upper back. Gently.

I flinched, but for no reason. It didn't hurt at all. In fact, it felt good. Welcome.

Again it whizzed through the air and landed on the other side of my back below my shoulders. Several more strikes landed similarly as I relaxed into the rhythm, forgetting entirely that I'd been nervous.

Gradually, each time he struck me, he swung

slightly harder. The increased pressure was welcome. In fact, I craved it. He didn't add to the force fast enough. I wanted more.

Suddenly, he switched to my ass.

I swayed forward with a gasp. The sting was delicious, but shocking.

"Stay still, baby. Don't move. It's important that I only swat you in the fatty areas. If you move, I might miss my target and hurt you."

"Okay."

"Okay what?"

"Yes, Sir." As soon as I spoke that word, I slipped into a place of submission one notch deeper than I'd been in. It was that easy.

"Good girl. May I keep going?"

"Yes, Sir." I craved it.

Several seconds went by while he rustled around behind me, and then he was back, and the next time I felt the leather hit my skin it was followed immediately by a second flogger.

I glanced over my shoulder. He held two now, working them in a sort of figure eight through the air so there was little pause between contact with my skin.

"Face front, Cheyenne. Hold still. This style is

THE GAME

called Florentine. How does it feel?"

"Amazing, Sir."

He chuckled and continued striking me across my upper back and then lower over my ass and thighs.

Instinctively I spread my legs wider. I closed my eyes. I was so wet. Incredibly turned on.

"You're enjoying this."

I was.

"Can you take more?"

"Yes, Sir," I whispered. I actually wanted him to continue.

His actions increased in speed and force until I found my head hanging lower in front of me and my back red hot with the burn.

He suddenly struck me four times in a row with sharp stinging slaps that made me moan, and then he stopped.

I heard the thud of the floggers hitting the floor, and then he was behind me, kneeling between my legs, his hands roaming up and down my body, rubbing the burning sting in my ass and back.

I was so horny, I could have come by his touch alone, and I willed him to reach between my legs. And then his hands were on my waist and he lifted me onto the bed on my hands and knees. I was shaking. I couldn't stop.

He disappeared for only seconds, and then I heard the tear of a condom wrapper and he was back.

He held me firmly as he thrust into me with no warning.

The shock was so much that I came immediately. My body pulsed around his cock deep inside me.

"That's it, baby. Let it go." He threaded his fingers into my hair and held my head firmly, tugging so that my neck elongated.

A deep moaned escaped my lips. My sated body wanted to ooze into the top of the bed and relax.

But Riley wasn't done with me. "Stay on your hands and knees, baby." He pulled almost out and thrust back into me, releasing my head to grab my hips with both hands. Fast and hard he thrust, over and over.

My first orgasm, not fully finished, turned into two and then three. Each one was more intense than the previous. The pleasure was more than I'd ever experienced, and I never wanted him to stop.

He didn't, at least not for a while. Instead he snaked one hand around to stroke my clit, driving me higher. I braced myself and thrust backward with his

The Game

rhythm so we moved in a choreographed pattern.

When Riley reached his peak, he paused deep inside me, his fingers working my clit so hard I came one more time while he emptied himself into the condom.

Completely out of energy, my arms and legs shook.

Riley held me up around the waist and slowly lowered me to the bed. He kissed my shoulder blade as he pulled out, leaving me sprawled open without the energy to move an inch.

He padded from the room and returned a minute later with a warm cloth that landed between my legs to stroke through my sensitive folds. When he was satisfied, he tugged my body so I lay the correct direction on the bed, climbed up beside, me and covered us both with the sheet. I was way too hot for any blankets and glad I didn't have to voice that because so far my lips didn't work.

I faded as he held me close to his side. "Sleep, baby. Rest." His lips landed all over my shoulder, soft kisses that lulled me into a deep sleep.

Chapter Twenty-Seven

I awoke with a start. A pounding noise penetrated my mind. The door.

Riley lifted his head off the pillow next to me and groaned.

"What time is it?" I mumbled.

"Three in the morning." He kissed my cheek and pressed into my back. "Stay here."

The pounding grew louder.

"That bitch," Riley mumbled under his breath while he dragged himself from the bed and then plucked his jeans from the floor and stepped into them.

We'd spent the late evening lounging in bed under the glow of candles, which we hadn't extinguished. The

The Game

room remained shrouded in the low glow of the flames. I sat up, tugging the sheet with me.

"Stay there, baby. I'll handle this."

I nodded. I had no intention of leaving this room. He could deal with his fucking ex without me.

He handed me his cell phone, pressing it into my palm. "Call nine one one. I'll keep her occupied until they get here."

I nodded and lifted his phone up to press the keys with shaky fingers.

As he shut the door to the bedroom, the operator answered. "Nine one one. What's your emergency?"

I took a deep breath and quickly explained to the woman about Christine Parson being at my boyfriend's residence banging on the door. This was easily confirmed while I spoke to the operator because both of us could hear Christine's high-pitched squeal of anger filling the house and seeping under the door to contaminate us with her venom.

The woman assured me someone was on the way and encouraged me to stay on the line.

I did, listening intently to the muffled voices outside the room when she wasn't screaming. I rarely heard Riley and assumed he was trying to pacify her and remain calm to give the police a chance to get there.

The voices grew louder, and I sat up fully, hugging the sheet against my chest and breathing heavily into the phone.

"Ma'am? Are you still there?"

"Yes," I whispered. I wasn't sure if Christine realized my car was out front in the street, and therefore I was probably in Riley's bed. But I wasn't going to take the chance and have her hear my voice.

She screamed again. I cringed, feeling helpless. Concerned, I dropped the phone on the bed and slinked to the floor to snag Riley's T-shirt and shrug it over my head. At least in an emergency I wouldn't be completely naked.

When something slammed into the bedroom door, I dashed to the adjoining bathroom and slid into the corner out of sight. The door to the bedroom flew open, and Christine's piercing voice filled the room.

"I know she's here. Why, Riley? Why would you want to fuck that whore instead of me?" she screeched.

I cringed, squeezing farther back to stay out of sight and glad I'd slipped from the bed when I had. The last thing I needed was a screaming match with his ex while half naked.

THE GAME

I snuck behind the open door and peered through the hinged slit as Christine stomped around the room. She a hand on her hip and spun around to face him. "Where is she? Hiding? You *asshole*," she shouted.

"Christine, calm down. We've been broken up for a year. Let's discuss this rationally."

Christine leaned down to grab one of the floggers. The floor was littered with our clothes and the floggers. She flung it across the room. It hit the far wall with a resounding thud. "Jesus, Riley. Floggers? Already? What kind of whore lets a man hit her this early in the relationship?"

I swallowed my anger and gripped my hands into fists, trying hard not to burst out of the bathroom and go after her like a rabid dog. It's what I wanted to do. Instead, I held my ground.

The phone still lay on the bed. I could see it, and I knew the connection was open, but all I could do was hope the police were close and the dispatcher was listening.

Christine flailed her arms around the room, and I wondered where Riley was standing. I couldn't see him. He must have been in the door frame.

And then I gasped and held my breath. She was

holding a gun.

Fuck.

She was more deranged than I thought. More than any of us thought.

Riley was intentionally making small movements in an effort to keep her from losing it and firing at him. No wonder she got by him and into the bedroom. The crazy bitch was waving a gun around.

"Let's go sit in the living room and discuss this. Work something out," Riley pleaded.

She laughed maniacally. "Work something out? You mean like I take Mondays and Wednesdays and that whore gets the other five days with you? I don't think so."

My mouth fell open. *I don't think so either, you fucking bitch.* It was painful enough knowing he'd ever laid a hand on her. I would spend my life blocking out the images.

"Why, Riley?"

"I don't know, Christine. Let's figure this out. Together. Come on." He was trying to lure her from the bedroom.

She glanced around, seeming to forget I was in there somewhere. And then she snapped out of it and lifted the gun, her finger poised to pull the trigger.

The Game

I screamed and she whipped my direction.

The gun went off.

I slid to the floor on instinct, hitting my head on the edge of the tub as I went down. The door swung almost shut. My face landed on the tile just past the door, giving me a view of the room. The pain was intense, but I fought to stay alert while the fading draw of being knocked out battled against my need to pay attention.

Riley emitted a deep primal growl as he ran forward into the room and slammed into Christine, taking her down to the ground and sending the gun spinning across the floor. It landed just outside the bathroom.

In a perfect world, I would have snagged it and saved the day, but in my world, my limbs wouldn't obey any command, and I lay there glancing between the gun and the struggle between my man and his ex.

A commotion filled the doorway, and I managed to flick my gaze to see several officers enter the room.

Riley held Christine down by sitting on her waist with his knees on her arms. She bucked beneath him.

The officers grabbed his arms and pulled him off. "We've got it from here, sir."

He glanced at first one man and then the other,

seemingly confused to find them in his bedroom.

And then he jerked his gaze to mine and jumped off Christine, screaming at the top of his lungs. "*No…*" His voice faded, even though that confused me as I watched him lunge toward me as if in slow motion.

****

My head pounded. I blinked awake, squinting toward the ceiling. The light was intense. I moaned at the sharp pain that washed through my body and left me close to vomiting.

"Turn her head to the side," someone shouted.

I blinked again to find Riley holding my face and tipping me to one side.

That hurt worse. I fought him.

He held steady. "Easy, baby. You hit your head."

I knew that. I remembered the tub slamming into me as I went down.

I curled onto my side on the bathroom floor as Riley grabbed a blanket out of someone's hand and tucked it around my frame.

I shivered in spite of his efforts, remembering I wore nothing but his T-shirt.

"Christine?" I asked.

"Police have her. She's gone. They already left.

The Game

Ambulance is on its way."

"For what?" I asked, squinting into the bright room again. "Did someone get shot?"

"No." He shook his head, smiling down at me with his lips. His brow was incongruently furrowed.

I was confused.

"You're hurt, baby. You need a doctor."

"Me?"

"Yes. Though you scared me to death when I saw you on the floor. You must have hit your head on the tub. I thought she shot you." He pointed at the door.

I lifted my gaze to follow where he angled his finger at the splintered hole in the door. Shit. That bitch did fire off a round. I was lucky she hadn't hit me.

"Jesus, she could have killed us both." I fought against his hold to sit up.

"Stay there, baby."

"Cold. The tile…" I shivered against the frigid floor.

Riley tucked his hands under me and lifted me into his arms. "Hang on. I'll get you to the bed."

When he gently lowered me to the mattress and tugged the comforter over me, keeping the blanket around me at the same time, I immediately felt better. I still shook violently, but I thought it was from shock more than pain.

"Sir, can you move down a bit. Let me look."

A paramedic leaned over me as Riley grabbed my hand and squeezed.

"What happened?" the man asked, flashing a light into my eyes.

"She hit her head when my fucking ex shot at her."

The guy glanced at Riley and then back at me. He turned me to one side and felt around the back of my head. "That's quite a knot, ma'am. Can you answer a few questions for me?"

"Sure," I whispered, cringing as he continued to poke the spot.

"Do you remember what happened, ma'am?"

"Yes."

"Good. That's a good sign."

"What's your name?"

"Cheyenne Decard."

"Do you know what the date is?"

"October fifth? Something like that."

"Good." He leaned back. "I think you'll be fine. I don't see evidence of a concussion, but that bump is

THE GAME

going to hurt like hell for a few days." He turned to look at Riley. "As long as she doesn't vomit or get disoriented, I think she'll be fine. Take her to the emergency room if there are any changes. But it's not uncommon for someone to faint when they hit their head like that, probably from the fear and the pain."

"You don't think she needs to go to the hospital?"

"If you're concerned, we can take her."

"Riley. No," I muttered, reaching out to grab his hand. "Just let me sleep. Please, babe."

He stared at me a moment and then faced the paramedic. "Okay." His shoulders slumped. "I'll stay up and watch her."

"That's all they'll do at the emergency room anyway. If she doesn't show any signs of confusion or extreme fatigue or an inability to wake up, you'll be fine."

Riley nodded as the man stood and headed for the door. With a squeeze to my hand, Riley followed him.

I listened as muffled voices filled the hallway and traveled down to the foyer. The police... The paramedics... Riley...

I closed my eyes and drifted into a light slumber, smiling a few minutes later when Riley slid into bed beside me and pulled me close. He lifted my head several inches and helped me swallow a pair of painkillers. "You scared the fuck out of me."

"Sorry." I would have said more if I had the energy.

"I was sure she shot you." He lowered me back onto the pillow, careful to set my head to one side and avoid the bump.

"I ducked too fast. I think I slipped. But I avoided the bullet."

"There is that." He held my face against his and inhaled long and slow. "I'm so sorry I brought you into this mess."

"It's over now. Right?"

"Yes." Thank God.

"I feel bad for her dad. He seemed like a level-headed nice guy."

"He is. And I hate that his daughter is such a whack job. She wasn't always this way. In the early days, she was sort of normal. In college we had a blast."

"Was it the BDSM?"

He shook his head. "No. That was gradual. As I grew more into the lifestyle, she faked like she went along with me. But she never really did, and unfortunately it took many years for me to realize she was faking it."

"Why would she do that?"

"She was a money-grubbing whore. All she cared about was finding someone to support her in the manner she was raised. I just didn't see it."

"She is beautiful. You must have been blinded by her looks," I teased.

He tensed next to me. "Is she? It's been so long since I found her attractive, I can't even see it. And her personality ruined any beauty she once possessed."

"I can see that." My voice trailed.

"Sleep, baby. I'll watch you."

"I'm fine."

"You will be." His hands roamed my body as if he needed the verification I was indeed whole.

I fell asleep to the feel of his warm hands.

****

When I opened my eyes the next time, the room was light. The blinds were partway opened and the sun leaked in through the slits. I turned to my other side and found Riley smiling down at me from a chair next to the bed. "How do you feel?"

"Better. Tired. Someone woke me up like ten times."

He smiles broader. "Just being cautious."

I reached up and rubbed my fingers over the lump on the back of my head. "Wow."

"Yeah. It's gonna hurt for a few days. I called your boss, by the way."

"My boss?"

He lifted a brow. "Yeah. You know. The guy you work for? Mr. Schultz. He sends his sympathy and says to take your time getting back to work." Riley leaned forward and took my hand in his. "Unless you want to quit and stay here as my concubine. I'm good with that too." He wiggled both brows, making me giggle.

I sobered instantly. "Ow. Don't make me laugh." And then I paused and spoke again, "He still wants me to work for him?"

"Of course. You do excellent work. He can see that."

"But I acted like a complete idiot."

"A deranged woman was out to get you. He understands."

"Not sure I can show my face there again." I flopped onto my back, careful to set my head down gently. I groaned.

"Does it hurt that bad?"

"No. I'm just thinking."

The Game

"Well, don't think so hard, then." He moved to sit on the edge of the bed next to me.

"My life's a disaster."

"Still? I thought we'd agreed to give this a shot. Your job is secure. Christine's in jail. What more do you need fixed?" He brushed a lock of hair off my forehead. He looked genuinely concerned for someone who forgot about my apartment.

"Riley, I don't have any place to live, and all of my belongings were shredded."

He scrunched his face again. "You don't need a place to live. You can stay here. I want you here."

"Here? In your house?"

"Of course. Unless you prefer the back yard, but it gets cold out there at night this time of year." His teasing voice soothed even though I wasn't sure his idea was a sound one.

"Riley, we've only known each other a short time. I can't move in with you."

"Why not? Who cares how long we've known each other? It feels right. And I want to grab onto that and never let it go."

I held his gaze for a long time. His plan was ludicrous. I opened my mouth to protest and came up with nothing.

Could I really move in with this man I hardly knew and set up house? And more importantly, what percentage of the time would he expect me to submit to him? No wonder he said we would be in constant negotiations. If he thought I was going to stay permanently, we would need to renegotiate several things right away.

"It's awfully soon for such a commitment. You aren't suggesting this because you feel bad for me losing my apartment, are you?"

"Hell, no. Actually the trashed apartment is just working in my favor. Making my life easier." He grinned wide.

Gah. How was I supposed to argue with him when he was so damn charming?

I nibbled my lower lip and considered his ridiculous proposition. Finally, I caved. "Okay, but only on a trial basis. Two weeks. Let's see if we can go that long without killing each other."

He nodded. "Done."

"And I'm not your slave. We'll need to negotiate what hours and days I'm willing to be in the role for you. It's fucking hot as hell, and I love it when you control me, but I also don't want to feel like I'm losing myself in the process. So, get flexible on that issue until we come to an amount of time we can both live with."

"Done."

I closed my eyes. "That was easy. Am I hallucinating?"

"Nope."

With my eyes shut and me fighting the need to sleep again, I continued to spill out my thoughts before they slid away. "And Riley?"

"Yeah?"

"Don't you ever go behind my back and pull a secret stunt like that one again. I'm not fragile, and I want to be in the loop on everything that pertains to me or us."

"Done."

"Again? Just like that?" I peeled my eyes open to meet his gaze again. "You're being far too agreeable. I might need to take your pulse again later."

He leaned down and kissed my forehead, his lips lingering for long seconds before he drew back. "Take my pulse any time you want, baby. I'll still be right here. Nothing will happen between us without your permission. Promise."

I felt lighter than I had in days as I let myself slip

Becca Jameson

into oblivion once again.

THE GAME

Chapter Twenty-Eight

One month later...

"We shouldn't have rushed this. It's crazy. *I'm* crazy. There's too much to do. And we only have two weeks left." Amy threw her hands in the air and stomped her foot. She looked hysterical in the short navy dress she wore that flowed around her thighs as she had her little mini tantrum. "Weddings cannot be organized in just seven months. I never should have agreed to such a short engagement." She shouted those last words while tossing her head back and angling her voice toward the hallway.

I held back my giggle by tucking my lips in and holding them with my teeth. I could see Meagan doing the same at my side where we both sat on Amy's couch. We'd come to Nashville last night for the big girls' weekend. Today we'd attended a lovely shower put on by her coworkers, and now we were set to go out for the evening.

Cade wandered into the room, grabbed Amy by the back of her hair, and tugged until her head tipped back and she met his gaze. "Baby, I'm warning you. Stop this nonsense. We're getting married in two weeks, and that's final. It's done. So, stop stressing over the details. It will be perfect. Whatever isn't done, we aren't doing. You've got flowers, a reception hall, a dress, a photographer, a minister, and ten thousand yards of some strange tulle. All I ever needed was you and a justice of the peace."

He gave her a warning glare that melted my heart. He was gruff sometimes, just like I'd found Riley to be, but he loved Amy to pieces, and all he wanted was to be married to her.

"Deep breaths, Amelia." He held her gaze while she obeyed him. "Good. The plans are perfect. No more stressing. Go out with your girls and have fun." He released her curls and nodded at Meagan and I before leaving the room.

THE GAME

I tried hard not to laugh.

At the last second, he grabbed the corner as he rounded to the hall and turned back. "Where are you women going again?"

"We didn't say," Meagan responded, sitting up straighter next to me as if a longer spine would give emphasis to her sassy response.

Cade pointed at Amy. "We have an agreement."

She rolled her eyes. "I know. I haven't forgotten."

And then he was gone.

"What's the agreement?" Meagan whispered, leaning forward.

"No men's hands on me."

Meagan laughed. "As if anyone would want another man's hands on them after Cade's."

"I know. Preposterous, right?" Amy stepped toward the kitchen. "Who wants a drink before we go out?"

I did. In fact, I wanted about three just to calm my nerves. I hadn't gone three days without Riley for the past month. Already I missed him. He hadn't been able to join me for this bachelorette weekend. I'd come to Nashville with Meagan, leaving him at home dealing with work issues. I had no idea what they entailed, but he'd been adamant at the last second that I should go and he would see me when I got home Sunday night.

I was loath to admit I already hated this plan. That's how far under my skin he'd gotten.

Amy returned with three wine glasses dangling by the stems in one hand and a bottle of something that probably cost more than my rent in the other.

If I had rent. Which I no longer did.

"How are you adjusting to living with Riley?" Amy asked as if she'd read my mind.

I shrugged, trying to be more nonchalant than I felt.

"It must be wonderful," Meagan responded, "because I never see her anymore."

Amy smiled. "Were you able to recover anything from your apartment?"

"A few things. It was a disaster. Riley hired people to go in and clean up the bulk of it before I got there. I did salvage mementos and some clothes. There weren't many items Christine hadn't taken scissors to."

Amy visibly shuddered. "I'm so sorry, hon. That blows. I hope they keep her off the streets and throw away the key."

"Her father actually offered to pay for the

damage."

"Really?" Amy took a sip of wine. "That was nice of him."

"Yeah. Riley turned him down of course, but it was a gesture. And that's what counts."

Meagan plopped back on the couch and took a long drink of the wine. "This is delicious. I've never been a wine snob before, but I could get used to this."

Amy angled the discussion back to me. "Are you happy?"

I smiled broadly. "Very. It's a culture shock, for sure, but I've never been happier."

"Are you still mad at him?"

I shook my head. "We have an agreement. He doesn't meddle in my job, and I don't freak out on him." I smirked. "At first I was leery. I felt like a moron going back to that office after the way I acted and how many people saw me."

"What ended up happening with the business proposal Riley had for your company?" Amy asked.

Meagan had already heard most of this, but I hadn't had the opportunity to chat as much with Amy in the last few weeks. "I didn't want to force him to take his business elsewhere because that would have hurt Talent

Marketing Group just to save my pride, but I also wasn't willing to take the project myself.

"Talk about a conflict of interests. So, I told Mr. Schultz to give the account to Stacy. She's over the moon. Riley still grumbles about it, but I had to take a stand and make it clear I was serious about him sticking his nose in my work."

Meagan reached for the bottle of wine on the coffee table and topped off her glass. "I would have loved to have been a fly on the wall when you had that discussion with him. He doesn't seem super flexible to me." She chuckled.

"That's an understatement, but I made it abundantly clear he needed to let me develop my own career. If he gets me special favors by marching into my office or buying it outright or whatever, I won't have any way of knowing if I'm even good at my job. And that's not who I am. I want to succeed without his help."

"I hear you," Amy said. "Cade and I went through the same thing. And now that I work for him, it's uncomfortable at times. I know people treat me differently since the owner is about to become my husband, but I've learned to live with it. I know I'm a valuable asset in my own mind, so I ignore the doubts of other. Most of the time."

"I keep trying to decide if I would want these astronomical problems you two have or if I should run from your sides and hide. Maybe I shouldn't even come to the wedding where there will be far too many rich dudes. Who would have thought it would be so much trouble to date a rich guy?" Meagan flipped her brown curls over her shoulder and stuck her nose in the air in mock snobbery.

"Don't knock it until you try it," Amy added. "There are bonuses to being with a man who doesn't have to count pennies at dinner."

"That may be true, but I still can't wrap my head around my two best friends in D/s relationships. How did this happen?" she teased.

I turned to face her more fully. "Listen to you with your perfect acronyms for dominance and submission. I'm so proud."

"Yeah, well, I thought I better study up on the lifestyle a bit so I'd understand you both better. I can't say I've figured it out, but I'll admit some parts are panty melting."

Someone cleared their throat behind us, and I glanced over my shoulder to find Cade's driver at the entrance to the living room. "I'm ready whenever you ladies want to leave." He turned and stepped back out to the foyer.

If I wasn't mistaken, his face was flushed. If he heard any of what we'd said, it wasn't surprising.

Four hours later, tripping over ourselves and laughing too loudly, Amy stuck her key into the front door and opened it. We all fell into the entrance to her condo and dropped our purses on the floor.

Amy was in the middle of a story, and she continued, grabbing the wall for support. "When Kelsie spilled her martini on the guy next to us, I thought he was going to have a coronary."

Meagan bent over at the waist in laughter. "Who would have thought by the end of the night he would ask her out."

We'd been with five of Amy's local friends, and they had all proven to be as fun and friendly as she'd insisted.

Holding on to each other and making no attempt to be quiet, we stumbled around the corner into the living room.

I should have realized the music in the condo was a bit louder than necessary for the time of night and the fact that there should have been just one man at home—

The Game

Cade. But my mind was a little slow, which left me stunned to find not just Cade, but several of his friends sitting around the long dining room table, cards strewn across the glass surface and every man holding a set.

Even more shocking was that Riley was there. I widened my eyes, a smile growing larger on my face.

He winked at me. "Surprise," he mouthed.

"Cade," Amy slurred, stumbling to his side. "You didn't tell me you were having poker…" she glanced around the table, "…with people from out of town."

Cade pulled her to his side and kissed her cheek. "Didn't want you to stress over it, so I didn't tell you."

"I would have fixed you snacks and shopped for beer and stuff."

"And that's why I didn't tell you." He grinned. "Bachelorette party, check. Bachelor party, check."

"I thought you were going out next weekend with the guys."

"I lied." He looked so pleased with himself.

I could totally understand his reasoning. Ever since Amy had met him, she'd become far more tidy than she'd ever been before. And she totally would have gone overboard preparing for this evening. Which the guys would never have found necessary. None of them would have even noticed her hard work.

Cade was a gem.

My man, however…

I narrowed my gaze as I strode to his side. The others waited patiently for this interruption to take place. I leaned in and set my lips on his ear. "What's your excuse?"

"For what?" He tugged me onto his lap, shocking me.

"Telling me you had to work all weekend," I added unnecessarily.

"Wanted you to enjoy your evening without checking your watch or leaving early. And don't try to tell me you wouldn't have done that. You totally would have."

He was right. And he was here. Bonus.

Riley kissed my neck and spread his legs, causing me to slip between them, holding on to his arms to keep from falling. "Kneel between my thighs under the table, baby." His words were whispered into my ear. Slowly. Distinctly. Broking no argument.

I swallowed hard and met his gaze. "Now?" All the alcohol I'd consumed fled my body, rendering me far more sober than I'd been moments ago.

"Now."

The Game

I hesitated. He'd never asked me to do anything like this before. Not in public. Not in front of people. Never. We hadn't even been to a club together, even though he'd suggested it several times. I wasn't sure I was ready yet.

It was one thing to submit to him behind closed doors. It made me so hot I couldn't deny the allure. But here?

Eight men were playing poker. The table was glass.

I was mortified as I stared at Riley, my mouth hanging open.

"Trust me."

Trust him? I did. Usually. He hadn't done anything to break that trust in the last month. But this was a huge ask.

Or demand rather.

What would the guys think? I didn't know any of them except Cade, of course, and Parker, who had obviously made the trip from Charlotte. How would I face these men at the wedding in two weeks after kneeling on the floor in submission to one of them?

I had a choice to make. And I needed to make it fast.

I glanced at Amy and gasped. She was already on

the floor between Cade's legs, her cheek on his thigh. Her eyes were closed. Her entire body was under the table where everyone could see her through the glass.

I surveyed the rest of the men. No one was paying any attention to Amy or me. They were all arranging their hands of cards, drinking something dark from low balls, or snacking on pretzels and assorted nuts.

Finally, one of them looked up and smirked at Riley. "Dude, we gonna play this hand or what?"

Riley shifted his gaze back to me and lifted an eyebrow. He said nothing else.

Where was Meagan?

I twisted in my seat to find her perched on the end of the couch staring at me. She had her lower lip between her teeth and looked surprisingly intrigued rather than appalled.

I blew out a long breath and oozed onto the floor between Riley's legs. Like I was made of some sort of thick fluid, I flowed into the spot he demanded, landed on my knees, tucked my hands behind my back, and leaned my cheek against his thigh.

All I could see was the bulge in his jeans that indicated he was aroused.

Good. I wasn't sure I would be obliged to do

The Game

anything about that arousal later when we were finally alone, but I was glad he would at least suffer.

I squeezed my eyes shut as it occurred to me I was suffering too. I wanted to be mortified. And in a way I was. On the other hand, what did I care what other people thought of our lifestyle? Clearly Amy didn't have a problem with it. And it was her house.

Which made me curious. Who were these men? Did she know them all? They couldn't be guys from the office where she was a high-powered employee by day. No way would she out herself like this.

I relaxed marginally as I let that reality sink in.

And then I flinched when I heard Cade's voice. "Meagan, do you want to join us?"

Join "us." What did that mean? I held my breath. Meagan was innocent. Way too innocent to witness this from her friends. I was suddenly more worried about her reaction than anyone else's.

What I needed to focus on was my reaction and how it made me feel to please Riley. Which at the moment was dubious.

I would do this. Play it out. Find out where it led. He'd asked me to trust him. I needed to give him the benefit of the doubt. He hadn't let me down a single time since the Christine debacle.

"I'm not very good at poker," Meagan confessed.

I could hear her voice closer to the table. She'd at least stepped forward.

"Oh, shit. Let me introduce you to the guys," Cade said. I could picture him pointing around the table as he spoke. "This is John, Stephen, Toby, Roy, Jeremy, and you know Parker and Riley."

"Yep. Well, Parker I've met briefly." I wondered if she was staring at him. He was formidable in his own right. Hell, all the guys at this table were.

"They're all members of the club Amelia and I belong to," Cade continued.

Oh. That was interesting. A BDSM club? Had to be.

I relaxed marginally, blowing out a breath. No wonder no one had looked surprised. Everyone in the room was in the lifestyle. Except Meagan.

A chair grated against the floor as it moved. And then Parker spoke. "You can sit with us and watch if you want. Or play. I'll be happy to give you some tips. Or hell, if you'd rather not be left out of the D/s scene, you're welcome to participate in that as well."

"What? Oh. Oh, that. No. No thanks." I could

hear her discomfort in her voice, and I felt it for her myself. This was crazy. Insane.

"Okay. Here. Sit. What do you want to drink?"

"I'm thinking maybe I've had enough to drink."

I smiled.

Riley threaded the fingers of one hand into my hair and squeezed in reassurance. I felt a bit like a cherished pet and he'd just given me an "atta girl."

Maybe he wouldn't be too pissed later for my hesitation before. Though I found that unlikely. He was probably plotting some way to punish me for not obeying his demands immediately.

Shock was my excuse.

Shock had been his main aim.

Parker chuckled. "Well, you aren't driving. And I'm sure you're beyond scandalized, so…"

"You're right. White wine would be fantastic."

"Coming right up." Another scoot of the chair against the floor filled my ears and then footsteps. Parker was right at home in Cade's condo. The condo that had been Riley's before he and Cade had swapped towns and residences.

"Here you go." Parker resumed his spot, and the game was back on.

"Hit me," one of the guys said.

I tuned them out while the game continued, becoming more sober by the minute.

It was late. The guys were on their last few hands. And less than half an hour later, they wrapped things up. Thank God because I was tired, my knees hurt, and I couldn't imagine staying on the floor like that much longer.

Riley took my hand and helped me stand. He turned me around to face the rest of the table and wrapped one arm under my breasts, hugging me close to his front while he pointed around the table to introduce everyone.

Each man smiled and nodded in turn.

"You did good, baby," he whispered in my ear. "Stay here while I see them out."

I lowered myself into his seat while he and Cade and Parker went to the front door.

Amy sat in Cade's vacated seat at the end of the table.

Meagan sat across from me. She nibbled on her bottom lip. "Interesting."

Amy giggled. "You wanted to see us in action."

"Interesting," she repeated.

The Game

I was still sort of mortified. In fact, my hands were shaking.

Amy reached over and grabbed my hand and squeezed. "You've never done anything like that have you?"

"No."

"Think he was testing you."

"I'm sure." I blew out a breath, not certain I'd passed that test or wanted to.

"What do you mean?" Meagan asked. "And would someone please tell me why you find that arousing."

Amy turned to face her. "Riley was testing Cheyenne's willingness to follow his directives in front of other people. It was brilliant since she didn't know anyone in the room and he never suggested she do anything besides kneel."

Meagan shivered. "Which is very weird."

"It's the most common sort of position in BDSM. Like the base, you could say. And exercising that right in public is a huge step."

"I didn't realize everyone at the table belonged to the same club, so I nearly died when he told me to kneel. And that was his goal, of course." I crossed my arms over my chest, still a bit unnerved.

"And this is sexy how?" Meagan asked.

Amy shrugged. "It's different for everyone, but pleasing Cade and seeing his expression when I do so is enormous. The way he stroked my hair or my face makes me feel cherished. Loved. It's so fulfilling." She turned to face me.

I held up both hands. "Don't look at me. That was a first."

"But how do you feel when you do it at home?" Amy asked.

"Yeah. She's right." I scrunched up my nose, picturing me on my knees while Riley fed me. We did that often. Or in the living room in the evening. "I guess it centers me and puts me in a particular frame of mind."

"What frame of mind is that?" Meagan asked.

"One where I get to let go of all concerns and turn them over to Riley for the hours we're in the scene."

"Uh-huh." Meagan sounded unconvinced.

I couldn't blame her. I had felt the same way just weeks ago. I heard the front door close, and the noise level from the foyer came to a halt.

Cade and Riley came back into the living room with Parker on their heels. They plopped down on three different pieces of furniture and Cade reached out a hand toward the dining area. "Come here, Amelia."

She rose and stepped to her fiancé.

I stood also as Riley motioned for me to join him. I was further surprised when he pulled me down beside him and sat with his arm around my waist like a perfectly normal guy.

He leaned in and kissed my earlobe. "So proud of you."

I turned a deeper shade of red that I could feel all over my cheeks and running down my neck.

Meagan turned her dining chair around to face us in the adjoining space.

I twisted my neck to see her. "Did you play poker? I stopped paying attention. Missed that part."

She laughed. "No. I watched. No way was I going to join in on that game. Those guys were serious."

"Those guys were all dominants," Parker added.

"That too." Meagan shivered. "They were intense. Is everyone at your wedding going to be in the lifestyle?"

"No," Cade stated, "You won't see many, and you won't be able to tell. Not in a mixed venue like that. People in the lifestyle are very careful not to offend those who aren't."

Riley flattened his hand on my back and trailed

his fingers up to my neck. "You did well. You trusted me."

"You tested me."

"I did." His eyes sparkled. "You passed."

"You tested me in front of Meagan."

"I did," he agreed again. "And still you passed."

"What if she was uncomfortable?"

Riley smirked. "I watched her like a hawk, baby."

"We all did," Cade added. "And she wasn't altogether uninformed. She knew about our lifestyle."

"Informed is far from experienced," Meagan added. "But I'll admit, I was fine. It didn't take me long to figure out Riley was testing Cheyenne, and Cade was using Amy to drive that point home. Did you all plan this for weeks?" She giggled.

Riley shook his head. "Nah. Just a few days. The poker game was planned for weeks. But it wasn't until we bumped heads about the participants that I realized I should seize the opportunity to push Cheyenne's boundaries." He squeezed my back and angled me toward him until I fell into his side.

"You should give it a try, Meagan," Parker suggested. "I'm a pretty good judge of people. You were turned on."

Meagan scrunched up her face again and shook

The Game

her head. "No thanks. That was all the BDSM I needed. I'll stick with vanilla."

I glanced at Parker, who stared at Meagan a bit longer than necessary, a smile lifting the corners of his mouth. I could see the interest there. Meagan was looking at her feet instead.

What were the chances three guys who had been friends since college could pair of with three women in the same boat? Slim. I shouldn't read anything into it.

I shook the thought from my head and turned to face Riley.

His look was full of hunger. "You willing to play some more in front of friends?"

Meagan jumped to her feet. "On that note, I'm going to sleep." She turned to Cade. "Thanks for letting us stay here. I'll see you guys in the morning." She left the room as if she were on fire, heading down the hall to the guest room she had occupied last night.

Parker stood also. "In the interest of keeping things less awkward for your new sub, I'll go to sleep also." He nodded toward me and made his way out of the living room too. I figured he was going to occupy the fourth bedroom, the only one not currently being used by any of us. Thank God Cade and Amy had so many rooms.

I tipped my head back to face my Dom. "What did you have in mind?" I should have been tired, but instead I was alert at his suggestion. If he wanted to test the waters, so to speak, there wasn't a single person I'd want to have witness me submitting besides Amy. She wouldn't judge. Hell, she'd even seen me naked more times than I could count.

Cade, on the other had, had most definitely never seen me naked. I shivered.

Riley set a hand on my back again and rubbed in circles. "In the lifestyle, people are not judgmental. Let yourself go with the flow. You know I won't ask you to do more than I think you're capable of."

"Yes, Sir." I hadn't referred to him as Sir in front of anyone until that moment. I turned to find Amy with her arms lifted in the air and Cade pulling her navy dress over her head. I was surprised to find her naked underneath. I hadn't realized she'd spent the evening without a bra or panties.

"Did anyone else touch your delectable body this evening?" Cade asked.

"No, Sir," Amy mumbled. She stood in front of Cade, facing him, her back to me.

THE GAME

"Good. The visual makes me cringe."

"I would never enjoy another man's touch anyway, Sir."

"I know that, baby."

Chapter Twenty-Nine

Riley's hand worked its way up to my neck, and he squeezed and turned me to face him. "Undress for me, Cheyenne. I've been dying to see your sexy body all evening."

God, I missed him. I'd seen him yesterday morning before we both left for work, but yesterday was Thursday, and then I'd come straight to Nashville and hadn't seen him Friday at all.

Yep. I missed him. Even his bossy attitude was welcome. Even in front of Amy…and Cade. I wanted him to control me. Dominate me. How far would he go in front of my friend? And his?

I stood before him and slowly removed my sheer

THE GAME

blouse, sliding each button through the hole until I slipped it off my shoulders and let it flutter to the floor. I unzipped my skirt next and let it pool at my feet.

Riley reached out a hand and hauled me closer until my belly pressed against his lips. He cupped my breasts with both hands and squeezed. "Love the matching panty set you never expected anyone to see."

"Thank you, Sir." I had only worn sexy matching lingerie since we'd started seeing each other. It had become a habit to always be prepared even though I hadn't expected to see him. It made me feel sexy and attractive knowing what I wore under my clothes.

Riley trailed a finger along the top edge of my bra, teasing the swell of my breast until I rocked forward. My back was to Amy. Her back was to me. It gave me some satisfaction knowing I didn't have to look her in the face while Riley played with me.

Riley smoothed his hands up my sides and around to my back. He unclasped my bra and then eased it over my shoulders and off my arms. With a precision I had not exercised, he dropped my bra on top of my blouse.

"Eyes on me. No one else is paying attention to you but me. Got it?"

"Yes, Sir."

"Good girl." He cupped my breasts again. I'd been aching for him to hold the swollen globes in his palms for over a day. And I was so glad he was here tonight to surprise me that I didn't frankly care who watched.

When he leaned forward and sucked a nipple into his mouth, I gasped.

His hands trailed down to my waist and then around to cup my ass. I swayed forward, losing my balance when he squeezed my cheeks and molded them in his hands. "Love the thong." He hooked his fingers in the sides and tugged the swatch of lace down my legs.

I stepped out of them.

"Spread your legs for me, baby."

I obeyed without question, biting my lip as I wondered how I would keep enough brain cells functioning to avoid making a fool of myself in front of the two other people in the room.

I was already losing the battle, considering I was lost in Riley world, putty in his hands. How far would he take me in front of Cade and Amy? Would he make me come?

My pussy was soaked. No denying that. It had been since I'd seen him sitting at that table when I stumbled in from the bachelorette party. My nipples

The Game

hardened as I grabbed Riley's shoulders to brace myself.

Amy moaned behind me, making me flinch. I'd nearly forgotten about her existence, and it soothed me to realize she was just as aware of mine. My job was to please Riley. I wasn't meant to have any concern for anyone else.

"Eyes on me, baby." Riley nudged my chin with his pointer until I lifted my gaze to his. He smiled warmly. "Good girl. So proud of you. I'll give you a choice."

I nodded subtly.

"You can either suck me off right here right now, or I'll fuck your sweet pussy with my fingers until you come standing in front of me."

My eyes widened. Interesting choice. Contrived. He knew it. If I sucked him off, he got all the pleasure, but I had my dignity in front of Amy and Cade intact. If I let him finger me until I came on my feet, I would feel like I won the lottery, but I would also lose myself and scream out in Amy's living room.

I chose number one. "You, Sir." Without hesitation, I lowered myself to my knees in front of him, unbuttoned his jeans, eased the zipper down, and let him spring free. I licked my lips. I loved sucking him. It was heady in a way I never would have imagined. Probably because no matter what I did to him, he ensured I received twice as much attention at his own mouth and hands.

He was simply like that.

I lowered my mouth and sucked his erection in between my lips so fast he gasped.

"Easy," he muttered. "Not a race."

I reduced the suction a fraction, gripped the base of his cock with one hand, and fucked him in and out of my mouth. I twirled my tongue around the tip and stroked it through the slit at the top until he groaned.

He bucked off the love seat, slamming his cock up into my mouth as though he were the one in control.

And he was. He always was. Even when I was on top, he was in charge. I couldn't give a blow job without feeling controlled.

Now was no exception.

Riley cupped my face and held my head steady as he fucked my mouth.

I had experienced this before, and I opened my throat and let him have his way. His flavor… The smell of his skin… It made me squirm and wish I could touch myself.

But he'd never allowed that without permission.

And besides, hello, Amy was behind me. I needed to shake the desire to masturbate from my head and control myself.

Though in reality it was futile to concern myself with whatever she was doing since she was as absorbed in Cade as I was in Riley.

I concentrated fully on the thick length in my mouth and hollowed my cheeks as I drew off him over and over.

Riley threaded his fingers into my hair on both sides and held my head steady while he took over, fucking my mouth deeper.

I closed my eyes and luxuriated in the feel of his smooth skin against my tongue.

It didn't take long. Moments later, he came, squirting down my throat in long pulses.

I swallowed him, loving the taste, loving the power I felt when he let me wrap my lips around his cock. It was one of the rare times I felt like I was in control of something, even though I knew it was a smoke screen. Riley was always in control.

When he pulled out, he cupped my face and lifted it to his. His gaze was serious, deep, penetrating. "I love you," he whispered.

I smiled and leaned forward, setting my cheek against his semi-erect cock. "I love you too."

Riley shocked me by standing up quickly and hauling me into his arms. He cradled me against his chest, tugged his jeans over his hips with one hand, and strode down the hall to the bedroom I'd already occupied the night before.

His overnight bag was on the bed. Clothes from earlier were tossed across the footboard. I smiled, loving the warm feeling of knowing he'd already infiltrated this space that had been mine and was now ours.

He tossed me on the bed, yanked off his jeans, and climbed over me. With his cock poised at my entrance, he brushed my curls from my face and cupped my cheeks. His expression was serious, intense. "You're mine."

I nodded.

I was his. In every way.

"Yes, Sir. I'm yours."

About the Author

BECCA JAMESON LIVES IN ATLANTA, Georgia, with her husband and two kids. After years of editing, she is now a full-time author. With over 40 best-selling books written, she has dabbled in a variety of genres, ranging from paranormal to contemporary to BDSM. The voices in her head are clamoring to get out faster than she can get them onto "paper"! She loves chatting with fans, so feel free to contact her through email, Facebook, or her website.

...where Alphas dominate...

Also by Becca Jameson:

Wolf Masters series:
Kara's Wolves (Book 1)
Lindsey's Wolves (Book 2)
Jessica's Wolves (Book 3)
Alyssa's Wolves (Book 4)
Tessa's Wolf (Book 5)
Rebecca's Wolves (Book 6)
Melinda's Wolves (Book 7)
Laurie's Wolves (Book 8)
Amanda's Wolves (Book 9) (coming spring 2016)
Sharon's Wolves (Book 10) (coming spring 2016)

Durham Wolves series:
Rescue in the Smokies (Book 1)
Fire in the Smokies (Book 2)
Freedom in the Smokies (Book 3)

Wolf Gatherings series:
Tarnished (Book 1)
Dominated (Book 2)
Completed (Book 3)
Redeemed (Book 4)
Abandoned (Book 5)
Betrayed (Book 6)

Emergence series:
Bound to be Taken (Book 1)
Bound to be Tamed (Book 2)
Bound to be Tested (Book 3)
Bound to be Tempted (Book 4)

The Fight Club series:
Come (Book 1)
Perv (Book 2)
Need (Book 3)
Hers (Book 4)
Want (Book 5)
Lust (Book 6)

The Underground series:
Force (Book 1)
Clinch (Book 2) (coming spring 2016)
Guard (Book 3) (coming 2016)
Submit (Book 4) (coming 2016)
Thrust (Book 5) (coming soon)
Torque (Book 6) (coming soon)

The Art of Kink series:
Pose (Book 1)
Paint (Book 2)
Sculpt (Book 3)

Claiming Her series:
The Rules (Book 1)
The Game (Book 2)
The Prize (Book 3) (coming 2016)

Stand Alone Books:
Blind with Love
Deceptive Liaison
Out of the Smoke
Awakening Abduction
Three's a Cruise
Wolf Trinity
Frostbitten
2015 BDSM Writers Con Anthology (Anthology)

Free Reads:
Lucky's Charms (Anthology)
Love in the Cards (Anthology)
Wrap (The Art of Kink, Book .5)